DESIGNER
DIRTY LAUNDRY

DESIGNER
DIRTY LAUNDRY

Solving Crime Through Style & Error

DIANE VALLERE

Polyester Press

www.polyesterpress.com

This is a work of fiction. Characters, places, and events are the product of the author's imagination or are used fictitiously. Any resemblance to real people, companies, institutions, organizations, or incidents is entirely coincidental.

No parts of this book may be used or reproduced in any manner whatsoever, including Internet usage, without written permission from the author, except in the case of brief quotations embodied in critical articles and reviews.

Praise for *Designer Dirty Laundry*

"...the book is enriched by the author's cleverly phrased prose and convincing characterization. The surprise ending will satisfy and delight many mystery fans."

-Kirkus Reviews

"Combining fashion and fatalities, Diane Vallere pens a winning debut mystery. With a fascinating look behind the scenes at what makes a department store tick, DESIGNER DIRTY LAUNDRY is a sleek and stylish read."

-Ellen Byerrum, author of the Crime of Fashion mysteries

"In DESIGNER DIRTY LAUNDRY, author Diane Vallere stitches together a seamless mystery. The story will have you on pins and needles. Samantha Kidd is a witty heroine that you will root for as she fashions a fresh stylish start in her hometown of Ribbon, Pennsylvania."

-Avery Aames, Agatha Award winner of nationally bestselling A Cheese Shop Mystery series

"A sassy tale told with warmth and charm, Diane Vallere's DESIGNER DIRTY LAUNDRY shows that even the toughest crime is no match for a sleuth in fishnet stockings who knows her way around the designer department. A delightful debut."

-Kris Neri, Lefty Award-nominated author of REVENGE FOR OLD TIMES' SAKE

"Overall, an impressive cozy mystery from a promising author."

-Mystery Tribune

"Vallere has stitched together haute couture and murder in a stylish mystery. Dirty Laundry has never been so engrossing!"

-Krista Davis, Author of The Domestic Diva Mysteries

Acknowledgments

A thank you goes out to everyone who supported me while writing this book: Amanda Spear Hartley, my first real critique partner. Thank you for getting it! Also to Kathy Whelan and Grace Topping for your valuable feedback. To the Chick Lit Writers of the World and the Stiletto Contest, for letting me know I was on the right track. To volunteer reader Richard Goodman, worth his weight in gold, Sergeant Derek Pacifico, for inspiring me with interrogation techniques, and editor Ramona deFelice Long, for incredible insights that made the story stronger.

To the Sisters in Crime Guppy chapter, for the ongoing support and cheerleading, especially Krista Davis and Daryl Wood Gerber. To Kris Neri, for calling this book funny, and to Ellen Byerrum, for calling it stylish.

To Gigi, for answering the questions I asked and for asking the ones I forgot about. And to Kendel, for a thousand and one things you helped with along the way, but most of all for your friendship. To my family for years—decades?—of support. And to Josh Hickman, for never acting like this was a big deal, which made it seem so much more doable.

Dedication

For my mom, Mary Vallere, and my dad, Donald Vallere,
for everything.

1

When you wear fishnet stockings to the grocery store, people tend to stare. Women look at you like you're affiliated with the sex trade. Men pretend they're not staring, doing so all the while. It's probably because they're thinking the same thing.

The last time I wore fishnets to the grocery store was weeks ago. It was then I met the man who changed the course of my life. Because of him I'd traded in the title senior buyer of ladies designer shoes at Bentley's New York to become the trend specialist at Tradava, the family-owned retailer in Ribbon, Pennsylvania. I'd given up an apartment in Manhattan to buy the house where I grew up. And now, because of him, I sat in a police station explaining my actions to a homicide detective.

I still couldn't pinpoint exactly when it all started to go wrong.

I changed clothes six times, then ultimately settled on the fashion uniform of black: satin motorcycle jacket cinched at the waist over a black lace camisole, pegged pencil skirt, fishnets, and stilettos. Elsa Klensch meets Catwoman. Patrick, the fashion director and my new boss, was bound to approve.

I topped off my look with a finishing blast of Aqua Net, powered up with coffee and a donut from a newspaper kiosk by my house, and headed to work earlier than I remember ever going to work before.

"I'm Samantha Kidd," I announced to the Latina woman behind the Loss Prevention desk at the store. "Patrick's new trend specialist. Do you know if he's here yet?"

"He's here but he didn't say anything about you." She picked up the phone and did a double take when she saw my fishnets. I heard the ring through the receiver. When no one answered, she hung up.

"Visitors gotta sign in."

"But I'm not a visitor, I'm staff. Today's my first day."

"You got ID?"

I reached into my handbag and pulled out a quilted leather wallet, then held it open so my driver's license showed through the plastic window.

"I meant a store ID."

"No. Not yet, anyway."

"That's a New York license," she said.

"You're right, I moved. But it's me, see?" I held the wallet up to my face and smiled at her in the way only a half-crazy person who is brimming with caffeine and adrenaline over starting a new job might. She reached her hands up and gathered her long wavy brownish-orange hair on top of her head then wound it around several times until it resembled a doorknob. The whole time she kept eye contact with me but didn't smile back.

She handed me a clipboard and a red ballpoint pen. *Samantha Kidd*, I wrote with a flourish. *trend office, 7:37.* I snapped my wallet shut and put it in my handbag, then hopped out of the way of a flatbed filled with merchandise and headed into the store. Aside from security and shipping, the store was quiet and I was on my own.

I wasn't a morning person. It was Day One of a new job and a new life, full of potential. My early arrival had less to do with my natural ways and more to do with my need to make a good impression. I was determined to be the best damn trend specialist Patrick had ever hired.

I wandered through the dirty gray hallway, through the shoe department on my way to the elevators, pausing by a round marble fixture that displayed a purple suede platform pump. My index finger traced over the black and white designer label that decorated the sock lining.

"Of all the shoes, in all the stores, *she* had to walk up to *mine*," said a husky voice behind me. I turned and faced the man whose name was stitched onto that label. The man I'd once fantasized about during a layover in Paris and almost kissed a couple of months ago after a particularly late dinner that involved a good deal of Sauvignon Blanc and an unexpected serving of lemon meringue pie. My judgment is severely impaired when there's lemon meringue involved.

Nick Taylor was a shoe designer. His showroom was charged with electricity, hot looks, and devastating style. His shoe collection wasn't bad, either. He was one of the few people I thought I'd miss after leaving Bentley's, that is, until I caught him flirting with the buyer from Bloomingdales and realized the only special thing we had was a gross margin agreement.

"You're a long way from New York. What are you doing here?" I asked in lieu of hello.

"Same thing as you, probably."

"I doubt that. I'm here to start a new job." I cocked my head to the side and crossed my arms, the plum-colored laptop bag that hung from my shoulder banging against my hip.

"First day? Let's get you into practice." He stood directly in front of me and held out a hand. "I'm Nick Taylor. Shoe designer and all around good guy."

I pursed my lips and took in his dark curly hair and his brown eyes, the exact shade of the three root beer barrels I ate in the car after finishing the donut. I met his outstretched hand with my own.

"Samantha Kidd. Former shoe buyer. Former angry New Yorker." I pumped his hand twice to emphasize the word 'former.' "Current trend specialist for Tradava, on the cusp of a new life."

He pulled me in, converting our handshake to an embrace. I lost my balance and fell against him. "I thought I might never see you again," he whispered in my ear. As we parted I checked my reflection in the highly polished doors of the elevators for smudged lipstick and errant crumbs. "So, Tradava?" He held his palms up and looked to his left and right at the store. "From the big city to the small town. I knew you'd land on your feet, but I didn't expect you to land here."

"You make it sound like I vanished into the night," I replied, blowing at a strand of hair that had gotten stuck in my lipstick. My cell phone buzzed from the depths of my handbag and I pretended not to hear it.

"You did vanish in the night. Out of my life, out of my dreams ..." He reached out an index finger and freed the lock of hair, a trace of red lipstick remaining on his fingertip. "And now I find you haven't even missed me. That hurts."

"So you took it upon yourself to stalk me. Good to know."

"C'mon, everybody needs at least one stalker in their life. It's good for the ego," he said.

Nick Taylor had captured the eye of more than one female at Bentley's and rumors of his love life often permeated the otherwise work-heavy market weeks. More than once I'd wondered what would have happened if I'd given in to my post-pie impulse to kiss him after that innocent business dinner last May.

"So, what *are* you doing at the store so early?" I asked, wondering at the luck of running into him on my first day.

"I have some outstanding business with the buyer," he said vaguely. "The only time he had available was this morning."

"Did security make you sign in?" I asked, nodding toward the back hallway.

"Sure. They make everybody sign in before the store is open."

The bell sounded. The doors attempted to open, then jerked shut. Nick stabbed the button with his index finger and the doors repeated their spastic motion. I had the other option to take the stairs but with a breakfast of highly concentrated sugar, fat, and root beer barrels coursing through my veins that wasn't going to happen.

The doors jerked open again and I jammed the laptop between them. They beat an irregular rhythm against the plum nylon case but left a resulting opening large enough for my fingers. By now I had exerted more energy than I would have on the stairs, but I was determined to get on the damn thing.

I quickly changed my mind.

In the elevator was a well dressed man. His jet-black hair was held perfectly in place with pomade and his mustache was neatly trimmed. He wore a taupe suit with a violet windowpane pattern, a brown and purple paisley ascot knotted around his neck, and a crisp white shirt that no doubt had been laundered and starched by a team of professionals. Even though his body lay crumpled on the floor, the shirt was barely wrinkled.

Patrick.

I yanked the laptop out from between the doors. When I stood back up, the room spun. I put a hand out to steady myself and lost my grip on the computer bag. It fell from my shoulder and landed on its side. A sound escaped my lips, my knees buckled, and I followed the laptop to the floor.

2

blinked several times and tried to focus. I was sitting on a sofa in the shoe department, leaning against Nick. My fishnets were torn over my left kneecap, so I crossed my legs to hide the tear. I scanned a pile of catalogs and magazines and strained to read the covers. After spelling out V-O-G-U-E I figured the worst had passed.

Nick pulled his cell phone away from his ear. "Are you back?"

"From where?" I asked, confused by more than his question. "What happened?"

"You passed out when you saw Patrick's body."

"Is he—he's dead?"

He nodded. "I couldn't find a pulse."

"Did you call 911?"

He nodded again. "Take a couple more minutes to relax. You went down like a ton of bricks."

Considering I was on a sofa about twenty feet from the elevator doors, the analogy was more humiliating by the evidence he'd probably carried me to my present location. *Mental note: lay off the donuts.*

"I'm fine now," I said, feeling anything but fine.

The second elevator bell rung and I turned back around. The doors slid open and a thin woman in a navy uniform stepped out carrying a collapsible gurney in her hand. She stopped in front of the elevator with Patrick's body and inserted a key in the control panel. Her hat was low on her forehead and I couldn't see her face. The reflective letters EMT on the back of her nylon jacket were more jarring than white shoes after Labor Day. I wondered how long it had taken her to get there, which made me wonder how long I'd been lying on the floor like a ton of bricks.

"It's my first day. If I'm going to be late, I should call someone." I rooted around in my handbag for my phone.

The EMT adjusted the bill on her navy blue hat. She coughed twice. "Today's your first day?" she asked in a scratchy voice. "What department?"

"His," I said, pointing toward the elevator. Reality hit like, well, that clichéd ton of bricks Nick had introduced into our conversation. I turned to Nick. The room spun again and I leaned down, dropping my head between my knees, trying to head-off a second black-out.

"You really go in and out fast, don't you?" Nick asked. His hand, warm through the fabric of my satin motorcycle jacket, gently stroked my shoulders. Truth was I'd never fainted before in my life. I slowly sat up.

The woman looked at us for a couple of seconds, then knelt on the floor. She grabbed Patrick's ankles and pulled them out so the fashion director was laying in a straight line. It looked like too big a job for one person and I stood up, not sure if one of us should offer to help. The EMT log-rolled Patrick until his body was on the gurney. She snapped one end of the gurney up, then came around the other side and raised it until it was level. She moved it into the elevator before jabbing a gloved finger at the control panel.

"Wait—the cops are coming. I think."

"Nothing anybody can do about it now," she said through a second stifled cough, then pulled a tissue out of a pocket and blew her nose like a foghorn. "Heart attack. Textbook." She tipped her chin toward her neck and cleared her throat. "I'm taking him out through the sub-basement. Less disruptive that way."

"911 routed the call to you that quickly?" Nick asked.

"Nah, he must have called from his office, I guess." She held up a cell phone then put it in her pocket and coughed again. "They happen fast." She tossed a brown sheet over Patrick's body, covering the cuff of his taupe and violet windowpane pants and his purple cashmere socks. Until he was covered, I hadn't been able to look away, and I knew, long after he was wheeled off, his image would stay with me.

I turned back to Nick. "I should tell security."

"They know. They let me in," said the EMT. She kept one hand over the elevator door to keep it open.

"The executive office, then." I dialed zero on the phone that sat in the middle of the shoe department. Several rings indicated the operators had no reason to show up hours early, like I had. My legs shook while I hung up the phone.

I plunged back into the cushions of the sofa, my hand still in my handbag, closing around a half-eaten candy bar. "There has to be someone around here. I'll go to the exec offices and let them know."

"You'll have to take the stairs. I'll have the elevators tied up for a while," said the EMT. She turned the key on the control panel and the doors closed.

"Are you sure you're going to be okay?" Nick asked.

"I didn't plan on this," I blurted.

Nick sank into the sofa next to me, our knees touching. "Kidd, there's nothing you can do now. Do you want me to walk you to your office?" He held out a hand. I rose to my feet without his help and looked around the shoe department, trying to get my bearings. He followed me into the stairwell. I grabbed the dull metal banister and started up the staircase. Halfway up the third flight, his footsteps stopped.

"You said you're working in the trend office, right?"

"Yeah," I said between breaths. I turned to face him, but he was looking down the stairs, his face clouded.

"They're on the seventh floor."

"I know. I already told you, I can get there myself," I said, between short, shallow breaths. My thighs were starting to burn, and I needed a gulp of air. *Mental note: reintroduce exercise into my life.*

"I'm going back to the shoe department to wait for the cops, let them know what we saw." He jogged down three steps, stopped, turned back in my direction and jogged up five to where I stood. "Only five more flights, then you can let your heart rate go back to normal," he whispered in my ear, without a trace of breathlessness, I noticed.

"Four and a half," I said, and glared at him, largely because it was the only response I could handle without proving he was right about my heart rate.

"Good to see you again, Kidd, even under these circumstances," he said, then jogged easily back down the three flights we'd already covered.

I scaled the rest of the stairs and only barely avoided hyperventilation before entering the trend offices. Fluorescent tube lighting illuminated the space, casting distorted shadows on the piles of notebooks, slides, and posters. Two desks in the office were covered with an assortment of action figures, fabric, colored markers, drawings, and a few other items I didn't recognize. Posters of Marilyn Monroe dabbing on perfume, Warhol's tribute to Jackie O, and a concert poster of Madonna lined the walls. I wasn't sure what I'd expected of Patrick's office, but eighties pop culture wasn't it. My interviews with him had taken place on the phone and outside of Tradava, and I was beginning to think he was not what he'd seemed, when an inventive string of curse words popped off behind me.

9

"Hello?"

"Who are you?" asked a green-eyed blond guy whose skin flushed red against a glowing tan.

I answered with a question. "Did you say something?"

The stranger scratched the side of his head and left a chunk of hair sticking straight out above a glowing blue light attached to his ear. "Who are you?" he asked again.

I sat down at the desk with the Wonder Woman action figure. "I'm Samantha Kidd. The new trend specialist." I waited, wondering if he was going to say anything. "Today's my first day. And you are ...?"

He leaned against the doorframe and smiled casually, as though he knew something I didn't. Given how calm he was I would bet that wasn't true. My first impression was skateboard dude, but he had an air of maturity lacking in the guys I watched on ESPN extreme sports. His scruffy hair seemed more chlorinated than salon-dyed, and his eighties concert T-shirt looked like it came from one of those expensive vintage-reproduction stores. Either that or the laundry pile, I couldn't tell which.

He remained silent, with a lopsided smile on his face, while I tried to find a spot for my handbag. I finally leaned it against my ankles and folded my hands on top of the desk. I was on edge already and his presence unnerved me even more. Truth was I didn't know where I should be or what I should be doing or who I should be talking to.

"Don't you need to be getting to your department?" I asked.

"I can't get to my desk right now," he said.

"Why not?" I asked.

"You're sitting at it."

"Isn't this the trend office?" I hopped out of the chair as if it were wired with a shock device. The chair knocked over my bag and four tubes of near-identical pink lip-gloss rolled out by my left foot. I bent down to collect them and felt my skirt split over my right hip.

"No, that's down the hall. This is the Visual office. I'm the manager, Eddie Adams." He pulled the Bluetooth device from his ear and tossed it onto the desk. It rolled in a semicircle until it bumped up next to Wonder Woman's red and white boots.

"I'm sorry. I made a mistake," I said. I looped my handbag over my arm.

Before I had a chance to move, we were interrupted by an exotic blend of black pepper and hyacinths. A reed-thin redhead in an off the shoulder leotard, black harem pants, and geometric earrings that fell to her shoulders and tinkled like wind chimes swept past us.

"Patrick?" she called out. "Patrick?"

"Patrick isn't with us," I said tentatively. It was an understatement, to say the least.

The woman disappeared into an office further down the hall. Moments later she returned to the hallway, stopping by a small desk. She flipped through a couple of cards on a Rolodex with one black fingerless-gloved hand while the other hand fiddled with one of her earrings. An overflowing hobo bag covered in silver zippers dangled from her elbow. Files and fabric swatches spilled out of the bag. She ran her fingertip along the card in the Rolodex, then left the desk and approached me.

"When Patrick gets here, tell him we're overdue for a meeting. The competition is right around the corner and I need to know where he stands."

I studied her face. Her red hair was bone straight, cut into an asymmetrical bob. A smattering of freckles peeked out from under a dusting of powder. She looked more effortlessly stylish than I had in any of the five outfits I'd considered wearing.

"I'm sorry—" I started to say in a shaky voice.

"Patrick isn't here," Eddie filled in.

"Never mind. I'll call him later," she interrupted and left.

"Do you know who that was?" I asked Eddie.

"One of the Patrick parade. There's a steady stream of designers coming in and out of here all day. Write 'Red was here' on a message pad, and he'll either figure it out or she'll come back."

I picked up a pen. I even went so far as to write the R from Red, before my hand started shaking so badly the pen fell to the desk. "I have to get out some air," I said, and ran out of the office. I stumbled back into the store. I wasn't sure where I was going, but halfway through the lingerie department my cell phone screen lit up with an incoming call from the same number as earlier.

"Hello?" I answered.

"Samantha Kidd?" said a female voice.

"This is Samantha," I replied.

"This is Brittany Fowler. From Full Circle Mortgage? There's a problem with your application. It seems you are no longer employed, a fact we didn't know when we approved your application?" She had a way of ending her sentences with questions that made me want to answer automatically.

"Well, yes but not really," I said. I'd been so wrapped up in impressing my boss at the new job that, for the last couple of hours, I'd forgotten about life outside of Tradava. Truth was, even though I gave my notice to Bentley's I still cited them on the mortgage paperwork. Gray area, I figured, since I knew I was about to start working for Tradava. Seems gray was not the mortgage lender's favorite color.

"I have a new job. At Tradava, in Ribbon, Pennsylvania." I said, slowly circling a fixture of nightgowns. "Someone from the store was supposed to fax a letter to you a couple of days ago."

"Hmmmm," she said, in the kind of the tone that suggested she wasn't happy with my answer. I reached the end of the fixture and headed toward a display of pantyhose. "How long have you worked there?"

"I just started today." I stood rooted to the spot, in the corner of the lingerie department, and stared at the carpet.

"Perhaps we could clear this up now if we could talk to your supervisor?" she asked.

"That's not going to work. He can't verify anything." I heard a sound behind me and turned. Eddie stood next to the nightie fixture, with a middle-aged man in a short-sleeved plaid cotton shirt and baggy Wranglers.

"There she is, Detective. That's the woman you're looking for. That's Samantha Kidd."

"Ms. Kidd, I'm Detective Loncar. Get your things and come with me."

3

"**D**etective?" I asked. The phone fell to the carpet. The man in the plaid shirt stepped forward and showed me a badge. "Detective Loncar. Ms. Kidd, it's about this morning. It's important we talk. Now."

"Can we talk here?"

"No." He turned on his heel, took a step, then turned back to face me. Red-faced, I scooped the phone from the floor and disconnected the call. I returned to the trend office and collected my bag, then walked with him too close for comfort out of the store. Employees had started to arrive, milling about the parking lot, and that humiliating walk past people I hadn't even met yet would be hard to overcome. It was like the first day at a new high school; I'd never get another chance to change this first impression.

I landed in a black and white squad car, which made the detective's plainclothes an ironic choice. It was hot. I unzipped the satin motorcycle jacket and exposed the black lace camisole I wore underneath. When we arrived at the police station, I followed him through the front doors, where a small group of cops eyed my Aqua Netted hair, my camisole, my torn fishnets. I zipped the jacket back up and dealt with the sweating.

In a small office, with dirty windows and a checkerboard linoleum-tiled floor in shades of gray and gray, Detective Loncar grilled me about what had happened that morning at Tradava. Sitting in a small, stuffy office with bright light bulbs and closed windows on an unseasonably hot day would elicit a confession from anybody, only I didn't have a clue why we were there in the first place.

"Ms. Kidd, what were you doing at Tradava this morning?"

"I work there. I'm about to work there. I just moved back to Ribbon."

"So you're new in town?"

"Not really new-new but new by your standards, I guess."

"And you're new to Tradava?"

"Yes, though technically I haven't started working there yet."

He made a note on a lined notepad. Pieces of torn off paper stood out at a jagged edge from the binding. I leaned forward to read his handwriting upside down. He shifted the notepad so I couldn't.

"Tell me about this morning."

"What do you want to know?" I asked. I wasn't trying to be flip. I was scared shitless, which, I've learned, prompts me to act unnaturally obtuse.

"What did you see?"

"Patrick, in the corner of the elevator."

"Patrick who?"

"Just Patrick. He only has one name. Like Cher."

He stared at me intently and I fought every instinct to look away. "What else?"

"An EMT arrived in a separate elevator and took him out of the store through the sub-basement."

"How do you know that's where they went? Did you follow them?"

"No, but it makes sense, doesn't it?"

He made another note. "Did you notify security?"

"No, the EMT did."

"Did you call 911?"

"No, Nick did."

"Who is Nick?"

"Nick Taylor. He was there too."

"Does he work for Tradava?"

"No. He's a shoe designer."

"And he was with you?"

"He was with me, but he wasn't with-with me. Did you talk to him? Didn't he tell you about me? We should have planned this better." I uncrossed my legs, revealing the tear in my fishnets. My left leg started hammering the floor, and I crossed the right leg over it to keep it under control.

"Planned what?"

"This morning. I mean, this. Now. Not this morning. We didn't plan anything this morning!"

"Ms. Kidd, do you and Mr. Taylor have a history?"

"Yes, well, not a history-history, but I know him."

"And do you know what Mr. Taylor was doing at Tradava this morning?"

"No." The detective waited for me to elaborate. I didn't. His questions mixed me up, and the answers, to more than one of them, eluded me.

"How did you get to the trend office?"

"I climbed the stairs." He glanced at my feet. "Yes, in these shoes," I added.

"Why?"

"Because they go with the outfit."

"Why did you climb the stairs?" he repeated without missing a beat.

"Because that's where I was supposed to be."

"The job you claim you were about to start."

"I don't claim it, it's true. Ask Human Resources."

"Mr. Adams told us he never saw you before this morning when he found you at his desk."

"I didn't know it was his desk. I'd never been there before."

"But you claim you were supposed to be working there."

Ah, we were back to that.

"Ms. Kidd, can you tell me anything else about what happened this morning?"

"What exactly *did* happen this morning?" I asked. He didn't answer. "I can't help you with details, Detective. With all due respect, I passed out as soon as I recognized Patrick."

"Do you have a habit of passing out?"

"No. I don't know. I mean, not usually, but I'm not in the habit of finding my boss dead in an elevator either."

He leaned back in his chair and flipped the pen upside down. He tapped the end of it on the table in front of him. *Tap, tap, tap. Tap, tap, tap.*

Our conversation continued to go round and round, arriving close to where it had started. Nowhere. Despite a month of the kind of planning that filled notebooks by day and Post-its by night, I was about as far off-base as I could have been, and it was starting to piss me off.

"Why am I here? Patrick had a heart attack. The EMT told me. She took Patrick out of the store through the receiving dock so there would be less attention."

Detective Loncar sat very still. After an awkward amount of time, I started to count. He shifted his weight when I hit seventeen but didn't speak until I reached twenty-two.

"Ms. Kidd, there was no EMT. There was no body. You keep telling me a man died but we don't have a corpse. You're here because I heard about a 911 call from Tradava, and when I got there I found out you're the only person who was at Tradava who has no reason for being there."

"What about Nick?"

"This Mr. Taylor you mentioned?"

"Yes, him. Why was he there?"

"For now let's focus on why *you* were there."

"I work there!" I said.

He didn't have to say it this time. I knew what he was thinking.

Despite my forthcoming attitude about what little information I had to share, I left as in the dark as I was when I arrived, with the mortgage company conversation nagging at me like a bad song from the eighties I couldn't get out of my head.

It was after eleven when I was returned to the store. All of the energy I'd put into impressing Patrick on my first day was gone, like the wind had been knocked out of me the moment I saw his body. Ever since our first meeting in the parking lot outside of Tradava I had been looking forward to working with him. But now that would never happen.

I slowed as I approached the store. Crowds of people stood outside, sharing cigarettes and talking on their phones. It looked like a fire-drill, only the odds of that were low. Eddie emerged through the crowd and jogged toward me.

"You want to tell me why you left here with a detective?" he asked.

"P-P-Patrick," I stuttered.

"Patrick isn't even here."

"H-H-He's not going to be here," I said. My voice shook as the words escaped my mouth. "Ever. He's dead," I blurted. I didn't care Eddie was a relative stranger. It was a relief to speak the words to someone who had a chance of taking me seriously.

Complete silence. They're right about that pin drop thing. "Patrick? Dead? How? Where?" His head jutted forward and his eyebrows shot up. A gust of air lifted his blond hair straight up, and, for a moment, caused him to look like a startled chicken.

"In the elevator." The fresh air countered the wooziness, but I wasn't sure how much of my morning I was capable of replaying. "Didn't you notice the elevators weren't working when you got here?"

"I take the stairs."

Great. I needed comfort food and this guy was probably going to bust out into yoga moves.

"How about we get out of here and you tell me what's going on?" he asked.

Crowds of people milled around the store entrance, and pieces of their conversation floated to my ears. *Who's she? Some new girl.* I hurried in my stilettos to keep up with sneaker-clad Eddie and separate myself from the staffers eager to gossip. For the moment, "some new girl" hadn't been identified, though by the way a few of the associates looked at me, torn fishnets and all, I was climbing the list of candidates. By the time we returned, that phrase would probably be embossed on my nameplate.

"I'd rather not walk through the store again today. Not until everybody leaves."

"Even if you wanted to, you can't. They made us all leave and they won't tell us if we can get back in. Nobody knows why. Come on," he said, and led the way to a Volkswagen Beetle.

Still a bit dazed, I followed him to a diner that sat at the edge of the mall parking lot. Minutes later, Eddie bit into an egg-white omelet while I considered whether or not my stomach could handle the four pieces of bacon I'd ordered.

"I can't believe he's dead," I said as I lined up the strips of meat.

"Have you known him a long time?"

"No. Why?"

"You sound, I don't know, really shaken up."

"He's Patrick. He used to be very influential in the fashion industry."

"You sound like he meant something *to you.*"

"He did mean something to me. He was my boss."

"Today's your first day."

I didn't know how to explain the Starting Over Plan to Eddie. How do you tell an almost stranger you voluntarily gave up a high profile job in the fashion industry because you weren't sure that's what you wanted out of life? That you had done your job so well you became the problem solver for everyone, only, when your own problem became the fact you weren't happy, you had no one to turn to? That when your parents announced they were moving to Los Angeles, you did the craziest thing you'd ever done and put in a bid on your childhood house without telling your family you were the buyer? It sounded crazy to me. I couldn't imagine what it would sound like to him.

An overwhelming sense of what-have-I-done kept me silent while Eddie flagged the waitress down for more coffee.

"Deets, please," he said.

"I don't know where to start."

"Start at the beginning."

While 'the beginning' was slightly ambiguous in terms of my life, the fact remained I needed to talk to someone. I gave him the highlights of the morning and wrapped up my story with a vague comment about Patrick's crumpled body. Since my portion of the observation ended there, it seemed as good a stopping point as any.

My cell phone rang and I recognized the mortgage officer's number. As I weighed the pros and cons of answering, the waitress returned to our table. "You two work over there, right?" She tipped her head toward the window that faced Tradava. Eddie nodded. She topped off our coffee and served up a reality check. "Crazy what happened this morning. A couple of officers said a call came in about a dead guy in the store but when they went to check it out, there wasn't a body. Crackpot 911 call, they thought."

"There was a body," I protested for the second time that day. "He had a heart attack." Like the detective, she didn't seem to believe me. The phone stopped ringing and I dropped it back into my handbag. "I'm not making this up." I finished.

She tipped her head slightly but said nothing. "Sounds fishy to me." She rubbed the back of her hand across her forehead. "Think what you want, but I bet there's more to this story than any of us know."

"Like what?" I asked.

She set the coffee pot on a nearby cart and put her palms face down on the table. "Routine heart attacks don't make bodies disappear. If you saw someone take a body out of the store, then I'd be willing to bet somebody was trying to hide something. Nothing routine about that."

"Are you saying you think Patrick was kidnapped?"

"I'm saying I think he was murdered."

4

I looked at Eddie, and suddenly the waitress's words struck me. *Murdered?* The word resonated in my head. "Murdered!" I said to see if it sounded any better as a part of a conversation. It didn't.

"You said you weren't alone when you found the body. Who was with you?" Eddie asked.

"Nick Taylor."

"The shoe designer?"

"You know him?"

"We carry his collection." Eddie's eyebrow twitched slightly. "So Nick saw Patrick's body too. I hope for your sake he talked to the cops. Otherwise you'll be the sole crackpot."

The sole crackpot. Another title I wasn't itching to add to my resume. Instead of asking the detective why Nick was at Tradava I should have demanded they get him to verify my statement. They'd do that anyway, wouldn't they? For the first time since moving out of New York I wished I'd paid better attention to the crime in the city so I knew what to expect from the cops.

Eddie paid our check, and I followed him to his car. He nestled his to-go cup of coffee into the cup holder and I pulled my cell phone out and listened to the new message. "Samantha Kidd, this is Brittany Fowler. We were cut off this morning? When I called you? We need to finish our conversation. Please call me back as soon as possible." I tapped the phone against my thigh while Eddie drove us back to the store.

"If you want to make a call, make it out here. No cell reception in our part of the building."

I flipped the phone shut. "I have to talk to Human Resources first, straighten a couple of things out."

He pointed to the store, where people still stood outside. "I don't think they're letting people back in yet." He scratched the side of his head and a chunk of blond hair spiked straight out. "Go home. Take a bath, relax, pretend the last twenty-four hours never happened. Try to forget about this morning."

As much as I would have liked to do just that, Logan would have been mad if he didn't get a gourmet meal. Logan has a bit of a temper, and has been known to punish me by, well, getting funky in my shoes when I don't feed him on time. Logan, of course, is my cat. My second favorite thing besides my cat are my shoes, which says a lot about me and my priority system.

It didn't matter the stuffy air in the police station had long since turned my straightened hair to frizz, or the events of the morning had left me looking more vice squad than fashion police. I drove to the grocery store, and endured the silent judgment from the cashier that suggested black lace and torn fishnets weren't *de rigueur* in the fifteen-items-or-less lane. I was in need of a magnum of wine, a box of pretzels, an hour-long shower, and a do-over.

"I'm a very respectable person, you know," I said to her as I handed over a twenty-dollar bill. She counted out my change but said nothing. I bagged my own groceries while a couple of older customers stared at me and I wondered if my fashion sense was helping or hurting my new life. If nothing else, it was getting me noticed.

As I carried my bag out of the grocery store, I couldn't help remember the last time I sat outside the grocery store, the day I first met Patrick.

It had been the last day of my vacation. I'd spent it in Ribbon, helping my parents pack a lifetime of belongings into recycled cardboard boxes before the movers came to empty the house and transport the boxes to California. I had planned to make the drive back to Manhattan the previous night but nostalgia kicked in, big time, and instead I stayed behind by myself.

The following morning I stopped off at the grocery store before starting the drive back to Manhattan. After loading the groceries into the trunk I unloaded Logan's carrier and walked with him to the park bench in front of the store. Side by side we sat, staring at an empty parking lot of a shopping center anchored by Tradava. The parking lot was set off by the marquee of a ninety-nine cent theater, the same theater where I'd gone on my first date. Logan yowled periodically in protest of the blue plastic cage.

"It's not often you see a women in tweed and fishnets outside of the market," said in a proper voice behind me. I turned around and there stood the most nattily dressed man I'd ever seen, and working in fashion, I'd seen my share. Navy blue suit with a chalk stripe through it. Pink shirt, pink ascot, pink pocket square. Pencil-thin mustache, black pomaded hair, parted on the side.

"I'm sorry, I'm a bit of a mess." I dragged my index fingers across my under eyes to eliminate any possible mascara smudges.

"That's impossible. You cannot be a mess when wearing Chanel. It's the rule." He smiled, and the tips of his mustache pointed up with the corners of his mouth. "Patrick," he said, extending his hand.

"Samantha," I replied in like fashion, but it felt incomplete. "Samantha Kidd," I finished.

"And who do we have here?" he asked, peering into the cat carrier.

"Logan." As if on cue, the little devil started to purr.

"Tell me, Ms. Kidd, what brings a fashionista like yourself to my corner of the world?"

"I'm thinking about buying a house here." I surprised myself with the words. "My parents are selling my house. Their house. The house where I grew up."

He studied me.

"It's not even a great house. It has wood paneling and shag carpet."

"How very 1974."

"I never remembered it that way."

"What way?"

"Seventy-four."

He tipped the cat carrier back and looked down his ski slope nose into Logan's cage. A black paw pressed against the inside of the door and Patrick gently stroked it with his index finger.

"Seventy-four was a good year. The maxi skirt. Wide ties and Qiana shirts."

"Platform shoes and bell bottoms," I added.

"The Russian peasant look."

"And Halston," I added with a smile.

Patrick picked up Logan's carrier and sat next to me on the bench. "What do you do, Ms. Kidd?" he asked while he and Logan played the finger equivalent of patty cake.

"I'm a buyer. Bentley's New York. Ladies Designer Shoes." I pulled a crinkled business card out of my breast pocket and held it out, as if to prove something. He placed it in his own suit pocket without looking at it.

"Are you serious about buying the house?"

25

It had surprised me that I was, but I simply answered yes.

"Ribbon is not New York, you know."

"I know."

"Are you trying to find something you lost along the way?"

I considered his question before answering. It wasn't that I'd lost something but what I had didn't feel right. "I'd like to find my own corner of the world, I guess."

He pursed his lips and nodded slightly, as if he liked my response. "See that store?" he pointed to the white brick building that anchored the strip mall. "That's Tradava. I'm their fashion director. As it happens, I'm in need of a trend specialist."

I knew the store. It's where I had gotten the red cotton pantsuit I wore on the first day of eighth grade. It's where my mom bought the charcoal gray and neon pink outfit I had worn on that first date to the movies. It's where I picked out my white eyelet prom dress. I didn't say any of this. Instead, I said the only I could think of.

"How soon can I start?"

He threw back his head and laughed. "Samantha Kidd, I like your style. Call me tomorrow and we'll work something out." He stood up and the creases fell effortlessly from his navy blue trousers. "Pleasure meeting you."

He crossed the parking lot to the store. I waited until he was all but a moving dot that disappeared into the doors on the side of the building.

"And so goes either my savior or some nutcase," I said as much to Logan as to myself. I stood up and carried the cat cage to my car. We started the drive to New York, not knowing we'd be back in the span of a couple of weeks.

What Patrick had offered me was a fresh start. My life was like fabric in the clearance bin. Sure, some of my yardage had already been used, but there was enough left on the bolt. With a little planning, and if I cut corners, I could still make something really fabulous out of it.

My new life is about four days old, counting last Friday when I celebrated in the empty house with a large pizza and a bottle of pink champagne. Saturday the boxes arrived, along with the reality that I lived in a seventies split level house with avocado appliances and shag carpeting. Yesterday I dug through the attic to see what kind of treasures Mom and Dad had left behind while a *That Girl* marathon ran in the background.

And today I found my boss dead in an elevator.

A slight pre-autumn breeze wafted through my open car windows and washed over me as I pulled into the driveway. Crabapple trees in the front yard had blossomed and discarded soft papery white flowers now covered the ground. Miniature apples lay scattered around the base of the tree, produce cadavers to be pecked at by birds and squirrels and chipmunks running through the yard.

Inside the house, I peeled off my Day One outfit, the one I'd so carefully selected when the biggest crisis in my life had been what to wear to work, and kicked it into a corner. After a hot shower meant to rid myself of the day's bad juju, I pulled on a silk kimono, then headed to the kitchen. I checked the messages on the brown faux-wood answering machine that sat on the counter in the kitchen next to a stained Mr. Coffee machine. The only call was from the mortgage lender and it was almost exactly what she'd said on my voicemail. There was nothing for me to tell her until I straightened things out with Human Resources so I deleted the message.

While Logan swatted a felt mouse across the linoleum-tiled floor, I flipped through the mail, past credit card applications and a catalog for customized stationery addressed to RESIDENT. My mind was racing with thoughts, and now seemed like a good time to sort them all out.

What if what the waitress said was true? Patrick's body had been at Tradava. I'd seen it. But if his body had gone missing, what happened was anything but routine. Why would someone murder the fashion director? And how? Patrick had a heart attack. The EMT confirmed it before she wheeled Patrick away. She said it was textbook and I believed her, although it was my first experience with a dead body, murdered or otherwise, and it occurred to me I didn't know what textbook was.

And it occurred to me if it wasn't for my desire to change up my life, I'd still be sitting at my desk in New York, recapping the previous week's business, fielding calls from my vendors about what sold and what didn't, planning my next set of appointments to look at new shoes, and working on budgets for upcoming seasons. I'd still be Bentley's number one employee, working sixty-five hours a week, trading my personal life for an extra percentage of gross margin. If life had seemed difficult then, in all my years at Bentley's, I'd never found a dead body.

Finding Patrick's body complicated just about everything.

While the shower had taken off the vice squad stench, it provided little in the way of comfort. My plan: Haagen Dazs for dinner, except I needed more than comfort food to get through the night. I needed answers. I called Nick's number.

"Nick?" I wasn't sure why it came out as a question. "It's Samantha."

"Kidd. I'm worried about you."

"I'm okay," I said, breathless for no reason other than the sound of his voice. I wound the curly phone cord around my finger until I came to a point where a kink interrupted the coil. I unwound to my starting point and repeated the pattern, stopping at the kink each time.

I looked out at the backyard where my dad had taught my older sister Sasha how to mow the lawn with the riding mower. She was twelve at the time; I was eight. I'd watched them drive in ever-shrinking rectangles over the back yard. It looked like fun. I asked him to teach me too. *You're not ready yet. You're just a kid* he had said, laughing at my request. To this day, I over-planned everything, making sure I was ready before I did anything. *You're just a kid.* The four most defining words of my life. It was why I'd moved to New York in the first place and become such an overachiever at Bentley's, all to prove I was an adult.

"Are you still with me?" he asked, reminding me that phone conversations generally require words.

"Do you want to meet me for dinner?" I asked abruptly.

"What did you have in mind?"

The clock read seven thirty. I was in pajamas, no makeup, wet hair. I could have spent the night with Logan, a carton of ice cream, a vat of wine, and an old movie. Nobody would have been the wiser.

"Meet me at Briquette Burger in twenty minutes," I said, throwing caution to the wind.

Eleven minutes later, the doorbell rang.

I know it was eleven minutes, because it takes me exactly four minutes to apply makeup, two minutes to run the requisite amount of serum through my hair, and five minutes to blow dry my natural curls into something I can live with. That's why I was still in my kimono when I answered the door.

"Hey, Kidd," Nick called through the door. "Can I come in or are you going to let me stand out here looking like a Peeping Tom?"

"Not a bad idea." I secured the sash on my kimono with a square knot and opened the front door. I looked at him suspiciously. My brain was already filled with questions, so you'd think it was full, but apparently there was room for things like *How did you know where I live?* and *Since when does Meet me at the restaurant mean Show up at my house?*

"How do you know where I live?" I asked, trying to make my voice sound casual.

"You told me all about this house last May. Remember, we went to dinner at that little French restaurant off of 57th Street? As long as I've known you, I always knew you were good at your job. But that night was the first night I think I ever saw you come alive."

I looked down, a slow blush warming my face. "You wrote the address down on the back of your business card and I kept it. I wasn't all that surprised when I heard you bought the place." He stopped talking for a couple of seconds, and when he started again, his voice was softer. "I'll never forget the way you looked that night."

"It was the pie," I said quickly, and turned to the refrigerator to get the magnum of wine. Truth? I never expected Nick to use my address, and here he was standing in the middle of my kitchen.

I splashed a bit of wine into two juice glasses left behind in the cabinet. "Did you talk to a detective this morning?" I asked.

"Briefly. He wanted to know what I saw. If you think about it, neither one of us saw much of anything."

"I saw Patrick. Dead. I *saw* him. You saw him too. Don't pretend you didn't, Nick."

"Kidd, Patrick's corpse never made it to the morgue. And since we're the only two people who claim to have seen his body, the cops think we're the likeliest two people to be involved in whatever it is we're saying happened. And since we don't know what happened, the whole thing is a little unclear."

I put the wine back into the refrigerator and shut the door. "So then, what's the problem? If nothing happened, why do I feel like a criminal? And if something happened, where is Patrick's body?"

"I mentioned you were there, but you had passed out. I thought they might not even call you down since they might have decided your statement would be useless."

"Useless?" That comment, though sort of accurate, was the icing on the cake that had already fallen. I swirled the wine around in my juice glass and set it back down on top of an existing countertop stain. *Useless.* A new word to layer into the soundtrack playing inside my head.

"Kidd, you've had a hell of a transition in the past couple of weeks." He reached a hand out to the satin collar of my kimono and loosely ran his fingers inside by my collarbone. "I can take your mind off things, if you're willing to hear my suggestion ..." As his voice trailed off his touch ignited my skin, like an unexpected spray of grease from a pan of frying breakfast meats.

"Bacon," I said, then felt my face grow hot. His hand fell to his side and I stepped away, trying to think straight. I picked up the glass of wine on the counter and took a gulp.

"Bacon?"

"Comfort food. Let me change. You're driving." I went upstairs to put on clothes. Regardless of what I felt at the moment, this was one night where I didn't want to be alone. At least not yet.

Half an hour later, we sat in a booth at Briquette Burger. It was a small restaurant about a mile from my house. It had been renovated since I was last there, but the yellow and red sign on top of the building was as I remembered it. Inside, the first thing I noticed was a refrigerated case of freshly baked pies. I looked away before I did anything rash. We took an available booth and I ordered a cup of coffee. Nick ordered the Briquette Burger Sampler. Neither one of us mentioned bacon.

"I keep thinking I know something about this morning. That we know something. But I can't figure out what it is."

"Leave it alone, Kidd. The cops will figure it out."

"But we were there. We saw Patrick before anybody. And the EMT came from nowhere, and she had a key to take the elevator down to the basement. She seemed so, so *normal* I didn't notice anything. Did you?"

"I noticed you passed out. I noticed you never thanked me for carrying you to the sofa. And I noticed a man was dead."

"I noticed he was dead too, but nobody believes us because *his body is missing*. That doesn't get to you?"

"It's not your business. It's not my business."

The waiter interrupted our conversation with hot plates of food. We finished most of the sampler platter, leaving only the fried eggplant. Nick paid before I could reach for my wallet, and we walked to his truck in a shared silence. He opened the door for me and I stepped up onto the sideboard, then stopped, and hopped back down to the loose gravel of the parking lot. I stood to my full five foot seven inches and looked up into his soft brown eyes.

"I could have walked, you know. To the sofa. After I passed out. I don't faint. I'm not a fainter. I would have gotten up in a second and walked to the sofa. You didn't have to carry me."

"You're not very good at accepting help, are you?" He stepped backward and walked to the driver's side of the truck. When we reached my house, he walked me to the front door, even though I said I could make it. I was crashing fast, despite all of the coffee. All I wanted was to collapse in my bed, to wake up, to realize it had all been a dream.

Nick fidgeted with the remote key to his truck while I unlocked the front door. "Kidd, I think you should forget about going back to Tradava."

"I can't exactly up and quit after one day."

"What's going down there isn't your business and you'd be smart to stay out of it."

"You know something, don't you?" I said, stepping toward him.

"I know what's happening there is none of your business."

"Jobs don't grow on trees, Nick. If you don't recall, I left behind a *very* nice job in New York with this as the anchor to my future. The man who hired me is gone. He wanted me to work on his team and that's what I'm going to do." Across the street, a light went on behind closed curtains. "Thanks for dinner. See you around." I wrestled briefly with the locks, then went inside and slammed the door shut behind me. It was a solid twenty minutes later when I realized Nick hadn't told me to quit my job. He'd told me to stay out of what was going down at Tradava.

And that suggested to me he knew more than he'd let on.

5

My alarm went off as I attempted to shut out the sunlight streaming through the bedroom window. I slapped a hand on the snooze button, vaguely considered reasons not to get up, and shivered as images from the previous day assaulted me. Worse than the reality of what had happened at the store was the realization that I had to go back. Today was Day Two.

If Day One is the day friendly co-workers escort you to your destinations and you're not expected to turn in any projects, Day Two is the day you try to prove your worth and accidentally walk into the broom closet. Day Two is never better than Day One, but compared to what I had to face today, the usual Day Two issues were just the tip of the iceberg. My Day Two would put me face to face with a whole store full of people who knew I was involved in the police investigation. And there was that troubling issue about verifying my employment.

I'd fallen asleep with the window open. The heat had broken overnight, and the air was crisp. Logan curled up on my pillow while I dashed from the warm bed to the hot shower. An hour later, my curly brown hair was tamed into submission thanks to the blow dryer and a couple of pumps of serum, and my pale skin glowed under makeup. My reflection stared back at me from the bathroom mirror. I mugged to the left, then to the right, then stared directly at my reflection and stuck out my tongue.

I pulled on a pair of soft gray and lilac glen plaid pants and belted a gray tweed cape over an ivory turtleneck. With dark purple patent leather pumps on my feet, I was ready. Fifteen minutes later I sat in the parking lot outside of the store. This time I knew there was no familiar face waiting to welcome me to the department. This time I knew I was on my own.

The façades of old department stores are impressive. They tower several stories over street level, promising unique and exciting merchandise within their walls. The illusion is shattered once you've walked through a store's employee entrance. You'll never anticipate that promise of glamour again.

This particular door had been painted gray at one time. Actually it looked like it had been painted gray many times over. I knew the routine; touch-up paint was slapped on every couple of years, never matching the original color. The kick plate at the bottom showed the dings and divots of flatbeds, handcarts, and maybe the toe print of a few disgruntled employees. Inside, one bulb flickered overhead, and the linoleum tile under my feet had yellowed with age. It was like a decorator's picture of Dorian Gray; this dismal passageway for the staff counterbalanced the glamour showcased inside the store.

I approached Loss Prevention and held up both hands. "I know, I know. Visitors sign in. I should get everything straightened out today." I signed my name on the next available line on the sheet of paper clipped to the clipboard. "I'm going to Human Resources now."

"They're not here yet. Nine o'clock," said the short Latina woman. Today her hair was flat-ironed and fell in an orange-brown sheath over her shoulders.

I looked at the clock on the wall. Again, I was too early. So far, being a morning person hadn't paid off.

I didn't walk to the elevators. Instead I took the stairs up seven flights, exited near the Intimate Apparel department and walked through the doors that housed the trend offices. A hush fell over the small group of people who milled around the hallway. This time I bypassed Eddie's desk and two doors later, entered a stark space that split off into two offices. One housed a large purple velvet sofa, and one was stripped clean. This was farther than I'd gotten yesterday, but still, I'd lay odds the empty one was mine.

It was quiet in this part of the store, but I didn't mind the solitude. A stack of pink While You Were Out messages accessorized my desk. *We need to talk to you. Contact us at the precinct.* A few phone numbers followed: office, pager, and cell. The next message read *Brittany at Full Circle Mortgage. Urgent.* Three more messages followed. All were dated with yesterday's date. I crumbled them up into small pink balls and lobbed them at the trashcan. Two of the five made it.

At the moment, I was glad the trend offices were in a separate part of the store. Outside the heavy glass doors that marked the entry to this wing, the buzz of gossip would soon turn to a roar, and I wasn't up for it. Not yet. I was still a stranger in a strange land, and until I could figure out how to feel as though I belonged, I wanted to avoid the store full of curiosity-seekers.

A knock on the doorframe interrupted my thoughts. A wood sprite in a mustard yellow velvet blazer that hung down to his knees met my startled stare. Matching yellow ear buds and iPod fed tunes directly into his head. His gravity-defying hairstyle suggested a heavy gel dependency.

"Hi. I'm *Michael*." He bounced back and forth between his feet, as though he could barely control his energy while standing still. A ketchup-colored scarf hung around his neck. He could have been anywhere from fifteen to twenty-five, and I envied him the ability to project that age range.

"I'm Samantha," I offered.

"I'm a *designer*. Did Patrick tell you about me?"

"Um, no. What can I do for you?"

I didn't know if it was possible this character didn't know about Patrick's untimely death, but I was beyond contributing to the gossip chain. Anybody asking for Patrick stood out on my radar.

"I'm here for my *portfolio*."

I looked around the office. I hadn't seen any portfolios and wasn't sure where Patrick would have kept them if they really were there. "I'm sorry. I'm not familiar with Patrick's filing system."

"I am. I'll get it." He bounced away toward Patrick's office.

"Wait!" I jumped up from the desk and followed him. "You can't go in there!" I called to his back.

"Here it is," he said, holding a flat black vinyl folder zipped shut around three of the edges. He reached into his pocket and lip-balmed himself while I stood there. "Are you one of the judges?"

"Judges of what?"

"The *competition!*" I must have looked confused. "Never mind," he said quickly, and bounded toward the heavy glass doors. I stepped into Patrick's office to see if anything seemed out of order even though I didn't know what to look for.

It struck me as odd Patrick had never interviewed me at Tradava. Our first conversation had been in the parking lot and our subsequent interviews had taken place over the phone and at local restaurants. When I'd asked him if he wanted me to meet him at Tradava, he'd been evasive. "I like to keep things less formal," he'd said. "There will be plenty of time at

Tradava once I've made my decision." And when I'd pressed him about that decision, he smiled. "I chose the wrong words. Once my decision is official, is what I should have said."

"So your decision has been made?" I'd asked.

"Let me be candid, Ms. Kidd. I need someone like you at the store, someone who loves fashion for fashion's sake. Designers must look to the past to envision the future, but many are in too much of a hurry to show their own point of view they fail to learn from those who have paved the way."

It was that night my plans to move to Ribbon felt real. He all but told me I had the job. The next day he called with an offer which I accepted. We discussed start dates and I gave my notice to Bentley's. He must have notified Human Resources, gone through the proper channels, unless he was the kind of person who felt like the rules didn't apply to him. I didn't know if he was that kind of person or not. Aside from those few meetings, I didn't know much about him at all. He'd maintained a public presence over the course of his career, but who *was* he?

Idly, I opened and closed file cabinet drawers and thumbed through piles on his desk. I found a set of keys by his monitor and tossed them from one hand to the other three times before I buried them inside my handbag. On the corner of his desk sat a Rolodex. It was open to a card from a local fabric store, Pins & Needles. I flipped to the card in front and the card behind and left it where it was.

It didn't surprise me to find the spinning business card holder on Patrick's desk. He was part of what we at Bentley's liked to call the old guard, the generation who preferred their contacts to be at their fingertips versus at the click of a mouse. Names of designers now famous were scribbled on dog-eared cards along with people I'd never heard of. I wondered about each name I flipped past. Who were these people? What had they meant to Patrick's career, to Tradava, to fashion?

I left Patrick's office and went back to mine. A cardboard carton stamped with a fancy bottled water logo lay in the corner, now filled with obsolete office supplies: a battery operated pencil sharpener, carbon papers, three-ring binders with the covers falling off. Faded empty walls surrounded the room, bright squares of paint showing off where pictures had hung. The shelves alongside the desk held fashion magazines and catalogs that were a couple of years old. I doubted I was going to get any valid information from them. Unless, of course, they had been there a couple of decades, since fashion tends to repeat itself.

Next I checked out the file cabinet. A monstrous gray fixture with four deep drawers, it stood by the inside wall of the office, stacked high with piles of paper on top. The first drawer was filled with files, old army green hanging folders so stuffed with paper the metal rods were barely able to support them on their beams. The plastic labels had cracked with age and the paper that had started out white was now the yellow usually reserved for legal pads. Handwritten titles on the labels read *Spring, Summer, Prefall, Winter, Runway.* The name in the upper right corner read *Aries,* and I wondered if my predecessor had identified herself by her astrological sign.

The next drawer was in much the same state of disorganization, though the folder titles were years past. The reports were the same format; this time *LESTES* was written in standard block letters. The third drawer contained more folders like the second. There was no name on the corner of the page, but the author had not minced words when critiquing a collection. Expecting no surprises, I opened the fourth drawer, but it had been gutted of all overflow and left empty.

Looking for a distraction from the one gruesome thought that seemed to keep coming at me, I scanned an issue of the *Style Section*, the fashion industry's weekly rag, that had been left on my desk. I opened it to a page marked with a lilac Post-it. *First Ever Design Competition. Winner receives $100,000 grant to fund start-up collection, guaranteed order from Tradava, six pages featuring collection in Tradava catalog,* *and unparalleled recommendations in the fashion industry.* Patrick's name appeared at the bottom as one of the judges, along with Maries Paulson, noted icon in the industry. The Post-it said: *This competition is our number one priority. Let's make it fabulous!* I wondered who the note was for.

A few pages later a *Where Are They Now?* article quoted Patrick, whose name was circled in red marker, speaking about designers who defined previous decades and renewed interest in their labels. I flipped back to the ad for the contest. The young designer who had stopped in earlier had mentioned it. So had the redhead from yesterday. It seemed as good a project as any to sink my teeth into. I flipped through the Rolodex and found a number for Maries Paulson. Four rings later my call went into voicemail.

"This is Samantha Kidd, trend specialist at Tradava. I was hired by Patrick, and I want to offer to help with what remains to be done for the competition. You can reach me at—" I stopped. I didn't know the Tradava number off the top of my head. As I was rattling off my home and cell phone numbers, Eddie rounded the corner of my office. He set two cups of coffee on my desk and slammed his finger down on the phone, disconnecting the call.

6

"**W**hy'd you do that?" I asked.

"You are a wanted woman."

"I am not!"

"Yes, you are. People are looking for you. The cops, some mortgage company, and the head of Human Resources."

"They think I'm easy?"

"What?"

"You said I was a wanton woman."

"*Wanted*, not *wanton*." He set two cups of coffee on the desk. "Who were you calling? What are you doing here?" he demanded in a low voice.

"I'm trying to do my job." I tapped the paper with my index finger. "Patrick was one of the judges of this competition. I thought I should volunteer, you know, on behalf of Tradava. The show must go on, and all of that. Why did you disconnect the call?"

"You *don't* work here." He glanced at the open Rolodex, then to the phone, then back to me. "You're calling people from Patrick's file and giving them your home number? What the—that's like stealing company resources."

"I *do* work here, and I would have left Tradava's number only I don't know it. I have it written down, somewhere, but it wasn't in front of me, and I thought I should give my own number instead of nothing. Now I have to call back and explain why I hung up half-way through my message." I opened and shut a couple of drawers, for no reason other than I felt like a fool and wanted to look busy. "Are you going to stand there all day?"

"The standard response to someone bringing you coffee is 'Good morning' or 'Thank you', but yours works too. Less expected." He sank into the chair in front of me and pushed one of the cups in my direction.

"Why did you bring me coffee if you thought I wouldn't show up today?"

"I was hoping you'd show even if I didn't think you would."

I pulled one of the Styrofoam cups toward me. "I haven't decided yet if it's a good morning."

"Have any cops showed up to talk to you?"

"Not yet."

"Sounds like a good morning to me."

His black and white checkered Vans complemented his Devo T-shirt. Now that I had more time to take in his total look, I realized this creative surf dude didn't end up in retail fashion by accident. He had an eye for details. I'd bet his long board matched his wetsuit.

"You don't remember me, do you?" he asked. He sat back in his chair and watched me watch him. He crossed one checkered shoe over the knee of his other leg and pulled his ankle up until it rested mid-thigh.

I studied his face, his body language, his demeanor, all the while repeating his name inside my head. *Eddie Adams ...Eddie Adams ...Eddie Adams ...*

"We graduated high school together." He raised his coffee cup toward me as though in toast. "I was only there for the end of senior year. I didn't get to know many people. Check your yearbook."

"The math test?" I asked, as a memory clicked into place. He nodded.

Eddie had been the new kid at school, starting halfway through senior year. There was a test in Calculus, and he scored the highest score. So had the captain of the football team, sitting to his left. Rumors that Eddie cheated started almost instantly. And, being the new kid, there was no one to come to his defense.

That was the year I sat in the back of the class. I'd been stumped on the seventh test question. So, instead of concentrating on my own exam, I'd been staring out at the classroom, watching everyone else scribble numbers and math symbols on the pages in front of them. And I saw him copy the answers from another student's test.

Not Eddie. The football player.

He'd just gotten a full scholarship to college. Getting caught cheating would have cost him his future. He did it anyway, and got away with it, and Eddie got suspended. I went to the principal's office three days later, told him what I saw, and demanded something be done. The school readministered tests to both boys. Again, Eddie scored well. He came back and finished out the year, and went on to art school. I'd asked the principal to keep me out of it, and I remember not knowing if Eddie had ever suspected I was the one who came forward with the truth, at least until months later when I read what he'd written in my yearbook. He was the last person to sign it, because I didn't want anyone else to know what I'd done.

The football player failed. And though I never told a soul what I'd done, I'd gained a lot of satisfaction in doing the right thing. You work hard, you get what you deserve. That lesson followed me my whole life.

"You stood up for me," Eddie said. An assorted bunch of miniature Sharpies dangled from a turquoise D-clamp he'd hooked to a belt loop on the side of his jeans. He jiggled the foot on his knee and the Sharpies clacked against each other like a colorful set of plastic janitor's keys. The yellow one popped off and landed on the floor.

"Have you been in Ribbon since high school?" I asked.

"I landed this job out of college. I've been here ever since."

A part of me wanted to push aside thoughts of Patrick's murder, the cops, the mortgage company, and Human Resources to get lost in our reunion, but before I could word the questions in my mind, Eddie tapped my cell phone with the bottom of his coffee cup.

"Weren't you listening yesterday? No reception." He glanced toward the ceiling. "These offices were never meant to be anything more than temporary. You won't get a signal. And store policy says you can't have one on the selling floor. Looks bad to customers."

I chucked my phone back into my handbag and peeled the top off my coffee, a puff of steam hitting my face. With full knowledge it was too hot to drink, I took a sip. Burnt my tongue. Patience is not my strong suit. Finally, I spoke. "Are you sure you want to be seen talking to me?"

"It's better than talking to Patrick's assistant, if you know what I mean."

"Who is Patrick's assistant?"

He gestured toward the balls of pink messages that accessorized the floor surrounding the trash can. "The guy who took the messages yesterday."

I wasn't following.

"Michael Dubrecht? The swishy guy who was here this morning?"

"He was here yesterday? I never even saw him." I sighed. "See, that's probably the kind of thing the cops would want to know."

"They do. They came around yesterday, talked to everyone who was here. Anybody here before eight thirty was

44

questioned. They closed the store so nobody could get in after that, and store management was pissed when they heard nothing actually happened. Significant loss of business."

I'd angered Store Management. I wondered how regularly they checked in with Human Resources about things like this.

"Do you remember anything?" he asked.

"Nothing more than I remembered yesterday."

He shrugged out from under the messenger bag still hanging across his shoulder and set it on the floor next to the errant yellow Sharpie.

"I think you know more than you think you know."

"I can't see how."

Eddie sipped his coffee. I mirrored his action, waiting for his questions to start. He set his cup down and leaned back, folding his arms across the Devo logo on his shirt.

"So are you going to tell me why you're really here?" he asked.

I froze, mouth filled with hot coffee, barely able to swallow. I coughed a few times after choking it down, and glared at him with wide, water-filled eyes. My twice-burnt tongue clumsily formed a retort.

"Here, where?"

"Here, Tradava, today, of all days."

"I told you. It's my job. Patrick hired me. Just because he isn't around doesn't mean I'm not going to show up for work. Maybe hiring me was his last wish."

Eddie bent down to retrieve the yellow Sharpie. "What's your background?" His voice came from somewhere by my feet.

"Shoe Buyer at Bentley's New York."

He sat back up and whistled. "Nice. You travel much? Go to runway shows?"

"Some."

"I'm not buying it." He tapped his palms on the rubber elbow rests of the desk chair.

"I'm not so sure I'm trying to sell something."

"You're telling me you left behind a buying career in New York to move to Ribbon? You traded flying to Paris and Milan for this? We're not exactly the fashion capital of eastern Pennsylvania, and Tradava is not exactly in the same category as Bentley's." He gulped from the coffee cup. "Nope, I'm definitely not buying it."

"Wait a minute." I leaned forward and grabbed my cell phone.

"No, seriously, people don't just up and leave jobs like that without good reason."

"Not that, this! You said there's no reception in here."

"You're a quick one, aren't you?"

"The elevators are right outside of the office. If Patrick was having a heart attack in here and tried to call 911 from a cell phone, the call wouldn't go through."

"True."

"Yesterday the EMT held up a phone and said Patrick called emergency himself. She was lying!"

Eddie slammed the palm of his hand down on the desk. "I knew it. I *knew* you knew more than you thought! What else do you remember?"

"I don't know." I stood up from the chair and started pacing around the office. "After I realized Patrick was dead I sat in one of the sofas in the shoe department with Nick. The emergency tech put a brown wool blanket over the body."

"How much time passed?"

"I don't know." I stole a glance at him.

"Estimate."

"I really don't know. I, um, passed out."

"No way."

"Way. And now I don't know what happened."

"You remembered that cell phone bit. You better tell that to the cops."

Eddie finished his coffee; I pretended to let mine cool. I wasn't eager to field more questions, especially now that I had information to share with the police.

"How long have you known Nick Taylor?" he asked next.

"Years. I bought his collection for Bentley's. We were kinda friendly, until recently."

Eddie gave me a knowing look. "Kinda friendly? Is that code for 'We were sleeping together' or 'we had a flirtatious business association'?"

"That's a little personal, don't you think?" My face grew hot. Truth was, our business relationship precluded anything other than dinner and the occasional two cheek kiss. Romances between vendors and buyers were seriously frowned upon at Bentley's so regardless of what I'd daydreamed about on that flight over Paris, I had accepted our relationship for what it was.

"So you had a flirtatious business association. What was he doing here?"

"He said he had a meeting."

"I wonder who with? The shoe buyers are all in New York for market week."

He was right and I should have known that. If I were still at Bentley's, I'd probably be in the middle of a tight schedule of showroom appointments trying to cull together next spring's assortments. That life felt more like a distant memory than something I knew.

"Besides, Tradava dropped Nick's shoe collection based on poor reviews. I heard the advertising team talking about it at a meeting last week."

"Would Patrick have written those reviews?" I asked, wondering again about Nick's cryptic warning.

"Maybe," he said. "But back to my earlier question, how well do you really know him? Have you guys spent time together outside the office? Do you know what kind of person he is?"

I wasn't sure where he was going with this so I followed along. "Occasionally we went to dinner together, but it was always business-related." *Ish,* I added to myself. "I don't know his deep dark secrets or anything."

"You think Nick Taylor has deep dark secrets?"

"Everybody has deep dark secrets. What do you mean?" I asked.

"Okay, does he know your deep dark secrets?"

"No. I mean, I don't have any, I mean," I paused, then gave up trying to defend my own secret-less life. "What's your point?"

"What was he really doing here yesterday morning when most people weren't even at work yet? Was it a coincidence he was with you when you found Patrick's body?" Eddie continued. "How much time transpired between you passing out and him calling the cops?"

"You're implying Nick had something to do with Patrick's death." I shuddered when I heard my words. "Why do you think that?"

Eddie sank his head into his hands. Chunks of blond hair stuck out between his fingers.

"I don't know." He leaned forward with interest. "You were at the scene of the crime. You were on hand for vital clues and important details no one else except Nick saw."

I remained silent. *It's only your second day on the job,* I told myself. What I wanted was for the rest of the day to go off without any more unexpected hitches, straighten out the hiring situation, and discover some trends. Nobody had warned me crimes of fashion were to be a part of my job.

Finally, I spoke. "I keep thinking I should remember something, but I don't."

"Are you sure you don't remember anything about that morning? Anything that seemed out of the ordinary?"

"It was my first day of work. I found a dead body. Belonging to the person who hired me. Whose body is now missing. What part of that *is* ordinary?"

"Good point."

I stood up and shook my left leg until the creases in my pant leg released. "I can't think about this now. I have to go to HR and get the hiring straightened out."

"You better be prepared to talk about what you saw, especially if you want them to move past the fact that you're the one who got the store shut down during business hours. It's going to come up." He tapped the desk in front of me. "Go through it with me, one more time."

I launched into my story for the millionth time: the elevator doors, the body, the EMTs, the cell phone, and the quick exit through the basement. And then I remembered something else.

"The computer."

7

"**W**hat computer?" Eddie asked.

"Patrick loaned me a computer, a small laptop, after he hired me. It's in a plum nylon case."

"Patrick didn't have a laptop. Patrick wouldn't know what to do with a laptop. He took notes. Longhand, and had Michael transcribe them."

"Then whose computer did he loan me?"

Eddie shrugged. "Why did he loan you a computer?"

"He wanted me to get a briefing on his current projects. He arranged to hand it off to me in the parking lot."

"Why didn't you just come up for it?"

"I don't know. He specifically said I didn't need to come to the trend offices. This was two days before I was supposed to start."

We stared at each other, processing what this might mean. I wasn't willing to accept the obvious answers. "How do you know Patrick didn't have a laptop?"

"He might have had a laptop, but it didn't belong to Tradava. Everybody in corporate got new desktop computers six months ago. There's that," he jerked his thumb in the direction of the office, "and a BlackBerry. All the directors and veeps got them. Anyway, people like Patrick aren't tech savvy. Did you look at it? What was on it?"

My breakfast of cold Pop-Tarts that I ate in the car flipped over in my stomach. I'd read over his newsletters, checked out his calendar, but other than that, nothing had struck me. But what if there was something else on the hard drive I was supposed to discover? And where was it now?

I pulled Detective Loncar's card out of my wallet and dialed.

"Loncar," he answered.

"Detective, it's Samantha Kidd. You said I should call you if I remembered anything else, and I did."

"Ms. Kidd. Where are you?"

"I'm at Tradava."

"What are you doing there?"

"I work here." Why was everyone having such a hard time with that fact? "Detective, Patrick loaned me a laptop I had the morning he died, but I don't know where it went." I waited for his response. There was nothing, for several seconds. Enough nothing for me to ask, "Hello? Are you still there?"

"Ms. Kidd. First you said there was a body, which we haven't seen. Then you said there was an Emergency Technician, who we haven't identified, and now you say there was a computer that went missing. Plus, you claim to have employment nobody can verify."

"I'm not making this stuff up, Detective. I'm *trying* to be helpful."

"Hold on, ma'am," he said. Instinct told me now was not the time to tell him I was too young for him to call me that. "Ms. Kidd, why don't you come down to the Human Resources department on the fourth floor? Maybe we can clear up a couple of things."

"You're in the store?" I asked. After confirming that fact, I hung up and faced Eddie. "I'm going to HR. I'll be back in a sec."

I took the stairs down to the fourth floor and exited the stairwell by Human Resources. Detective Loncar stood talking with a woman with a gray pixie haircut. A chunky blue necklace hung around the neck of her Nehru-collar shirt. Perfect timing, two birds, one stone, and all that.

I stepped around the side of the escalators. Their words were quiet but so was the store.

"She's on her way down. She said she works here."

"I don't know what she wants or why she keeps returning, but we have no record of her interviewing here, let alone working for us. These awful things she keeps saying about Patrick, about him being dead, well, I don't know why a person would make such gossip up, but it's disturbing. Her presence yesterday morning seems as suspicious to us as it does to you."

I leaned back against the wall, suddenly lightheaded and dizzy. The ground shifted under me in an unexpected bout of vertigo. I peeked back around the corner. The detective checked his watch, then scratched his head behind his ear. "I'll take her to my office and we'll see if we can't figure out what she's up to. Let's wait inside, I don't want to scare her away."

Too late for that, detective. I was three feet from the down escalator, as soon as they stepped into the office, I sidestepped to the escalator, picked up the stairs on the third floor, and bypassed the security entrance for the customer doors that faced the lot where my car was parked.

I broke all kinds of speeding laws driving home. I sat in the driveway with the windows down, breathing deeply the scent of withering lilac buds that barely clung to branches on the bushes alongside the house, willing my thoughts and my racing heart to calm down, already. I pulled my cell phone out and called Nick. The one person who knew there had been a body.

My call went into voicemail and I left a message. "It's Samantha. It's—" I pulled the phone away from my ear to check the time but couldn't see it because a second call was coming through. Brittany Fowler needed to get a life. I put the phone back to my ear. "It's important. Call me when you get a chance. I need to talk to you."

I went into the house and pressed the play button on the answering machine.

Beep! "Hey Kid, it's your mom. Just wanted to check in on you and see how you were doing. Things are good on the west coast. We're going to the beach now so don't try to call us back. Love you!"

Beep! "Hello, Ms. Kidd, this is Maries Paulson. Please call me at your earliest convenience. I'd like to meet with you to discuss Tradava's role in the upcoming designer competition."

Beep! "This is a courtesy call is for Samantha Kidd. This is the video store. You have an overdue rental. Please bring the movie back to avoid accruing late fees."

Beep! "Ms. Kidd, this is Brittany Fowler from Full Circle Mortgage. Can you call me back today please? I really have to talk to you about this application."

A lot of people wanted to check in on me. People I didn't necessarily want to talk to. The best way to avoid any additional calls was to avoid the phone. I grabbed the movie, left my cell phone on the counter on purpose, and locked the door behind me.

I needed something familiar. I drove to the strip mall with the video store and left the car running while I dropped the DVD case into the wall slot. Instead of pulling out of the lot, I sat in an empty space and inhaled the scent of lunch meat coming from the hoagie store three doors down.

They didn't have strip malls like this in New York. Where at special times of the year like now the air was perfumed with the scent of Capicola, Provolone cheese, and lilacs. I turned off the engine and followed the scent to the counter of the sandwich shop where I ordered a hoagie big enough for two: twelve inches of hard roll seasoned with oil and oregano, and filled with four different kinds of lunchmeat, Provolone cheese, lettuce, and onion. I snagged a large bag of potato chips and a carton of iced tea and stepped to the register to pay. My appetite may have been slightly larger than my stomach, but I needed that sandwich. It might clog my arteries, but it would clear my brain. And at the moment, clarity was what I needed. No distractions like missing bodies or untimely police visits or angry mortgage companies—

"I see you got your appetite back," said Nick from behind me.

I turned around and searched my crowded mind for a comeback but didn't want a repeat Bacon incident so I kept my mouth shut.

He looked as good in a crisp white shirt and jeans as he did in a suit. Before he could make another comment on the size of my lunch, the cashier reclaimed my attention with the total. The twenty in my wallet would barely cover it. I hoped against hope the flush warming my face was not apparent.

"Looks like if I want to spend some quality time with you I'll have to kidnap you from the hoagie store."

"Wouldn't want you to commit a felony," I said, perhaps too quickly.

"Fine, then I'll kidnap your lunch." He snatched the bag from the cashier who thought he was being playful. "Play along, and nobody gets hurt," he said in a low whisper. He placed a firm grip on my elbow and steered me out of the sandwich shop before I could respond.

8

"What do you think you're doing?" I asked.

"You're coming with me." He held up the bag. "Insurance."

We left the store, Nick holding my lunch hostage. He turned to the right. We walked down the sidewalk together in silence, approaching the video store. For a brief moment I wondered if he was going to turn me in for harboring stolen movies, but when we passed it, and his fingers continued to bite into my upper arm, I wondered something worse.

We passed three additional storefronts before he paused in front of a vacant one. "In here. This place looks deserted." He handed me the bag of food and pulled a credit card from his wallet. "I'll pop the locks open so we can get inside. Nobody will even know we're here."

Panic set in. He was right. Not only did nobody know we were there, but nobody knew I was with him. I tried to remain calm on the outside, but inside I freaked out. What did I really know about Nick aside from what I'd picked up when we worked together? I mean, how many shoe designers actually know how to pop open a locked door with a credit card, and how many have the guts to do it during business hours?

His choice of words hammered an ominous refrain inside my brain. *No one will know we're here. I'll kidnap you. You're coming with me. Insurance.*

He was having trouble with the lock. Daydreams while flying over Paris notwithstanding, I knew if I was going to get away it would have to be now. My weapons for defense were limited: a carton of Icy Tea and a hoagie.

I pulled the carton of tea from the bag and took a step back on the sidewalk. My foot hit the edge of the curb and I lost my balance. I fell backward, dropping the food. Nick turned and grabbed me, his bear-claw hand easily circling my small wrist. He held tight while my feet sought stable footing. The carton exploded on the sidewalk and instantly the air was scented with lemon. I planted one foot underneath me, then the other. His grip relaxed. He bent over and picked up the bag of food. A puddle of brown liquid seeped onto the sidewalk and headed for the toe of his brown oxfords. He sidestepped the stream and handed the Visa card to me.

"Kidd, relax. If it bothers you that much I'll use the key." He fumbled around with the change in his pocket, pulled out a key, and unlocked the door.

I was confused. He held the door open, but I didn't move. I looked around the inside of the vacant store, but all I could see were stacks of white boxes along the back wall. Shoe boxes.

"They're not going to bite, you know," he said. I couldn't be sure, but it seemed like he was more nervous than I was.

I looked inside again. I still wasn't 100 percent sure we should be there, but I was at about 85 percent. Before I dropped the tea I was only at about 35 percent, so things were going the right direction. Curiosity trumped caution.

Nick looked somehow different than he had at the hoagie store, or at Tradava, or even out front. He looked proud. He turned away from me and looked at the walls, the floor, the ceiling. His hands were in his front pockets, jiggling his change. He faced me. "Your opinion means a lot to me."

"My opinion about what?" I asked.

"My new showroom."

He placed his hand on the small of my back and guided me inside. It dawned on me slowly that there were a lot of things about Nick I didn't know, not the least of which was why he'd been spending so much time in Ribbon. When we stopped, the time seemed right to ask some questions.

"Your new showroom?"

"Yes. Well, satellite showroom. Satellite showroom slash store. Imagine it like this," he said, and stepped forward. "A desk up front, white laminate." He walked to the middle of the room. "Tables here and here." He waved his hands to either side, "so buyers can work the collection. I picked up two dozen frames from an art supply store. After I paint them, they'll go on the walls around display shelves so I can showcase my samples."

"White?"

He nodded. "Yellow rod lighting by the ceiling, to give the place a glow. I can't decide about the floor. White carpeting, which might be a nightmare, or exposed cement."

"Hardwood. White wash it."

"Tom Sawyer-style?"

"Why not?"

"It's not a bad idea."

I joined him in the middle of the room while he looked around. "Why Ribbon? Why now?"

"A lot of reasons, actually. It's cheaper. It's not that far of a drive from New York City, and I show at the market center when I'm there. My collection has always done well here, and now that I've scaled back my distribution, it seemed a natural to start small. Thanks to stores like Tradava, there's name recognition, a built in audience. And my dad's here, alone, since my mom passed away."

"Did Patrick know about this?" I blurted out.

"Yes." He looked back and forth between my eyes and his brows pulled together, as though he was calculating a really big tip. I waited for him to elaborate, but he didn't. Instead he covered a bare patch of carpet with sheets of white tissue paper, then set the lunch in the middle like a picnic. "He's the one who suggested it. I'm not sure if it's the right decision. Some people think I'm making a big mistake." He pinched the Visa card and pulled it out of my hand, then tucked it back into his worn brown leather wallet. "Even when I use the keys I feel like I'm breaking and entering."

I took a step in his direction and squeezed his hand. "I think you made the right decision. You're a talented designer. There's no way you won't succeed."

He looked down at me and squeezed back. "I had a feeling you'd like it." My stomach rumbled again, removing all sentiment from the moment. "Enough about my business. Let's get you fed. I don't want to be the person who stands between you and that hoagie."

We sat down on the floor and split my sandwich. He didn't seem to be concerned his showroom was going to smell like potato chips and Capicola, so I didn't point it out. Our lunchtime conversation covered the details of his new venture. Countless business dinners had taught me he favored a martini during the social hour, had eyes the color of milk chocolate fondue, and vacationed in Hawaii once a year, but they left me short on his creative aspirations. Other than casual business conversation and the occasional innuendo, I didn't know much about him, a small fact I'd rarely considered until I realized I thought he was capable of kidnapping me.

"So this is it. A store with my name on the front," he added.

"That you are incapable of breaking into."

"Apparently I'm not cut out for a life of crime."

"So you keep telling me." I raised an eyebrow.

"Seriously, I felt bad about what I said last night, when I told you to stay away from Tradava. It might have sounded like I was lecturing you."

"As a matter of fact, it did."

"Let's talk about something else."

I bit into a potato chip with a snap. "Are you nervous?"

"Nervous? Sure. But excited too."

"But what if ..." My voice trailed off. I was knee-deep in my own sea of self-doubt and wanted to know I wasn't alone.

He looked down at my hands, crumbling the chip. "If it's important, you make it work, right? I know there'll be a lot of challenges along the way, but you do what you have to do. If something gets in the way, I'll deal with it and move on. That's what you should do."

His words hit me harder than I expected. My throat tightened and my face got hot. I stared down at the chip bag, letting my hair fall forward. *Move on.* I didn't want to move on. I wanted to make this work. Why didn't he understand that?

"Do you have a restroom?" I asked abruptly.

"Sure. Back of the store, to the right."

I stood and smacked my hands against each other, showering the tissue paper with tiny potato chip flakes. I passed the piles of shoe boxes and a closet-sized reception nook and entered a small office that smelled like cookies. I scanned the desk and spotted a Vanilla-scented plug-in air freshener. A navy blue blazer hung from the back of a chair. There were no signs of a restroom around. I started to back track, when I spied a familiar plum laptop bag on the floor of the office next to the desk chair.

Nick had Patrick's computer.

I bent sideways at the torso, in the kind of limbering-up waist exercises common on aerobics videos, checking that Nick was still out front. He was. I extracted the small laptop from the bag and looked around for a way to smuggle it out of the store.

"Kidd?" he called out. Shit. I flipped my tweed cape up and shoved the flat computer into the back of my waistband. My pants, now fighting both stolen office equipment and an unhealthy amount of lunchmeat, dug into my waist. When I rounded the corner, Nick stood in the doorway, talking to a pretty brunette. I pressed myself against the wall and strained to overhear their conversation.

"Will I see you tonight?" she asked.

"Not tonight. Something came up. Tomorrow?"

"I don't know if I can wait that long. You can't change your plans?"

"I don't think it would be a good idea. She doesn't know about us yet and that's a good thing."

Behind me, the door to the restroom slammed shut thanks to an unexpected cross breeze. Nick and the young woman turned toward the noise and I ducked into the reception area. The laptop wedged in the back of my waistband shifted lower into my tights. I had to get out of there.

When I returned to the showroom, Nick was alone. "You okay?" he asked.

"You have a lot of nerve, Taylor," I said. "First you warn me to quit my job, then you take my lunch, then you pretend we're all friendly, but clearly, we're *not*."

He leaned against the wall and smiled. The crinkles in the corners of his eyes made him look infuriatingly good. "What did I do this time? Put the toilet paper on the roll the wrong way?"

I was in no mood for his playfulness. I stormed past him to the makeshift picnic and loosely wrapped the rest of the hoagie in wax paper then shoved it into my handbag. Whereas I would have liked to depart on a highly witty note, brevity and the computer in my pants won out. "See ya around, Taylor."

I headed toward the door but Nick jogged past me and blocked my path. He wore confusion like a Halloween mask that distorted his features, and I vowed at that moment not to trust his facial expressions.

"Did I miss something?" he asked.

"No more than I did," I replied cryptically. I was *this close* to confronting him, but it seemed more important to get it home, to see what I was intended to see in the first place, before letting him know I was onto him.

He opened the door, allowing me room to pass. I concentrated on the tea stain on the sidewalk out front instead of making any more eye contact.

"So, when I see you at the Tradava Gala on Sunday, will we be past this, or not?" he called to me as I stormed past him.

"The what?" I asked.

"The Designer's Debut Gala at the museum. You're going, right?"

"Wouldn't miss it for the world," I said as I unlocked my car.

Now, I just had to figure out what the hell he was talking about.

B ack at my house, the leftovers went in the fridge and the laptop went on the dining room table. The beauty of the hoagie is that, unlike a new job, it's just as good on Day Two. The machine blinked with a second round of messages.

Beep! "Hello, Ms. Kidd, this is Maries Paulson. Please call me at your earliest convenience."

Beep! "This is a courtesy call for Samantha Kidd. This is the video store. You returned an empty box to the store. Please bring the movie back to avoid accruing additional late fees."

Beep! "Yo, it's Eddie. Hit me back when you get a chance." He left his number on my phone.

Beep! "Ms. Kidd, this is Brittany Fowler. If you don't contact me to resolve the issues regarding your mortgage, I'll have no choice—" I pressed delete mid-sentence.

I returned Maries' call first, and almost immediately, a sultry, scotch-and-cigarettes voice came on the line.

"Ms. Paulson, this is Samantha Kidd," I said. "I work in the trend office with Patrick. Worked," I corrected myself, cringing. Good thing she couldn't see my face.

"Ms. Kidd, how may I help you?"

"In light of Patrick's—in light of what happened, I wanted to offer my help with the competition, and with the Gala," I added as an afterthought.

"You mentioned in your message yesterday you worked with Patrick. Do you know where he is?"

"You don't know?" I asked, shocked. But of course she didn't know. According to everyone but me, there was nothing *to* know. But I knew. I knew what I saw. I didn't want to talk about it anymore, but it was a fact, nonetheless.

"I know we are facing a string of very timely deadlines and I've been unable to reach Patrick for the past three days. Are you acting on his behalf? Did he share his thoughts on the competition with you?"

"Only briefly," I said, looking at the computer on my kitchen table. Patrick had a file at Tradava and notes on the computer. Surely I'd be able fake my way through enough knowledge to pass as a professional. And if Maries treated me as though I worked in the trend office, then Tradava would have less reason to doubt my claims of employment. All in all it was a pretty sub-respectable bit of self-negotiating. I wasn't exactly proud of myself. "I'll be working from home for the next few days, but I'm available to help with whatever you might need," I finished.

She took down my address and phone number and promised to be in touch.

I took off my cape and draped it over the back of the kitchen chair, then booted up the laptop and went directly to the file manager. Patrick had mentioned the competition when he handed over the computer. I thought back to that conversation.

"Tradava has indulged me with an annual design competition, and it's my top priority. This will be the first time we've attempted something on this scale. We've invited residents within a sixty-mile radius of Ribbon's epicenter to show us what they're made of, or rather what their wardrobes are made of."

"Do you want to brief me on the competition?"

"I don't want to bore you with the mundane details of orchestrating this project. My hope is to discover a talent within our city, put Ribbon on the map."

"Do you think anybody will pay attention? Ribbon is not New York, you know," I said, repeating the same thing to him he had said to me in the parking lot in front of Tradava the morning we met.

"I believe the hundred thousand dollar prize will make people pay attention." He handed off the small laptop and I was on my way.

A series of folders lined the left side of the screen. The first folder contained old files of Patrick's trend newsletter. I'd read them a few nights ago but perused them again in case I had missed something, though I was still not sure what I was looking for. I discovered little more than Patrick's droll take on the demise of couture, and his *bon mots* of commentary about such pressing issues as the hemline to high heel ratio advisable for the modern woman.

The second folder was titled RUNWAY, and, as expected, contained slides and background information for different runway shows. I sifted through additional files for travel expenses and budgets for the office, along with a few spreadsheets that projected how much inventory Tradava owned in different trends, and how much volume they anticipated from these of-the-moment categories.

As I clicked around the excel file, I couldn't help think about what it would have been like to work for him. We'd talked for close to an hour about fashion week and going to "market", the frenzied window of time when designers launched their collections each season and opened the doors to their showrooms for buyers to place orders. He had lit up when we talked about the fast pace of the New York fashion industry. Patrick had been a fixture on the New York runway circuit until sometime in the eighties when he left the Big Apple and took the position as Fashion director at Tradava. Though he didn't share his own reasons for changing his life, he was the first person who appeared to accept my decision to change mine, no questions asked. I selfishly wished I would have had the chance to work with him, to carve my own niche out of the trend office at Tradava as part of his team.

The doorbell distracted me from my research. I closed the laptop and pulled a couple of newspapers over it. An elegant woman draped in black stood on my front porch. I recognized her immediately and opened the door.

"Ms. Kidd?" she asked. I nodded. "Maries Paulson." She swept past me, a cloud of cashmere and Chanel No. 5. Oversized black sunglasses obscured most of her face. She did not take them off. Her head was covered with a turban that looked so chic I wondered if it were time for the style to made a comeback.

"I hope you don't mind the unexpected visit. I'm more troubled by Patrick's absence than I led you to believe. I can't believe he'd leave me, our competition, with so many details left—"

"Ms. Paulson, Patrick didn't abandon you, at least, not by choice."

I explained what happened on Day One at Tradava. Out loud, it sounded crazy, but Maries didn't act like I was insane. She pulled a white monogrammed hankie out of her quilted Dior handbag and dabbed at her eyes under the large black sunglasses.

"May we sit?" she asked. I gestured to the kitchen and she led the way.

"I'm sorry. Patrick was a dear friend of mine. He was an amazing man. I'm sure you knew that."

"I actually didn't know him well. You—you believe me, don't you? Why do you believe me? Nobody else does."

"Ms. Kidd, Patrick anticipated something like this would happen. He received a couple of threats and alerted the police."

"What kind of threats?"

"Threats to cancel the design competition, that something would happen if he didn't."

"What kind of something?"

"He never said." She pulled the glasses off and for a moment she focused on me as if for the first time. The eyebrows were drawn on and the lipstick was as red as a tomato-shaped pincushion. Her bright blue eyes appeared muddled through the tears that pooled in her lower lids. I'd place her in her seventies, but I was guessing she'd deny it vehemently.

"The police paid him little mind." She adjusted her cashmere wrap. "If the police kept that information from you, it only means they are worried about how they will look in the eyes of the public when the news becomes common knowledge."

Admittedly I've had very little experience with death and consolation. I remained silent while she composed herself, still wondering what had brought her to my door. I offered her a glass of iced tea, which she accepted.

"He saw himself in you, you know," she said.

"He talked to you about me?"

"You impressed him, and that's not easy to do."

I looked at the pile of newspapers on the kitchen table. Thankfully, the laptop was out of sight. I didn't want Maries to know so soon after her friend's death I was trying to break into his files, especially after learning I'd impressed him.

"I wonder if you would consider looking into his murder?"

"I think the police should do that," I said automatically.

"Simply put, the police don't understand the intricacies of the fashion world like we do."

"What makes you so sure he was murdered? As far as I know, the police haven't found his body. Maybe they're right. Maybe he orchestrated the whole thing because he needed to get out of town."

She reached inside her handbag and pulled out an interoffice envelope. "What happened to Patrick is only the beginning." She pulled a stack of applications out of the envelope and set them on my table. "Patrick and I were judges of a design competition. This, you know. These are the applications and profiles of the contestants. I have reason to believe the killer may be one of those people."

"Then you have an obligation to turn this over to the police," I said, pushing the pile back toward her.

"Ms. Kidd, you're being myopic." She pulled her glasses down a second time and touched the inside corner of each eye with a tissue. "I suppose, if I want you to see the big picture, I should share with you a bit about Patrick's past, about what brought him to Tradava."

She leaned back. Her black cape flowed over the arms of the chair. For all of her presence, she appeared exhausted. I sat in one of the other chairs and leaned forward.

"Patrick was a legend for a very long time, until one day, he was not. There came a point when his opinion was no longer relevant. sensed it. He knew he was becoming a dinosaur."

"Is that why he moved to Ribbon?"

"He chose to re-envision his role in the industry he loved. By moving to a smaller town, to Tradava, he chiseled out a new home for himself. No one with his credentials had ever worked for Tradava. He was a big fish in a little pond and at that point in his career, it suited him."

Big fish, little pond. Patrick and I had talked about the same thing during one of our interviews. *Find a way to remain relevant and you can live the life of your dreams,* he had said.

"When Patrick first dreamed up the competition, it was a way for him to be a voice again. To help the next generation of designers. I've been asked to judge many a competition over the years, and I've always said no. The only reason I said yes this time was because of Patrick. I owe my career to him."

She paused to take a sip of tea. The ice cubes clanked around in the glass. "He approached Tradava and they agreed to underwrite the competition and the reward. He convinced them it would be a great way to get out from their current reputation as a mass-market retailer, and claim a portion of the fashion trade he so loved. Part of the reason they had hired him was to bring his cachet to the store, and I'm sure he felt he must deliver on the promise of his connections."

"But what happened?" I interrupted.

"As the economy took its toll on the store's business, the board of directors determined they couldn't foot the bill for what Patrick had in mind. They pulled out, but he wasn't willing to let it go. He procured funding from another source, and Tradava agreed to sponsor the gala. Publicity for them, and a private donor would allow Patrick to have the competition he wanted. He considered it a win-win." She paused again, swirling the iced tea around in the glass but didn't take a second sip. Small beads of condensation trickled down the outside, forming a wet circle on the faded cotton placemat in front of her.

"Last week, I received a phone call, demanding we cancel the competition."

"Who was it? What exactly did they say?"

" 'Kill the competition before it's too late'," she said.

"Too late for what?"

"I don't know. I told Patrick, and he advised me to tell the police. That's when he told me he'd received similar phone calls."

"What did the police say?" I pictured Detective Loncar, in his Wranglers and plaid shirt, being asked to take seriously a threat over a design competition. The image was anachronistic at best.

"As I told you, the police have paid no attention to Patrick's concerns. This morning, I received a second call. A demand for one hundred thousand dollars, the competition prize, to be delivered by me at the Designer's Debut Gala. The caller said 'What happened to Patrick was a message'. Without knowing more, I'm afraid we might both be in danger."

"We?" I asked.

"You and me. The last thing the caller said was a warning. 'Go to the police again and the trend specialist is next to die.' "

10

I don't understand," I said, because the overwhelming evidence pointed to the fact that I wasn't the trend specialist, even though I continued to argue I was. Maybe it was time to give up that argument.

"I don't know who Patrick was involved with or where the money was coming from."

"Do you know where it is now?"

"In the bank, I imagine. I'm beginning to think he turned to an unconventional source. Whatever information he kept hidden, he would have kept at Tradava. With him gone, you represent the trend office and have access to his files." Her gloved hand fingered the brooch on her cape. "Someone doesn't want us to proceed with this competition. Please consider getting involved. Without more information, I don't know which way to turn."

"But you are cancelling the competition, aren't you?"

"This competition is Patrick's final legacy. I will not be bullied into cancelling it. I owe Patrick that much." She stood from the table and pushed the chair back under. I followed suit, only left my chair jutting out as I followed her into the living room.

"Ms. Paulson, there was a designer in Patrick's office the morning he ... that morning. I didn't catch her name, but she was tall, thin, with bright red hair—"

"Oh yes. Ms. Stevens. She's insignificant in the grand scheme of things." She waved her hand as though shooing away a fly. "Ms. Kidd, will you help me?"

I looked down at the shag carpet to avoid making further eye contact. "I'm sorry about your friend, but I'm trying to start a new life in Ribbon and have had a couple of challenges of my own. I think it's best I concentrate on doing the job I was hired to do and putting what happened to Patrick behind me."

In my head, I politely tacked on another suggestion that she go to the police, but I couldn't speak the words. She seemed firm in her belief the police wouldn't help and promised to let me know if she received any additional threats. She left as abruptly as she arrived.

What was I doing? I was involved in a murder, thanks to a job I most likely didn't have. There should have been nothing keeping me in Ribbon. Screw the fact that I'd grown up in this house. I'd always heard you can't go home again, and because I tried to go home again, I was being punished. But where was I going to go? If I couldn't make the mortgage payment, I would be little more than a squatter on the property, and besides, something told me skipping town wasn't going to help me in the credibility department, especially when it came to my new friend Detective Loncar. After what Maries Paulson had told me, my path was bound to cross with the detective's path, sooner rather than later.

Long after Maries Paulson drove away from my house, I turned my attention to the folder she left behind. There were two stacks of paper inside, each secured by a binder clip. The first was thick. I flipped through it with my thumb. The second pile held only four pages. The letters A through D were carefully printed in purple marker on the upper left corner of each page, circled with Giotto-like precision. A Post-it on the smaller pile read FINALISTS. I fanned the finalists out over the table. Four names, along with answers to questions on inspiration and experience, stared back. Amanda Ries, Clestes, Michael Dubrecht, and Nick Taylor.

Nick was a finalist in the competition? There was more wrong with that than right. He was already a professional designer. He hadn't mentioned any of this on the countless opportunities he had to tell me, and he'd been the one to take Patrick's computer.

He was hiding something.

Maybe Maries Paulson was right. Maybe Patrick's murder did have to do with the design competition. I returned to Patrick's computer and double-clicked a file titled DESIGN COMPETITION. The computer prompted me for a password.

I don't know what I had expected, but it certainly wasn't that.

I didn't know enough about Patrick to crack his password in the first seventeen tries. I thought, not for the first time, if I wanted to understand why Patrick had been murdered, maybe it was time for me to get to know Patrick better. And I figured the best place to do that was at Tradava.

I changed into faded jeans, a black turtleneck sweater, and some rubber soled black booties with chains hanging down around the heels. Investigative style, I might have called it, if I were writing an expose instead of planning a B&E on Patrick's office.

There's a certain skill set common to retail buyers. Sometimes you have to be creative. Sometimes you have to be analytical. The problem with this mental makeup is sometimes you lack the common sense normal people take for granted.

When it came to creative, analytical problem solving, my cup runneth over. When it came to common sense, my glass was half-full.

The late September heat wave had broken with an unexpected thunderstorm, and raindrops pelted the windshield and the empty parking lot. The occasional flash of lightning illuminated the lack of activity around the store's exterior. Aside from a woman in mommy jeans running toward a minivan, a hunched-over lady pushing a stroller through the lot, and a mall employee hoisting a lumpy bag of trash into the dumpster, the lot was deserted. The store staff had probably dwindled down to minimal coverage on the selling floors. I wondered if Eddie was anywhere in the store.

As the rain picked up I ran as fast as my impractical but sassy boots would allow, then entered the store through the main customer entrance, closer to me than the associate door. I remained relatively dry.

I passed the shoe salon and the elevators on my way to the escalators, which I rode until I was at the fifth floor. I ducked into the stairwell and hiked up two more flights to the trend offices, the one place I was pretty sure I wasn't allowed to be, and I felt more and more like a criminal with every passing step. I pulled the keys I'd lifted on Day One out of the bottom of my handbag but kept them hidden in my palm.

After a deep breath, a couple of sideways glances, and three keys that didn't fit the locks, I found a match. The door swung open and I stepped inside and headed to my stark office where I put my handbag down and looked around, wondering what to do next.

I'd searched the file cabinet yesterday. I'd been through the files on the floor as well. In fact, all of the items remaining in the office had been given my once-over, and I'd learned nothing. But someone connected me to Patrick, and the only tether between us was Tradava and a job I probably didn't have.

Outside his office sat a small yellow desk with a phone, a lava lamp, and a bundle of purple number two pencils stamped with the name Michael. A sketchpad lay next to a tear-off calendar featuring quotes by tough-talking women. I slid open a drawer and found a manila file folder inside, containing clippings on several designers along with a copy of the *Style Section,* the industry newsletter that covered events, shows, trends, and designers. I flipped it open a couple of pages and found myself staring at a picture of Nick and the woman from in front of his new showroom. I read the caption: *Nick Taylor and Amanda Ries: compatible competition?*

She was the woman from Nick's store and she was one of the finalists.

Dark, smooth hair that matched the shine of her lip-gloss hung in a delicate waterfall to her impossible waist. Porcelain skin set off by arched eyebrows and a low neckline that revealed nothing but perfection. She filled out the gown she was wearing, a chic halter that plunged to her navel, revealing the intangibles of life: great cleavage and no sign of tummy rolls, tan lines, or stretch marks. She was not the type you invite for a picnic with hoagies and chips.

Of course Nick would be with someone like her. Why wouldn't he? He was a talented shoe designer, attractive, funny, and full of charm. No wonder he didn't want me as a date. She could wear a bias-cut fabric like nobody's business and her hair was frizz-free. Somewhere after noticing her ability to accessorize, a fat tear droplet hit the newsprint and distorted the copy.

Somehow seeing *this* woman, looking perfect, next to Nick, was too much. Not only did I not have the guy, but I also didn't have a job or a paycheck. What I had were two new friends: a homicide detective and a mortgage officer. I imagined a conversation between the two of them: Why no, detective, we didn't know she was involved in a murder investigation. Did you know she lied on her mortgage application? I think that speaks to character, don't you?

I wasn't here to find out about Nick's social life. I was here to find out about the man who should have been my boss. I shut the newspaper and moved into Patrick's office. Vintage *Vogue, Bazaar,* and *Elle* covers hung on the walls. Photos on the shelves above the desk showcased a younger Patrick in various settings with various, then-starting out, now-legendary designers. Outdated outfits helped identify the decades, but Patrick was like a fashion Where's Waldo, wearing some version of the same outfit in every photo. His black hair, neatly parted on the side and his waxed mustache, seemed to have become his trademark in the early seventies and remained a constant, much like the plaids and checks and stripes I had recognized when I saw his body crumpled on the floor of the elevator.

I reached out to the Rolodex. It was still open the card for Pins & Needles. I wasn't sure if this was what Red had been looking at when she flipped through the card file yesterday or not, but it was worth investigating. I pocketed the card like I'd seen so many detectives do on TV.

Next, I rifled through his inbox, looking for something, anything that would clue me in to his personality. Midway through the stack, I paused, spotting a mini-fridge tucked in the corner next to the purple sofa. Leaving no stone unturned, I abandoned the inbox to see if it was stocked.

The mini-fridge held a pitcher of lemonade, about a dozen bottles of Pellegrino, and several somethings hand-wrapped in gold foil. Further investigation exposed individually wrapped chocolate and caramel sweets, neatly piled in stacks: two stacks of six and one stack of four. A sucker for symmetry, I took two from the stack of six for myself.

I poured a glass of lemonade and bit into a caramel confection, then opened and closed his desk drawers, eventually finding a folder labeled DESIGN COMPETITION. I pulled the crisp white folder from the hanging pocket inside the drawer and laid it open on the desk. A small piece of paper from inside the folder fluttered to the floor. I bent down to retrieve it. Written on a page from a monogrammed tablet with an elaborate P in the center was a note in Patrick's fluid handwriting. I read slowly at first, then again, and again.

I'm wracked with guilt over my recent behavior. This is not what this business is about. New talent needs a proper home. I cannot sit by and watch anymore. I leave it to you to look in vogue and correct my legacy. I fear I won't be around. This is not about the money, it is about the creativity. Friendship and loyalty do not have a price, and I was foolish to think otherwise. If this is the new business of fashion, it will go forward without me; my only regret is that I turned to the wrong people to achieve my final goals.

I set the paper down on top of the other pages in the folder and thought about what this meant. Patrick had left behind a note that indicated his guilt about something. But what had he done? And one sentence gave me the chills. *I fear I won't be around.* Maries was right. He had known.

I scanned the note again. Words like *money, regret,* and *the wrong people* stood out like bandanas on a display of silk scarves. He was trying to tell me something.

Unexpectedly, my vision blurred. My heartbeat whooshed in my ears, loud and rhythmic, making it hard to hear anything other than the pounding of my pulse. I stood up and felt along the corners of the desk for balance as my vision swam, distorting the details of the office in sideways, stretched images. Something was wrong with me. My heel caught on the edge of the carpet and I grabbed at Patrick's inbox, pulling it off the desk and scattering the contents over the floor. I landed on the pile of papers, closed my eyes, and faded into blackness.

I awoke with a start. A yellow Post-it fell from my cheek and fluttered to the carpet. I didn't know why, but I was on the floor of Patrick's office. I blinked several times and tried to figure out how I'd gotten there. My head ached.

I crawled to Patrick's chair and planted my hands on the soft black leather. After a few motivating breaths, I pulled myself into it. The office was dark, illuminated only by emergency lights from the hallway. I pulled the desk phone close enough to read the display. One thirty seven. As my mental faculties faded in and out, one thing became clear.

I was trapped in the store.

A clap of thunder crashed overhead, an audible punctuation mark to my thoughts. I was trapped in the one place I wasn't supposed to be. If caught by the wrong people, this would not look good. Considering I was trying to find out details about a murder during off-hours in a store where questions surrounded my employment, the wrong people were numerous.

My paranoia kicked into overdrive. Having worked (or not) for this store for a sum total of about twelve hours I realized this might not be the kind of behavior they encouraged. Not only that, but I didn't know vital facts about their operation, things like what kind of overnight security they had. I strained my ears to listen for the sound of bloodhounds or some other equally frightening dogs, sniffing away for intruders and became suddenly aware of my movements, wondering if the store had invisible light beam laser grids I'd seen so often in movies. I didn't hear sirens but didn't want to risk it.

Think, Samantha, think. I tried to settle on a plan but couldn't formulate a clear thought. I rubbed a sore spot on my temple and let my vision adjust to the darkness. This was the second time in two days I'd blacked out. But this wasn't like seeing Patrick's body in the elevator. This had been different. My mind was fuzzy, like fleece after it's been laundered. I fished my cell phone out of my handbag, but Eddie was right. No signal. Still groggy, I moved to the purple sofa and curled up under a pashmina someone had left draped over the back.

Someone shook me awake. I opened my eyes and saw purple velvet. Immediately, my body went rigid, and I whirled around, hand in a ball, ready to strike the person behind me. I swung and Eddie caught my fist. When I relaxed, he did too. With effort, I sat upright. The office was light. I had spent the night asleep in the store. My heart pounded in my ears and adrenaline raced through my body.

I rubbed my eyes, smudging mascara accidentally. I sat quietly, searching for the best way to explain how I'd come to be asleep on Patrick's sofa behind the doors of a previously locked office.

"You've been here all night?" Eddie asked before I worked out my explanation.

I nodded.

"Then you don't know."

"Know what?"

"Everything's changed. Someone found Patrick's body in a dumpster behind the store."

11

ddie ushered me out of Tradava, past store security, and to his car. I didn't put up a fight. He drove to the diner and led me to a booth in the back by the kitchen. We flipped our coffee cups over and a waitress filled them. Before either of us spoke, we each drained our mugs. Me from a need to snap out of the zombie-like trance I'd found myself in, and Eddie, probably, from caffeine addiction.

"Who found him?" I asked. He'd been patient with me, allowing me space to wake up, to collect my wits, and to try to feel normal, though the idea of Patrick's body being discovered in the dumpster would keep me from ever feeling normal again.

"Michael Dubrecht. He said there was a meeting scheduled for the design competition, only, nobody else showed up. It's on page four." He pushed a newspaper in my direction. For the moment, I ignored it.

I took another swig from my coffee mug then opened up to Eddie about what I knew. "Maries Paulson came to visit me yesterday." I detailed her visit, including the part about the funding, the extortion, and the threats about going to the cops.

"She's probably right about the murder being connected to the competition. You know what killed him?"

"Heart attack?" I said, though I already suspected this to be untrue.

Eddie shook his head. "He was strangled with seam binding." He waved the waitress over and ordered an egg white omelet and plain wheat toast. She turned to me and I waved her away.

"Where'd you hear that?"

"I already told you how I get my information. Store gossip."

"And you trust it?"

He leaned back against the vinyl booth. "Michael ran into the store and told a guy in security. He's dating the counter manager for Clinique. One of my staff members was working on a new fragrance display next to her department." He shrugged. "Most reliable source of information in the industry, if you ask me."

Eddie's news left me at a loss for words. Last night I'd thought nothing about going to the store. I thought nothing could happen. Now I find out a body was dumped less than fifty feet from where I'd parked my car. Talk about too close for comfort.

Eddie continued with other important facts of the previous night.

Point A: Because of the thunderstorm, the building had been close to empty. The skeleton crew of managers had most likely left as quickly as possible, making it an ideal night for someone looking for an opportunity to dump a body.

Point B: Patrick's candy bars and fresh-squeezed lemonade were as legendary as he was. More often than not, visitors to his office scheduled appointments in the afternoon when they were guaranteed an offer of a snack.

Point C: There were no laser beam grids in the store, but the killer had managed to get in there once before and might very easily have been there again.

He didn't mention a point D, but it hung in the air: I'd been sneaking around at Tradava during the night when Patrick's body had been dumped. Some folks might find that suspicious.

I told Eddie about the designer profiles sitting on my dining room table. "Michael is in the file. And Patrick was strangled with seam binding, and I can't think of anybody who walks around with seam binding except for maybe a fashion designer. Somebody who entered the competition was going to walk away with one hundred thousand dollars. So, if you think you have a chance of winning, why kill the judge? That makes it seem like it's one of the people who had no chance of winning. Maybe one of the designers who wasn't a finalist." I slouched down in the booth. "And that's the bigger pile of candidates. Worse, now Patrick is dead, nobody knows where the money was coming from or where the money is. Maybe someone already took the money and skipped town."

"So we should try to figure out who skipped town?"

"Sure. We can systematically try to track down over a hundred different designers who may or may not hold a grudge because they did or didn't final in the competition. And as soon as we find out who is missing, we can call the cops." But there was something wrong with that logic. Everything I'd taken to Detective Loncar had to do with what couldn't be found. Patrick's body, the laptop, and the EMT. Patrick's body had turned up, and I had the laptop, which ironically endorsed my statement and made me look guilty at the same time. To introduce a hundred thousand dollars that was missing along with a designer who was missing would do little more than encourage him to file me under C for Crackpot or P for Person of Interest. My best bet was to steer clear of the police. All the way around.

The waitress returned with Eddie's food. She set a small plate with two strips of bacon in front of me, then smiled and held a finger up to her mouth, and tipped her head toward the man by the cashier. I assumed he was the manager and she was the angel of mercy who had delivered me the unexpected bounty of breakfast meat. I picked up a piece and snapped it off between my teeth.

"Remember Red? She said something about the competition. I asked Maries about her and she said she was insignificant." I thought for a second. "And don't forget, she's just one of the strange people who were traipsing around that morning."

"What strange people?"

"Red, Michael, Nick," I ticked off, then bit into a second piece of bacon.

"Red came in asking for Patrick. Michael was Patrick's assistant, and as far as I can remember, Nick didn't actually come into the office."

"What are you saying?"

"That there's nothing strange about any of those people being at Tradava. The only strange person is you."

"I resent that."

He changed the subject. "What else did you find last night? Anything in Patrick's desk or files?"

"No I actually found *nothing* in Patrick's desk."

"How can you find nothing?"

"There was a space in his desk drawer where something had been but wasn't there. How much space do you think a hundred thousand dollars cash would take up?"

"What else was in the drawer?"

"Desk drawer stuff. Old calendar pages, mechanical pencils, paper clips, flu medicine. And a big empty space."

"Bigger than a breadbox?"

"Big enough for a lot of dough, that's for sure."

"You think he kept the prize money in cash in his desk drawer?"

"I don't know what to think."

"You want to know what I think? You need to go home and get some sleep. You aren't looking your best right now."

"Sleep—that doesn't make sense either. How did I fall asleep at Tradava? I don't pass out. Before two days ago I never passed out. Is there something special about the air quality in Ribbon since high school? Is it thinner? You have it piped in from the Pagoda?"

Eddie ignored my questions. "Go home. Take a shower. Lay low. This will all blow over."

We slid out of the booth and he threw a twenty on the table by the bill. I fished two ones out of my wallet and tucked them under my coffee cup. The tip was almost as big as the bill, but I liked knowing, in the middle of everything else that was rapidly going wrong with my life, that there existed a waitress in a diner who was willing to slip me some bacon when I most needed it. I gave Eddie a head start and ignored his advice to lay low. Instead, I drove to the fabric store.

"I'll be with you in a minute," said the plump woman measuring fabric on the cutting table at Pins & Needles. She wore a red taffeta smock buttoned up the front over a white cotton shirt and black pencil skirt. A pair of gold scissors hung from a chain around her neck. A white plastic nametag that said Florence was pinned to her shoulder.

The shop was long and narrow, and the walls were lined with bolts of fabric sandwiched tightly on high-gloss white shelves. Bust forms stood like sentries around the store, draped with silk, chiffon, plisse, and cashmere, secured with little more than an array of pins. The entire interior was like a time warp; I half expected Edith Head to step out from the stockroom.

"Now, how may I help you?" Florence asked while attaching a small hand-written price tag to the yardage of fabric she had carefully measured moments before.

"Can you tell me where I can find the seam binding?"

She pointed across the store. "Notions are with the zippers and thread. Past the fixture of gabardine."

I eased past the cutting table and followed her directions to the wall of notions. A small fixture about the size of a doghouse was pushed in a corner and stocked with zippers, bias tape, and the item I'd come here to find: seam binding. I pulled a package out and turned it over in my hands.

"Are you finding everything okay, dear?" asked Florence, who had silently reappeared next to me. I glanced at her feet, in sensible shoes with rubber soles. If I were going to take up sneaking around, I might need to find out where she bought them.

"I'm not sure. I think this is what I'm looking for."

"You don't know?"

"No, not really."

"Not a lot of people still use it, though it's been a hot seller lately."

This piqued my interest. "Why would that be?"

"I imagine it's because of the competition. A few of the designers have been in here to purchase it."

"I didn't realize the competition was so well known."

"My dear, Ribbon isn't the biggest city in Pennsylvania, but Patrick's competition has given us something to talk about. Don't let the smock and the sensible shoes fool you, I run this fabric store, and I have a longstanding love affair with fashion. My business is based on it. If I didn't know about the competition, people would question my expertise."

"Do you know the designers?"

"Of course! Most of them are regulars."

"Is Michael Dubrecht a regular?"

"Oh, that Michael is such a nice boy. Always shops the remnants. He has such grand ideas but not very much money."

A bell rang at the front of the store and Florence excused herself before I could continue asking questions, though, I wondered how long Florence would gossip with me if I'd simply stood around rattling off names of suspects. I needed a better plan, more concrete questions. Lost in my thoughts, I left the store and started the drive home.

Two traffic lights from the store I saw a small BMW turn right at the intersection. It could have been black, it could have been gray, and it could have been navy blue. I was less interested in the color of the car than the color of the hair of the driver. Red.

I did an illegal U-turn when the light changed and hoped the Ribbon police force was out trying to catch murderers and not watching for traffic violations. I weaved through traffic, looking for a black, gray, or navy blue sedan. I found it just as it made the left hand turn into the Pins & Needles parking lot.

Red parked in a space close to the front door. I parked by the rear of the lot. Aside from her license plate number and the fact that her car was black, gray, or navy blue, there wasn't much I would learn by sitting there, watching her parked car, so for the second time that day, I headed inside.

"Back so soon?" called out Florence as the bell chimed over head. She stood inside the cutting table, measuring off a bolt of cobalt blue silk jacquard.

"I forgot my list," I said, waving an old receipt I'd grabbed from the center console before coming back inside. I returned to the Notions aisle. When I rounded the corner, Red stood by the seam binding, filling her basket with packages.

Her brilliant hair hung to the side of her face. Her ankle-length dress bore the asymmetric and angular lines of a Japanese designer, but she'd cinched it at her waist with a leopard-printed patent leather obi belt.

"Stocking up?" I said as I approached.

She looked up from the fixture, noticeably startled by my voice. "I didn't realize anyone was there. What did you say?" She looked at her basket. "Oh, seam binding. This is the only store that carries the kind I like."

"I didn't realize seam bindings varied that much. What's so great about that brand?"

"Most of the newer ones are rayon but this one is polyester. I like the feel of it in my hands. Not everyone uses seam binding, but you'd be amazed at what you can get away with when you use it."

Interesting choice of words. "Are you a designer?" I pressed.

"I like to think so, but the jury is still out from the rest of the world. I own a boutique at the Designer Outlet Center." She reached into her handbag and pulled out a business card. I glanced at the name: Catnip. Underneath, in a neat cursive font, the card said 'Ribbon Designer Outlets', followed by an address, phone number, and email. There was no name on the card. As I took it from her hand, she stared past me, across the store. I turned to follow her gaze but saw nothing. "I have to leave," she said abruptly, abandoning her basket by my feet.

She ducked out the door that faced the back alley, leaving the tinkling of chimes overhead in her wake. I still didn't know how she was connected to Patrick but this time I knew where to find her. I picked up a package of seam binding and turned it over in my hands. One dollar and thirty cents. Seemed like a small price to pay for a murder weapon.

12

When I returned home I dumped my handbag on the floor inside my front door and powered up the laptop. I called to Logan, but he didn't appear. A noise emanated from behind the door to the basement. When I opened it a bolt of black fur shot past me. Food or litter box? Logan bee-lined for the food bowl, which meant there was probably a small mess in the basement. I headed down the rickety stairs to find the spot he had chosen to leave his mark. A sickening smell hit me and I turned on the light switch, gasping at the sight.

Only a few days ago I had sat in front of the house looking at the lilac bushes. Gazing fondly at the crabapple trees. Recalling summer nights, sitting on the porch swing with my dad. I'd managed to edit the leaky basement from my memories, had forgotten a storm of any magnitude would turn the concrete floor into a murky indoor swimming pool, ruining anything not at least two feet above floor level.

The rising water level claimed paperback books, back issues of fashion magazines, and broken TV sets left in a state of disrepair ages ago. I wondered, not for the first time, why I was trying so hard to make this work. *Just pick up the phone and call your old boss,* said a voice inside my head. *Ask them to take you back. Better yet, call mom and dad. Tell them you need their help.* As I watched my childhood belongings swirl around in the muck, I knew I wouldn't make that call.

Thoughts of the sixty hour work weeks, the daily battles with my landlord and dry cleaner, the inconvenience of paying to park in a garage where I couldn't get my car when I needed it flooded my mind like the water flooding the basement. They made up a patchwork maxi-skirt of reasons for why I'd been so willing to leave. A belly full of cupcakes and a giant card signed by my peers had been enough of a send-off. I had made the decision to start over for me. I wasn't going to throw it all away over some soggy cardboard boxes.

I had a flashback to my early years when it was the family responsibility to carry buckets of water out of the basement and realized what I had to do. My dad's rubber fishing waders were propped along a wall in the garage and I pulled them on, even though they were a few sizes too big. I trudged down the stairs and located a bucket.

Several hours and inventive curses toward the previous owners later (I'd suspended familial loyalty within the first half hour of work; there was a little thing called 'disclosure' they'd ignored when they sold me the house) the water level had waned from feet to inches. Autopilot had replaced exhaustion. The rancid smell of decades-old memories and waterlogged mildew turned my stomach. I'd done what I could, for now. I hiked back up the open wooden steps. Logan sat at the top of the stairs, cleaning himself. He made a lazy attempt at a meow, as if to say I should consider cleaning myself up too. I peeled off the wet everything: boots, socks, clothes, underwear, and left them in a trail to the bathroom where I showered. The last thing I remembered was collapsing into my bed in the buff, completely oblivious to the sun shining through the curtains.

I woke with Logan swatting at my head. I pulled on a Dick Dale T-shirt over a fresh set of undies and padded to the kitchen. As I rounded the corner, the doorbell rang. I let out an inhuman sound and hid behind the wall. My mind filled with warnings not to open the door to strangers, and I armed myself with a bread knife.

"Kidd, it's Nick Taylor. I know you're in there, I heard you scream. Will you open the door already?"

For the second time in as many days I slammed the laptop shut and covered it in a pile of newspapers scattered on the table. I opened the door, forgetting I was still grasping the bread knife. He took a step backward. His eyes darted to the hand holding the knife then grew darker as his gaze shifted to my lower half.

"What are you doing here?" I asked.

"May I come in?"

"No." *Don't trust him!* sounded in my head. I stood in his way, one hand on the door, the other on the frame. I was a one-woman bouncer in a guitar-god T-shirt and cotton panties.

I was in my panties.

My face flushed with embarrassment. "Wait here," I said quickly, jabbing at the air between us like a swashbuckler with the world's smallest sword. I slammed the door in his face and ran upstairs, jumped into a pair of jeans that had been in the corner, and returned downstairs. No need to abandon my weapon now, I thought, and trained the bread knife on him while I opened the door again. "What do you want?" I asked.

He scanned my body before looking me in the face. "I forgot to give you this when you were in my store." He held out the plum laptop case. At least one of us knew it was empty. At least one of us chose to keep that fact to ourselves in pursuit of more important information.

"Where did you get that?"

"You left it behind at Tradava. After I walked you to the stairwell, I went back to the shoe department. That's when I saw it." He extended the bag toward me and I took it. I searched his face for an indication he knew it was empty. I got nothing.

"Thank you," I said. I set the laptop bag on the end table.

"It occurred to me that you saw it in my office at the store, and that's why you were so mad when you left. But then I thought if you *had* seen it, you would have asked me why I had your laptop. So, I don't know why you stormed out."

I needed to distract him, and for a brief second regretted not being able to play the T-shirt and panties wild card. I stepped back and let him pass.

He stepped closer to me, close enough that we were sharing the same air. He brushed his warm finger under my chin and tipped my head back. "I heard about what happened last night. Are you okay?"

I looked directly into Nick's root-beer clear brown eyes and lied my heart out. "I'm fine." I walked to the sofa. He followed. We both sat down. Nick was waiting for some kind of explanation, and there was the smallest possibility I owed it to him.

"I'm curious. Were you this crazy when you were a kid Kidd?" Logan hopped up onto the spot between us. "Or when you worked for Bentley's?"

"What's your point?"

"I'm not sure I would have trusted your taste level or strategic thinking if I'd known," he said.

"I don't recall you complaining when I wrote your orders."

"Back then I just thought it was good business. I had no idea you were nuts."

I sank deeper into the green velvet cushions, ignoring the broken spring that dug into my left butt cheek. "Do you ever think about your childhood? About whether or not you're the you you started out to be?"

"I'm not sure I follow."

"I worked at Bentley's for nine years. I started as a sales associate and left as a buyer. I was promoted every two years into some really great positions. Only, none of them was enough. I should have been thrilled every single day to get up and say I was a buyer for a store of their caliber, but I wasn't."

"Is that the real reason you changed your life?"

"I was about to drive back to Manhattan after helping my parents move. I didn't want to leave. I met Patrick that morning, in the parking lot outside of the grocery store. He told me about the trend specialist job and, well, and now here we are."

I leaned back against the cushions of the sofa and stared at my fingers, still pruney from dealing with the water in the basement. "I didn't expect it to be easy to start over, you know? But I thought it would be fun." The phone rang in the background. I expected Nick to ask if I was going to answer it. He didn't. After four rings the faux-wood machine clicked on.

"Ms. Kidd, this is Brittany Fowler from Full Circle. We need to talk."

I kicked my heels against the sofa like a ten-year old, then stood up and went to the kitchen. I hit the delete button, then turned off the machine. "I have to get some new things around here," I said to Logan, who stared at me from the floor.

Nick stood up and walked into the kitchen. "Can I do anything? To make things easier for you?"

"There is one thing," I said. Before he had a chance to answer, I continued. "The Gala? With everything that's been going on, I misplaced my invite. Can I go with you?"

"Not that you don't have a charming way of inviting yourself along, but I already have a date for the Gala."

"I didn't mean to imply it would be a date," I started.

"Good, because I'm going to be busy that night. I guess you'll have to find your invite."

"You're one of the finalists!" I blurted out. His clear brown eyes caught mine and held them for an intense couple of seconds. "Can't you get me in?"

"Kidd, maybe you should sit this one out."

I thought about what Nick had said at the hoagie store. *When it's important, you figure it out.* If I could focus on one problem, I would. Unwelcome tears coated my eyes. I wanted to blink them back but blinking might have caused them to spill down my cheeks and I wanted that even less. I tipped my head back and stared at the ceiling, doing little more than establishing tracks of tears that ran from the outside corner of my eye into my hairline.

"Something else is bothering you. What's wrong?"

"It's the house. The basement floods."

"I find it hard to believe you ended up with a flooded basement after one thunderstorm."

"You don't believe me? Come on," I said. Several joints popped when I stood and I glared at him to keep him from commenting. He fell into step behind me. My dad's hip-waders sat in a puddle on the kitchen floor next to the door to the cellar. I pulled the door open and hit the light switch, shocked to see the water level had risen again.

It couldn't be! I had spent too many hours lugging water up the steps and outside. I threw on the lights and stepped halfway down the staircase. The water-logged boxes of vintage fashion magazines my mom had left stacked by the walls of the basement had busted open. The issue that glided past me was the same cover Patrick had hanging on his wall of his office. It, like dozens of other volumes, floated across the floor like dead fish. I watched it bump up against the wall. That's when I saw a green garden hose, dangling through a broken window, pouring water into the room.

"I'll be right back." I pushed past Nick, through the garage, and around the side of the house. A green hose was screwed into the outside spigot by the back door, the water turned on to full force. I closed my palm over the round metal valve and twisted it several times until it was off. I followed the length of the hose to the back of the house, only to find the other end threaded into a broken window at ground level. It all meant one thing.

My flooded basement wasn't an accident. Someone had wanted me out of commission.

13

I returned to the garage, pulling the heavy door down and throwing the locking mechanism. Nick stood by the cellar. I would not make eye contact with him. I would not let him see how much that had gotten to me. I was smart. I should have spotted the broken window and the rubber hose earlier. And because I didn't, I was going to have to deal with a flooded basement. Again.

Nick's attitude changed. If it wasn't for the crinkles in the corner of his eyes, I'd have broken down right then and there. The crinkles kept me in check. Because I didn't believe a person like Nick, with root-beer barrel eyes that crinkled in the corners would be laughing at me if things weren't going to be okay. He draped his arm around my shoulder. "It's just a house, Kidd. It isn't a sign. It isn't a message. Sometimes with old houses, things go wrong."

I only wished I could believe him.

My cell phone chirped from the nightstand table. How had I ended up in bed? Nick had come over to check on me. I remembered that much. He'd helped me drain the basement for the second time that day. After we were done he'd guided me up the stairs to the bedroom. A glance under the sheets at my undies confirmed Nick had seen me in my panties two times in one afternoon. A flood of more important thoughts pushed that one to the side. The broken window. The garden hose. The vandalism.

The fact that someone who would do these things knew where I lived.

The sun headed toward the horizon but there was enough light to see. I climbed out of bed and followed Logan to the bathroom. My reflection matched my condition: gray around the edges. I dressed in jeans and a heavy gray cowl neck sweater. After pulling on navy blue Wellies, I went outside to the back of the house.

When I looked at the broken window from the inside, it was like my vision had a zoom feature. All I could focus on was the break, the jagged edges, the hose snaked through the hole. Now, I wanted to find something else.

The window was about two feet wide by one foot tall, broken in the corner. It was at ground level, surrounded by a metal semi-circle window well. The inside ground of the well was covered with small pebbles and mushy leaves. A rock sat to the side. Maybe it had been used to break the glass. Maybe not. At this point, it was hard to say. The surrounding ground had been tamped by footprints, probably my own, that wouldn't tell me anything.

I returned to the kitchen and sat at the table, staring out the back window. Someone had been right outside that window while I was passed out at Tradava.

I should call the cops. Report the vandalism. Maybe it wasn't connected. Maybe it was a neighborhood prank, a couple of juvenile delinquents getting their kicks by messing with the new resident on the block. And that would be a totally reasonable reason to call the police. I would not mention the competition. I would not mention Patrick. I'd say enough to get a patrol car assigned to the neighborhood, to look out for my well-being. Detective Loncar probably wouldn't even learn of it.

I went back inside and dialed 911.

By the time the squad car pulled alongside of the curb, I was convinced I'd made a mistake. It wasn't an act of vandalism by bored high schoolers, and Nick was wrong about it being a freak old house thing. Someone was sending me a message. I was preparing myself to lie like a rug when someone knocked on my door. It was Detective Loncar.

"Why are you here?" I asked, looking behind him for a couple of fresh-from-the-academy cops.

"Ms. Kidd, you called 911?"

"I did."

"What seems to be the problem?"

"Isn't this a little minor for you?"

"When a person of interest in a homicide calls the cops, word gets around. Especially when that person appears to be avoiding the cops." He pushed his elbows behind his back and tipped his head from side to side, as though he was cramped from spending too much time in the car. Come to think of it, he'd arrived pretty quickly. Was he in the neighborhood? Had he picked my call up off of a scanner? Was this tantamount to illegal entry?

"Person of interest? I'm a suspect?"

"You sure have been acting like one," he said. "May I come in?"

"I'd like to wait for back-up."

The detective stopped his limbering up routine and coughed. He covered his mouth with a balled up fist, then patted down the outside of his windbreaker. From an inside pocket he pulled out a cough drop and bit the end of the wrapper, pulling the lozenge into his mouth.

"Back-up?"

"You're not going to force your way in, are you?" I asked.

"Ma'am, that's not the way this works. You called me, I'm here. If you got a problem, you have to tell me. I'd suggest you do, because the call's been documented, and I don't think you should make a habit of placing 911 phone calls for no reason."

"Boy who cried wolf, and all that," I added, to show I was following.

"Making false 911 calls is a misdemeanor."

Our standoff by my front door ended right around there.

"Follow me." I walked the detective around the side of the house to the broken window with the hose fed through it. "When I came home this morning, the basement was flooded. I know it rained but not enough to flood it like it did. After I drained the basement I noticed the hose dangling through the broken window."

Loncar stooped down by the window well and looked at the broken glass. He stood back up, pushing his palms against his thighs until he was upright. He turned to the left, then the right, shielding his eyes even though he wore dark sunglasses. A breeze ruffled his crew cut and for a brief second I thought, *he's taking me seriously. He's going to help me. I made the right decision, calling the cops to report the vandalism.*

"You said 'when I came home this morning.' You didn't spend the night here?"

And then I thought, *dammit.*

"I, no, um, well, I didn't say that—"

"Ms. Kidd, if you were here, I'm guessing you would have heard the glass break, or you would have heard the water in the basement before it filled up to two feet of water. So I'm assuming you weren't here."

"No, I wasn't here."

"What time did you get home?"

"I think it was around nine."

He looked at his watch. "It's four thirty now."

"I drained the basement, then I had a visitor, then I drained the basement again, then I took a nap."

"And then you called in your emergency."

I nodded.

"Ms. Kidd, may I suggest in the future if you feel something is an actual emergency, you rearrange your schedule in order to make the call on a more timely basis?"

"I didn't know it was an emergency until it flooded a second time."

"And then you took a nap."

"You don't believe me, do you?" I asked suddenly.

"Your credibility is not at stake here."

He took a couple of pictures of my broken window and garden hose and jotted something illegible from my upside-down perspective in a small flip-top notepad. "Anything else you want to tell me, ma'am?"

"Aside from the fact I'm too young to be called ma'am?"

"Are you going to tell me this has something to do with Patrick's murder?"

"Absolutely not," I said in a voice that suggested I'd greatly improved my lying skills. "But I do think it's a good idea to send a patrol car around regularly. You know, in case whoever did this comes back."

He flipped the notebook shut. "Be smart, Ms. Kidd. Lock the doors and get that window fixed." He pointed to the broken window with the corner of the notebook, then tucked it into his back pocket. "And if you suddenly determine it *is* related to Patrick's murder, call me." He pulled out his wallet and extracted a business card. I didn't want it, but I took it anyway. It was the polite thing to do.

I followed him to the front yard. I wasn't sure of the protocol for 911-slash-homicide-detective house calls, and wasn't sure if I should have offered him a cup of coffee while lying to his face. Too late to make a good impression, I stood by the garage door while he backed his car out of the driveway and drove away.

I pulled the sleeves of my sweater down over my hands and wrapped my arms around my body. As the sun dropped, so did the temperature, leaving a chill in the air that rivaled the one in my bones. I went back inside and double-checked every lock on every entrance. I angled the green velvet sofa against the front door and sunk into the well-worn cushions.

Someone was making life very difficult for me and I didn't know why. What did I have that someone wanted? I rubbed my hands over my face and took a deep breath, realizing how badly I needed a second shower. I dropped my hands to the cushions by my side and stared into the kitchen where the computer sat next to a pile of newspapers.

Patrick's computer held the key. It must. It was the only thing I had that someone else might want. And for some reason, he'd made sure to loan it to me. Those conversations with him were starting to haunt me.

Patrick had asked me to meet him in the parking lot outside of Tradava the day before I started.

"I would have come to your office," I said.

"I enjoy the chance to get out every now and then." He handed me a plum messenger bag. It had a cross-chest strap and I couldn't imagine Patrick in his dandy attire ever wearing it.

"My former employee's idea of a gag gift," he said.

"Is there something specific you'd like me to review?"

"My current projects are saved on the computer. I'll expect you to be versed in them and offer your opinion when asked."

I took the bag and fought the urge to duck under the cross-chest strap in his presence.

"Samantha, there is something I need to discuss with you before you start." He sat on the bench next to me and we looked out over the sea of cars in the lot. "Working at Tradava will be very different for you after your life at Bentley's. Are you prepared for that?"

After all of our talk about choosing our paths, his question surprised me.

"Different, how?"

"At a large store you can become somewhat invisible. At Tradava, people will see you. Our store team looks to us to give them a taste of the glamour of our industry, even if we don't see it ourselves. Your problem solving skills and creativity will serve you well here. You will be noticed."

"That's the question, isn't it? Be someone in a smaller environment, or be no one in a larger environment. Big fish, small pond, or small fish, big pond."

"The eternal argument."

"Have you argued that argument?" I asked.

"Countless times."

"Have you won?"

"To myself, I have. To the industry, I can't be certain."

"Does that bother you?"

"Only on rare occasions." He stood from the bench and shielded his eyes, then turned to face me. "I look forward to seeing what you bring to the trend office, Ms. Kidd. I trust you'll be able to figure out a thing or two on your own."

I stood up too, and shook his hand.

That was the last time I saw Patrick alive.

I carried the laptop bag from the kitchen back to the sofa and stared inside. Aside from a stack of Patrick's business cards wedged into a small pocket, the interior was empty. But the more I thought about that conversation, the more I thought Patrick had expected me to figure something out. I pulled the stack of business cards from the pocket and dealt them one by one onto threadbare sofa cushion. When I flipped them over, on the back of the last one, was written *LiVo72*. I went into the kitchen and typed the code into the password field. The file opened up. It was the easiest thing I'd done in two days. And now it was time to discover what was so important that Patrick had hidden it in the first place.

14

The file on the Designer Competition sprung to life in front of me. The first column said ENTRANT. Under it was a list of names. The first name was CLESTES, followed by fragmented commentary: *This is the work of a stylist, not a designer. The addition of a textile artist does not carry the collection. There is no DNA. Maries likes use of color and architectural elements.* I continued down the page. MICHAEL DUBRECHT: *Needs time to develop. Interesting ideas. Is this talent or a fluke? Maries disagrees. Thinks there is nothing there.* AMANDA RIES. *Fresh perspective. Innovative use of fabrics. Strong sense of design, proportion, color. New. Commercial. Ageless. Timeless. ORIGINAL. Shows much promise. This collection will be BIG. Maries says this collection could rewrite fashion history. I suspect she is right. Keep separate from Clestes to avoid clash.* The last line on the file said NICK TAYLOR: *disqualified.*

Patrick had gone to great lengths to keep these notes from public viewing, or any viewing for that matter. His opinion of each designer was obvious, but that wasn't what struck me. I already knew he and Maries were the judges, and so did everyone else. Of course there was going to be criticism.

The real question was why had Nick been disqualified? And what was he doing in the competition to begin with?

I looked over Patrick's notes one more time. If what I thought was right, one of these people had a lot to gain if they knew they weren't going to win the competition. I had to find them. Because if one of these designers had found the money, they were going to be awfully hard to find. And hiding Patrick's body for a couple of days would have given them a head start before the police figured out what they did and started looking for them.

I pushed stacks of unopened mail and newspapers around the table until I found the envelope Maries had dropped off. Inside were profiles on each of the designers. Four finalists, and a thick sheaf of papers for those who hadn't moved to the final round. I looked at the top application on the larger pile. The upper right corner was stamped with a grid. Dates and notations had been filled in: *Application fee processed. Collection sketches received. Feedback supplied with thank you for entering.* Next I looked at the pile of finalists. Nick's application was on top. The same grid was stamped in the same place. *Application fee processed. Collection sketches received. Finalists notified.* I flipped past Nick's page to Michael's. *Application fee waived. Collection sketches received. Notified.* A small, hand-drawn smiley face was next to the last word.

So Michael hadn't paid his entry fees. I didn't know what to make of that. Had his position as Patrick's assistant earned him a free pass? And had that free pass included finalist status?

I flipped through the pages. There had to be something in there someone would kill for, but I couldn't help wondering, seriously, if I was in the middle of a gigantic hoax that had gone awry. This was fashion. Outside of Gianni Versace, the words "homicide" and "high style" didn't belong in the same sentence. It was a stretch to think someone whose name was in this file had killed to keep it from being seen.

I set the pages on the table and looked back at the screen. If I was looking at what Patrick had wanted me to see, then the message was lost on me. I clicked around on a few different cells, then discovered a hidden tab. I unhid it and stared at a new page of information.

Rucci
Cavalli
Gucci
Gabbana
Missoni
Armani
Pucci
Piana
Miuccia
Donatella

It didn't take much more than a passing knowledge of fashion to recognize the names of famous Italian designers, some living, some not. Some working, some not. But what did they have to do with Patrick, why were they in a protected file on his computer? The more I discovered, the less I knew. It was a frustrating place to be.

I called Eddie and asked him to bring me food. I returned to the computer and clicked on cells at random. There had to be something else, something I was missing. Twenty minutes later, Eddie pounded on the door. I closed the file and shut down the computer, then spent a couple of minutes moving the sofa away from the front door. Eddie leaned in and looked around the interior before entering. One hand held a Tradava shopping bag, the other carried a stack of white Styrofoam takeout containers. He set the Tradava bag on the sofa.

"You won't believe what's happened so far today."

"You already know?" he asked. "You seem so calm."

"Calm? I'm freaking out. After I left you, I came home. Somebody had broken into my house. And Nick came over with the laptop—well, the laptop bag—he had it the whole time. He thought it was mine, and he took it for safe keeping."

"Dude," Eddie started, but the amount of information I had to share was in direct relation to the amount of caffeine I'd had, leaving him no opening to the conversation.

"So, I called the cops to report the break-in, and the homicide detective came over. What is this, Chinese?" I asked, taking the Styrofoam containers from him and moving into the kitchen. He remained in the living room. "Can you imagine if I was here last night instead of Tradava? Somebody was here, at my house."

"Dude, sit down and be quiet for a second."

"Sorry, sorry." I pulled an eggroll from one of the containers and bit into it. "Thanks for bringing this. I'll make it up to you, I promise, after I figure this thing out."

"I think you should move on."

There was something about how he said that last part that caught my attention. I set the eggroll in the lid of the Styrofoam container and leaned back.

"Move on? You want me to move on?" I said calmly. He didn't speak, which was smart on his part because I wasn't done. "I moved here under the illusion that Tradava was going to be my source of income. Now my boss has been *murdered*, I'm a *suspect*, and I'm going to *lose the house* if I can't prove to the mortgage company that I have a job. Yesterday somebody *broke a window* and *flooded my basement*. I used to live in an apartment overlooking, well, overlooking a bunch of other apartment buildings, but the windows were made of glass. Right now my window is made of duct tape. Why does everyone keep telling me to move on?"

He looked down at his hands, completely avoiding eye contact. When he spoke, his voice was low. "Dude, the detective was back at the store. He knows Patrick was murdered and now he thinks Tradava was the crime scene.

Somebody tipped him off that you went there last night and his team found your fingerprints all over."

I balled up a paper towel and threw it at the trash can. It bounced off the rim and landed on the floor by a muddy footprint. Logan swatted it under the oven.

"That's it, right? I mean, enough with the bad news already. That's all there is. Right?"

"Not exactly."

"What else could possibly have happened?"

"They found an EMT jacket stuffed in the bottom drawer of the file cabinet in your office."

15

"I looked in that drawer yesterday morning. It was empty," I said. Was that really only yesterday? It felt like a lifetime ago.

He pulled a newspaper clipping from a cargo pocket and held it out. "You need to start being careful. If that drawer was empty, then that jacket was planted. Recently. It doesn't look good for you."

I took the clipping and scanned the story. *Fashion Director Murdered* was the headline. Lines like, "suspicious characters in the store on the morning of the murder," "overwhelming class evidence," and "closing in on a suspect" gave me chills.

"Even if you're not guilty, you seem to keep coming close to the killer. Sooner or later the cops are going to find the actual murderer. Until then you have to be careful. Okay?" When I didn't answer him immediately, he spoke again. "I brought you a one month supply of the *Style Section* to catch you up on the fashion world, since you're supposed to be some kind of expert." I ignored his attempt at humor. He pulled a mini bottle of wine out of the bottom of the bag. "I don't want to encourage you to drink alone in your state, but this might help you forget what happened."

"But it did happen, Eddie. No amount of pretending can make it go away."

"Dude," he said quietly.

I sat back, no longer hungry. By telling the detective about the vandalism, I'd told him I wasn't home last night. Worse, someone else knew I wasn't home last night. The someone who had left Patrick's body in a dumpster. The someone who had vandalized my window. The someone who was out to frame me.

"You need this?" Eddie asked, holding out a receipt.

"For what? Dinner? Just tell me what it cost and I'll give you the money."

"No, the food's on me. This was on your floor."

"Where's it from?"

"Fabric store," he said with a full mouth after having bit into an eggroll. Logan hopped up on the table and I picked him up and put him back on the floor. He yowled and walked away. "Did you buy out the store? Is your strategy to wipe out the inventory, cut off the murderer's supply?"

"What are you talking about?"

"How expensive is that stuff anyway?" He pushed the receipt toward me with his elbow.

I picked it up and smoothed it out under my palm. The receipt was from Pins & Needles. It was damp and smudged with mud.

"Seventy-four dollars of seam binding." I flattened it out with the side of my hand. "I must have tracked this in from behind the house." I set the piece of paper on the table next to the Moo Goo Gai Pan.

Eddie finished off another eggroll and stood. "You sure you're going to be okay?"

"Sure. As long as the sofa's up against the front door, I'll be fine."

"I'll call you tomorrow. Every hour on the hour. I'll give you until 11:00 to sleep in."

"Dude," I replied.

After Eddie left, I examined the receipt he'd found on the floor. Someone who had been in my backyard had spent seventy dollars on seam binding. I suspected the talkative store manager at Pins & Needles would remember such a sale. I located the business card I'd swiped from Patrick's Rolodex and called the store.

"Thank you for calling Pins and Needles. This is Florence," said a friendly voice.

"Hi, Florence, I was in the store earlier today, and I was wondering if I could ask you a few questions about seam binding?"

"Who are you?" she said, her voice suddenly flat.

"Samantha Kidd."

"No! What are you doing? No!"

"Excuse me? Florence?"

"Get away from me!"

"I—Do you know who I am?"

"I'm going to call the cops if you don't leave!"

"Don't call the cops! Wait—leave where? I'm at home. What's going on?"

My ear filled with several muffled sounds, then a clunk. "Florence?" I said. There was no response. "Are you there? Florence!" The only thing I heard was more clunking. I disconnected and redialed the number. Busy signal. I tried three more times with the same result.

I dialed information and asked her to ring the number. After informing me of the related charges for such a service, she placed me on hold. Within five seconds she was back, confirming my suspicions. The phone was off the hook. By now I realized why the brief conversation with Florence sounded off. She hadn't been talking to me.

I hung up then started to dial 911. I stopped before the second one. What if I was wrong? This would be my third 911 call in less than a week. I pulled on the navy blue Wellies, grabbed my handbag, and ran to the car. Traffic on the highway was light enough to get me to Pins & Needles in a matter of minutes. I pulled into the vacant lot and parked slightly off center between a couple of lines painted on the macadam. I ran to the front door and pulled on the handle. The door was locked and the store was dark.

I slapped my palm on the front door aggressively. "Florence! Florence! Can you hear me? Are you in there?" I yelled. I pressed my ear up to the door of the shop. The only sound I heard was a faint tinkling of chimes.

Chimes. Like the kind I'd heard earlier over the back door.

I raced around the back of the store. Red taillights glowed at the edge of the parking lot, then disappeared onto Penn Avenue. It was too far away for me to make out necessary details and I wasted no time trying. I yanked the door open and ran inside.

"Florence? Florence! Are you in here? Are you okay?"

It took a couple of seconds for my eyes to adjust to the darkness. As quickly as I could, I moved through the store with my hands in front of me. A body jumped out at me and I screamed. It fell over and I tripped. It was one of the bust form dummies draped in fabric. I kicked it out of the way and stood back up. Slower, I moved to the cutting island where Florence had been earlier that day. I put my hands on the counter and made out the appearance of the phone base. I reached across the counter and found the curly cord, then pulled it toward me until I had the receiver in my hand. I set it back in the cradle.

Movement from the ground startled me. I peeked over the counter. A roll of black and white pinstriped gabardine rolled across the floor. I looked in the direction from where it had come. On the floor, bound, gagged, and blindfolded, sat Florence.

"It's okay now. I'm here to help you," I said.

I crawled over the counter and knelt down on the floor. First I pulled a wad of fabric from her mouth, then pulled the blindfold from her eyes. She looked scared at first. "I'm not going to hurt you. I was on the phone when whoever did this to you did this to you."

"Scissors," she whispered, and held up her wrists. I froze in place when I saw the tight lilac seam binding biting into her flesh. "In the drawer by the register."

I cut through the cords on her wrists and ankles. Indentations remained long after the fabric strips fell to the floor. "Can I get you anything?"

"You can hand me the phone. I'm calling the police."

"The police—" I started to say, then stopped. If Florence called the police, she could tell them she was on the phone with me when she was attacked. I shifted to all fours and felt around for the cordless phone.

"What are you going to tell them?"

"I'll tell them who attacked me."

"You know who it was?"

She leaned to the left and reached under the counter. "Whoever it was dropped this." She held out a business card. I leaned close so my eyes could make out the details. Sure enough, I recognized it. It was one of Patrick's cards, only Patrick's name had been crossed out.

Unfortunately for me, my name was written in its place.

16

"Florence, that's me. That's my name. I'm Samantha Kidd, but I didn't do this to you."

"Hand me that phone, young lady."

I handed her the phone and watched her dial 911. I stood up and looked around the store. I knew I wasn't going to stick around to hang with Detective Loncar, but I wanted to make sure she was safe. Aside from the army of bust forms that guarded the store, we were alone.

"This is Florence Ingram. I am at Pins & Needles on Penn Avenue. Someone came into my store and threatened me and tied me up. Please send a police car." She stopped talking for a moment. I could hear the other person talking but like a teacher in a Peanuts special, the words were indecipherable. I waited, not sure if I should stay or go. "A nice young woman, Samantha Kidd, came in to help me. Yes, she's still here with me. Yes, I'll do that." She hung up the phone.

"Samantha, why don't you have a seat with me? The police will be here shortly and it seems they'd like to talk to you."

I'm sure they would. "I can't stay. I don't know who did this to you, but I promise I'll find out."

"The police specifically asked for me to make sure you stayed with me."

"I know—" I stopped. Avoiding Detective Loncar was high on my priority list but not as high as abandoning an innocent woman who had been attacked. Besides, I reasoned internally, if I stuck around, I might be able to learn something from her statement.

I helped Florence into a folding metal chair and filled a Dixie cup with water for her, then settled in next to a bolt of green paisley and waited. Someone had taken things up a notch.

Eleven minutes later swirling blue and red lights illuminated the windows of Pins & Needles. Florence tried to stand, but I could tell she was still shaking. "I'll let them in," I said.

I braced myself for whatever Detective Loncar was going to say to me when I opened the door, but he wasn't one of the two uniformed men in front of me.

They both looked younger than I would have expected police officers to look but that might have been based on my recent interactions with the detective. One was about half a head taller than the other, with a smattering of freckles across his face. The other was Mexican, with dark curly hair and the beginning of a mustache.

"You called 911?" asked Mustache.

"Florence, the owner did. She's waiting inside." I led the two uniformed officers to the center cutting table. Florence wasn't there. I looked around in the darkness, not sure where she'd gone, until suddenly the store was bathed in light. The sudden change made me shut my eyes, then blink rapidly until my sight adjusted. Florence appeared from a door in the back of the store.

"Hello officers, I'm the one who called you, Florence Ingram. I'm sorry if I startled you, but I don't like sitting around my store in the dark."

"Ms. Ingram, can you tell us what happened here?" asked Mustache.

I stood off to the side while Florence described the attack. I wanted to hear her statement, to see if anything stood out, but the officer blocked us and kept his voice low. I picked up only the basic facts: she had been straightening the store before closing when the phone rang. After answering the phone, the lights went out. Someone jumped in front of her, shoved a wad of cotton batting in her mouth, and bound her wrists with seam binding.

"Were you here with Ms. Ingram?" asked Freckles.

"No, I'm the one who was on the phone. I thought she was talking to me when she was really talking to the person attacking her."

"So you heard her being attacked?"

"I heard her asking what someone wanted. I thought she was talking to me."

"Maybe she was."

"No, she was talking to the person in the store, weren't you, Florence?"

"I'm a little mixed up between the phone call and the attack. I'm sorry, but I don't remember much about the phone call."

"I told you who I was and your voice changed. You said 'Get away from me' then you said you would call the cops if I didn't leave." I turned to Freckles. "I thought she was talking to me."

"Why would you think that?"

"Because I was on the phone with her!"

"Ms. Ingram, can you corroborate that?"

She held out the business card she had shown me. "The person who attacked me left this behind." Freckles took the card and rubbed his thumb over the edge of it.

"I'm sorry, ma'am, I didn't catch your name," he said to me.

"Samantha Kidd. Yes, *that* Samantha Kidd. Only, I didn't drop that card and I didn't attack Florence. I came to the store when I realized what happened and I waited until you arrived to make sure she was okay. Would I do that if I had attacked her?"

"Ms. Kidd, what's your contact info?"

I rattled off my phone numbers, home and cell. Considering I'd stopped carrying my cell phone to avoid contact with the mortgage company, I figured there was no harm. I suspected I'd be hearing from Detective Loncar shortly but didn't suggest that to them. They were getting paid to make those kind of deductions, and at the moment I was unemployed. I had a stronger sense of people needing to work for their paychecks these days and didn't feel like cutting them any slack. They sure weren't cutting me any.

I took surface streets home, my mind abuzz while I drove. For now, the cops were treating the attack on Florence as a burglary. But it was her card, the one Patrick's Rolodex had been open to, that had led me to her store, and it was my name handwritten on a Tradava business card left behind at the scene of the crime. There *was* a connection, I could feel it. Now I had to find out what it was. Because the cops would be looking for a connection too, and even I had to admit I was in the middle of something. If the cops were looking to connect the dots between the murder, the attack, and me, there were dots aplenty.

When I got home I pushed the sofa in place in front of the door and wedged two wooden dining room chairs between the sofa and the hall closet. Tracks from the feet of the sofa were starting to tear at the shag carpeting, but I didn't care. I wanted to feel safe. I shut down the computer, folded up the calendar pages, and put anything else related to Patrick in the junk drawer, then poured a generous glass of wine.

In my former job, the one I'd left behind, I'd demonstrated I was a problem solver. It was on every review I received. My problems these days were as big as they came and it was time to see if the executives at Bentley's really had seen something of that skill set in me.

Logan rubbed against my ankles and I scooped him up, held him close, and nuzzled my face into his shiny black fur. He licked at my fingers. The warmth of his body vibrated against me. I carried him to the bedroom and dumped him onto the comforter. I tore my clothes off and dove between the sheets. So far, my move to Ribbon had been a disaster, but tomorrow was another day. Logan crawled on top of my chest and extended his paws so they touched my chin.

"The only person who can take care of me is me," I said to the furry black generator purring on my chest. "Starting tomorrow, I'll show the world what a risk taker I really am." I closed my eyes and failed miserably at getting sleep until the rising sun told me to stop trying.

Eddie started calling at eleven. I didn't tell him about the fabric store. I told him I was fine. I told him I was laying low. I told him I would not get into trouble. I told him all of this while sitting in my car in the parking lot of the Ribbon Designer Outlets. And after I hung up, I turned off the phone and stashed it in my glove box.

Patrick had said Ribbon was not New York and on some level that's why I liked it. Ribbon was neither a booming metropolis nor a small town but resided somewhere in the middle. Its population had been on the decline since sometime in the thirties, but it had its own Pagoda on a hill overlooking the city. It was home of the first outlet mall in the country but had the fifth highest crime rate of cities its size. You had to search far and wide to find good Mexican food, but it had the best pretzels money could buy.

Ribbon is not known to many people who aren't from the Tri-state area, but those who do know it think fondly of it for two reasons: the pretzels and the outlet malls. Pretzels are a staple, ready to snack on at basketball games, picnics, and quilting bees. Okay, I haven't actually been to a quilting bee, but if I were to attend one, being raised in the eastern Pennsylvania region, I'd be pretty upset if they didn't offer me some pretzels. We proudly call ourselves the pretzel capital of the world, offering an unparalleled assortment of the salty snack.

As proud as we are of our pretzels, we are even prouder of our outlet malls.

The off-price outlet mall can be traced to Ribbon. The first of their kind in the country, discount shopping venues on Moss Street and Penn Avenue offer everything from jeans to home furnishings to Japanese fighting fish. You could pay a couple hundred dollars to get a discount Ralph Lauren ensemble that originally cost closer to a thousand, or you could pay ten bucks for a velvet portrait of Elvis. I wanted neither a velvet Elvis nor a Japanese fighting fish. Today, I wanted information, but I had no idea what it would cost. I consulted the mall directory and located Catnip in the grand maze of retailers. Instead of heading there directly I ducked into a few shops along the way and charged up a respectable amount of merchandise so as to look like a non-threatening customer. Three return policies (confirmed) and one phone call to the credit card company verifying I wasn't shopping with a stolen Visa, I reached my destination.

Catnip had softer lighting and far fewer customers than the other stores in the mall which indicated two things: exclusive merchandise and higher prices. Designer clothing, even severely discounted and bought off-season, cost more than a lot of people were willing to pay. Red stood by a fixture, adjusting a display of leather skirts so the hangers were each an inch apart. She looked over her shoulder and said hello seconds after I entered the store, then moved to a table of cashmere twinsets and refolded the lavender stack.

Her striking red hair swung easily around her face in a blunt cut bob. She was either less than one percent of the population, or had a great colorist; I couldn't tell which. Tall and lean, with a body that was less curves and more angles, she approached me with confidence. She didn't acknowledge we'd met before. With an armload of packages, I looked like the perfect customer, and on a slow day, she wouldn't want to risk offending me. She offered to hold my packages behind the counter and I took her up on the offer, because it would be a lot easier to focus if I weren't bogged down with bags of merchandise I already knew I couldn't afford.

I headed for the designer racks, trying to hatch a plan to chat her up, but she beat me to it.

"You look like you're losing your steam," she said.

"I think my last cup of coffee has officially worn off. All that's left is a desire to accessorize," I said casually, flipping through a rack of satin blazers marked 75 percent off.

She laughed. "A desire to accessorize can provide a lot of fuel, I know that first hand."

She was good at making small talk, which must have helped her store move its higher-priced product. That might help me get her talking about other things, like why she was at Tradava the morning I'd found Patrick's body, and what her connection was to the competition. I waited for her to acknowledge she knew who I was. She didn't.

She motioned to the racks that stood toward the front of the store. They were peppered with signs identifying their creators: Donna Karan, Gucci, Escada, Nina Ricci. Other, smaller fixtures surrounded them, a mixture of merchandise from lesser known designer collections.

"Your assortment is fantastic," I commented. "I'm not familiar with a few of your collections. Is this one new?" I asked, pulling an olive green satin army jacket from a fixture signed *Clestes*. It was one of the names in the design competition.

She took the hanger and held the jacket in front of her. "One of a kind-handmade couture." She brushed her hand against the fabric twice, smoothing out invisible creases.

"Clestes," I said slowly. "Is it a man? Woman? "

"Both. It's a male-female team. Mostly unknown. He designs the textiles, she designs the patterns. I don't think their timing was very good, but I do love the clothes. Would you like to try it?"

"No," I said a little too quickly. "Olive green isn't my color," I added.

"Perhaps this is more your style?" She held up a pinstriped suit from a neighboring rack.

"That's fabulous!" I exclaimed. I snatched the hanger from her and ran a finger down the black satin piping that set off the lapel. It was a menswear-inspired jacket, but the subtle feminine touches made it sexier than a sheer black lace dress. There was no label inside, only a couple of threads to indicate that one had been removed. "Who designed it?"

"I don't know. This came from a lot of designer apparel I bought, sight unseen. The price for the lot was worth the gamble. Now, what size should I pull for the pants?" She asked.

Red stayed by my side as I shopped. Every time I got close to bringing the conversation toward Patrick she redirected my attention back to shopping. I finally admitted I was too tired to try anything on, and she took that as a cue to direct me to the register. As we continued to talk, I wished I'd met her under different circumstances, where I could invite her to lunch and we could talk about fashion instead of murder.

"You know a lot about the industry," I commented, mentally weighing my word choices, looking for a way to bring Tradava into the picture.

"I was thinking the same thing about you. Where do you work?" she asked.

"I'm the trend specialist at Tradava," I answered in an oh-what-the-hell moment. "Remember, I was there when you came looking for Patrick, the morning he—" I stopped talking when I saw the color drain from her face.

She turned around, put my selections on a small fixture, and punched a code into the register. As she started scanning the tickets I knew she was violating Rule #1 of customer service by keeping her back to me. If her behavior up to now had been any indication, it seemed something I'd said had shaken her up.

"What do you think about Patrick's murder?" I asked point blank.

She straightened her shoulders and lifted her chin slightly. With the back of her hand, she pushed her hair off her forehead and looked toward the stockroom doors then looked me dead in the eyes.

"You want to know what I think? I can't say I'm surprised. Sooner or later, if you make that many enemies, the odds turn in favor of something like this happening."

17

The brakes slammed on my shopping trip. If it hadn't been a metaphor, the store would have smelled like burning rubber.

"How well did you know Patrick?" I asked.

"Well enough to know he probably had it coming."

Our conversation was interrupted by a tall muscular man with tattooed forearms and sideburns who called out to her from the stockroom. "That detective you called is on line two."

"Excuse me," she said to me and walked away.

She'd called Detective Loncar? When? And why? Maybe she *had* recognized me from the morning at Tradava. Maybe she'd been chatting me up the way I thought I thought I was doing with her. But no matter what, if Loncar was coming to her store, I didn't want to be there when he arrived. He would have learned about my involvement in the attack at Pins & Needles by now, and might not understand my reluctance to return his calls. I wasn't ready for that face to face conversation but despite five or six shopping bags of merchandise, I hadn't yet gotten what I came for.

She returned quickly. "I'm sorry about what I said. I've never been Patrick's biggest fan." She twisted her fingers in the long strand of pearls around her neck. It was the first nervous habit I'd noticed, and it had started at the mention of the police. "Can I get you anything while you continue to shop?"

Information, I thought. *I need information more than I need anything at this entire mall.* My interest in fashion was definitely *not* insignificant at the moment and I had to figure out a way to keep her talking.

"You were at Tradava the morning he died," I said, pushing the conversation in the direction I wanted it to go.

"Fashion's a big industry but a small world."

"And how did Patrick affect your world?"

"I'd rather not talk about Patrick," she said. By now the necklace had become a knot. We stood facing each other, separated by a table of clearance cashmere sweaters and the kind of static you'd get by rubbing the sweaters against a balloon.

"Look. I know he has a great reputation in the industry, but I'm not one of his fan club. I think my assortments are better than what I see at Tradava, but I have to play the game just like everyone else, and at the moment, respecting Patrick is the name of the game." The man from the stockroom waved her over. "Excuse me again," she said for the second time, leaving me by the clearance rack.

I flipped through a couple more fixtures, then carried the pinstripe suit and a purple fedora to the cashier. I wondering where she'd put my purchases and if she'd notice if I fled the store and left everything behind.

Red returned before I could leave and totaled my purchases. She set the receipt in front of me, along with a pen, and set to work tissuing the hat.

"Do you need help carrying everything out to your car?" she asked politely.

I couldn't leave without getting her to tell me more about Patrick. I needed a plan. I scanned the interior of the boutique and I got an idea. "That would be great. But as long as I'm here, I probably should try on that Clestes jacket. As the trend specialist for Tradava, I really should be familiar with the experimental designers as well as the mainstream ones."

"I think you've done enough damage for one day." She picked up the packages behind the counter and walked ahead of me to the back door. I jogged a few steps to keep up with her, then pointed to my small black car in the corner of the lot. When we reached it, I popped the trunk and took the bags from her.

"Your store is great. I really mean it. I'll definitely be back."

She reached up to the lid of my trunk and slammed it down over the pile of packages. "I don't know what kind of game you think you're playing, but I don't want your kind of business."

"Excuse me?"

"I know you're not the trend specialist at Tradava, and I know you spent the last hour trying to get me to talk about Patrick. You've been ferreting yourself into the design competition and I don't like it. I have more to lose than I have to gain, so we're done here. The cops are on their way, and if you don't want to talk to them, you better leave." She stepped away from the car. "Consider that merchandise final sale, and find yourself another place to shop."

In a stunned silence I drove home. It wasn't until I sat in front of my house, next to a passenger-sized seat of fashionable booty I questioned her unwillingness to talk.

It took me four trips to get my packages into the house. Well, three to get the packages inside, and another to round up Logan, who had decided the open door was a chance for him to test his freedom. Fortunately for me, when Logan escaped, he didn't get farther than a few feet out the door, wondering which way to go. Looked a lot like the way I was feeling.

It was late afternoon, and it was time for me to process what I knew. Time for me to think. I carried the packages to the bedroom and went back down stairs to check the answering machine before I realized I had turned it off. I switched it back on and was halfway up the stairs when it started ringing.

"Dude, where have you been?" Eddie said when I answered.

"I turned off the machine. Nobody good calls me. I mean, except you."

"You might reconsider when you hear why I'm calling."

"Why are you calling?" I asked with reservations.

Silence filled the phone line, until he spoke again. "Loss Prevention called a meeting with all of the Tradava executives. We've been instructed to call them if you show up or claim to work there."

I wasn't sure I heard him correctly. Of course, the glass I dropped when he said that shattered on the floor, which might have affected my hearing a little.

"Say that again?"

"I don't think I have to."

"No, I don't think you do."

After we disconnected I crossed the kitchen to the pile of fashion newspapers Eddie had dropped off yesterday. The copy on top was the one I'd flipped through during the night I spent at Tradava, the one with the picture of Nick inside. I used it as a dust pan, rounding up the broken glass shards from the floor, then threw it away and went upstairs to escape.

I filled the bathtub with water and poured in a couple of scoops of powdered milk. Time passed without notice. Without phone calls, without interruptions. It was almost like the beauty police knew I needed these moments of solitude and had run interference with the outside world. I guess that might make them the beauty football team instead of the beauty police, which was fine by me, since I was avoiding the police. Didn't football teams run interference?

My thoughts ran in an abstract pattern, resting occasionally on my predicament but quickly moving onto other topics. Who killed Patrick? Would I look as good as Nick's date at the Designer's Debut Gala? Did I need to look for another job? Should I cap off my night of pampering with a glass of wine?

The answers were pretty simple. I didn't know, better, probably, probably not. The bathwater had lost most of its heat and the milk was starting to curdle. My fingertips shriveled to a pink raisiny texture and the stress had long left my body. The bedroom, now strewn with new clothing, assaulted me with buyer's remorse. Until I worked out the job situation, I had no business shopping. I belted on my robe, turned my back on the room and went downstairs. I fished the *Style Section* out of the trash and set it on the table. Nick wasn't the only one whose picture was in there. Amanda Ries was in there too, and it was time for me to learn how she was connected to Patrick's murder. I tapped one finger on the picture of two models in red coats on the cover and dialed Nick's now familiar number.

"Nick Taylor," he said. Unnecessary since his caller ID probably told him it was me.

I forced pleasantries into my voice. "It's Samantha," I said. "Kidd," I added, to match his professionalism. "Who is Amanda Ries?"

"Leave it alone, Kidd." He hung up.

I called him back.

"Nick Tay—"

"Why won't you tell me?" I demanded.

"—Lor. With whom am I speaking?"

"Cut the crap, Nick. What are you trying to hide from me?" There was a long stretch of silence. "If she's your date for the gala, just say so. And if she's involved in a homicide, I'll find out."

"I'll see you at the museum. Good-bye, Samantha." He disconnected a second time. I tried to crumble the newspaper up into a ball, but it was too big. I threw it across the room like a Frisbee.

Next, I called Tradava and asked to be connected with the Visual department. Eddie answered on the second ring.

"When do you get off work?"

"I've been trying to leave for the past two hours."

"Can you meet me for dinner? Brother's Pizza, my treat."

"Be there in twenty."

I picked the crumbled up newspaper off the floor and smoothed it with my hands, then rolled it up and stuck it into my handbag. I pulled a tweed hat over my ponytail and zipped black boots up over my jeans, then left.

When Eddie arrived, he walked right past me. I waited until he doubled back, then lowered the newspaper I held in front of my face. "Psssst. Over here."

He dropped into the booth opposite me. His eyes moved back and forth between my face and the hat. Okay, maybe I'd failed at the less eye-catching part of the agenda. Chianti bottles dangled over our heads and velvet-flocked paisley wallpaper cocooned us from the twenty-first century. The flame to the candle between the oregano and crushed red pepper threw off an eerie red glow, thanks to the faceted glass dome around it. The original wood tables had remained in place since the seventies; kids probably came here to find their parents' initials carved inside a heart. If they ever tore out the interior for a renovation I could redo my basement in retro pizza chic.

I pulled the *Style Section* out of my handbag and pushed it toward Eddie. Coffee grounds smudged the face of the model on the left of the cover. "Page seven."

He unfolded the paper and flipped the pages. "It's a good thing my picture never ends up in here," he said.

"Why?" I looked across the table and gasped. Amanda the goddess's face, no longer a picture of beauty, had been creatively defamed with little more than a felt tip pen. Her perfectly whitened teeth were blacked out and a set of horns was perched atop her head. The lines had blurred but the message was clear. Somebody didn't like Amanda. And considering I was the one in possession of the newspaper, it seemed like someone was me. Embarrassing as it was, I reasoned to myself, it could be worse. I could have cut out a picture of my head and pasted it on her body.

I slammed a hand down over the doodling. "That is Amanda Ries. She's a finalist in the competition, and we haven't seen or heard from her. That's suspicious, right?"

"Is that what you're all hopped up about? I would have thought it was the fact that she's pictured with Nick or that she used to work for Patrick."

18

"She worked for Patrick?" I asked. I remembered the word ARIES on files in the cabinet. A. Ries. It was so obvious now. I wondered what other obvious things were right in front of me. "When? Did you know her? Are you friends?"

"Slow down, camper. She worked for him for a couple of years. I don't think they really got along. I don't think they *didn't* get along either, but I don't think they made a real connection. She used to cover the accessories market and a few of the smaller designer shows Patrick didn't want to attend. I heard they had a big blowup when he wouldn't listen to her critique of one major runway show. She even went over his head to the executive committee but they sided with him. She didn't show up for work for two weeks and everybody thought she abandoned her job."

"That's how she left?"

"No, she came back like nothing happened. It was weird. People used to talk about her freelancing occasionally but after she came back, it was like, don't get caught talking about Amanda. I don't know what she did during that time. I think

Patrick pushed her out the door. Like, it was Tradava or whatever she was doing on the side but she had to make a choice. He wouldn't allow her to do both. Conflict of interest, I think. There was no room for advancement at Tradava if she kept working for Patrick."

"So if Patrick was out of the picture, she'd be in line for a promotion? I still think this sounds a lot like a motive." I wouldn't have minded if we found a tidy way to hang the murder on her, since it would clear me of all wrongdoing and get my job back, and leave Nick available for ten to fifteen years. Maybe less for good behavior.

"Why didn't you tell me this before?"

"Before when? Before two days ago you were a signature in my high school yearbook. Besides, I don't spend a lot of time in those offices. My home base is in the Visual workshop with my staff. They actually work when I'm around."

"Doesn't this make her a legitimate suspect? She had means. She had opportunity. And Nick won't tell me anything about her."

"What's her motive?"

I pulled the folder of designer bios out of my tote bag next, extracted one sheet of paper, and slapped it down on the table.

"There's her motive," I proclaimed, my index finger repeatedly stabbing the paper between her name and the purple A had been written on the corner of her application.

He looked over the information on the page. "She says here Patrick is the one who encouraged her to enter the competition. Explain how that would make her want to kill the man?"

"Okay, so it isn't really a motive. But she's in the competition and she was in the right place at the right time. No one would have suspected her coming and going. Why do I have to find a better motive? *I* don't have a motive! How can I be under suspicion and Amanda not?"

"She was employed there. Any evidence of her presence was probably written off as normal."

"And she doesn't work there now, so nobody bothered to see if she skipped to Canada with a hundred G's in small bills."

A pizza appeared on our table, as if by magic. Eddie pulled two slices apart and slid one onto a paper plate, shaking crushed red peppers and oregano on it. He paused briefly to acknowledge my stare, and tipped his head to the side. "I called ahead and ordered. If I left it up to you we'd never eat." He tore off a piece of the crust and bit into it, letting his slice cool on the plate.

"Whoever killed Patrick didn't seem like the murdering type." I said, ignoring Eddie's unexpected foresight. "Otherwise he would have known he was being threatened, or someone else would have noticed something suspicious. It must have been someone Patrick knew and trusted, someone who didn't seem out of place hanging around Tradava. And the EMT jacket in that bottom drawer, that's weird. Who could have gotten into my office without being noticed? Employees, that's who. Amanda. Michael. Both on the list of designers." I bit into the tip of a slice and immediately chugged water to cool my burnt mouth. "My money's on Amanda."

Eddie had a faraway look in his eyes. and I could tell he was looking for flaws in my logic. We kept our voices low. Gone were the jokes and sarcasm. Details were a little too close to home now. Spread out in front of us was the assortment of designer bios, and pieces of the disjointed puzzle were starting to fit together like mismatched panels on a quilt.

"What about security?" I asked.

"At a pizza place?"

"No, security at Tradava. Don't they keep track of who comes and goes from your wing?"

"Security is there to protect the merchandise from being stolen from the store. They don't watch our wing. It's our responsibility to lock the doors if we don't want people to walk in."

"Nobody seems to take that seriously."

"Michael took the responsibility *very* seriously, but he said his keys were missing."

"When did he say that?"

"This morning. He came in and I asked him."

"But they were in the office the day I started."

"How do you know that?"

"Because I took them."

"Sam!"

I tore a piece of crust from the slice of pizza on my plate and dabbed it in a pool of grease. "Get this. He didn't have to pay any entry fees for the competition. And the woman at the fabric store says he only shops the remnants because he's broke. He was there the morning Patrick was murdered, and he was there when the body was found. That's a lot of coincidence. How come he's been missing since Patrick's murder? That's suspicious."

"He's not missing. I just said he came in this morning. Besides, I never saw him as homicidal."

"It's always the ones you don't suspect."

"So we have another person with means and opportunity. What does his bio say?"

I flipped through more applications until I found Michael's. The purple circled C had bled through the paper.

"Wait here," I said.

I left Eddie at our table and went to the restroom. After locking myself in, I pulled my cell phone out and called the number on Michael's application.

"MD designs," answered a high-pitched male voice.

"Michael, this is Samantha Kidd. We met a few days ago at Tradava, in the trend offices."

"Um, yes. I remember." His voice quivered, but I couldn't tell if he was nervous or if it indicated an unfortunate residual note of puberty he'd never outgrow.

"Michael, I need to meet with you. Regarding the competition."

"You have nothing to do with the competition."

"That's not entirely true," I said. I paused for the briefest moment. When no counter-point followed, I continued. "I've reviewed Patrick's files and I have a few questions. Where and when can we meet?"

"What do you want?"

"I want to talk about the money."

"The money is in a safe place, and the person who is entitled to it will get it."

"You know where it is!" I said, perhaps a bit too enthusiastically, as indicated by the click on the other end of the phone. "Hello? Hello?"

This was news, big news. Michael knew something nobody else did. Which bumped him up several steps on the scales of suspicion. I noted the address listed on his application and headed back to the table to share the news with Eddie. Problem was, he was no longer alone. Nick sat across from Eddie with a slice of my pizza in front of him.

"Fancy meeting you here," he said.

"If I didn't know any better I'd say you've been following me."

He shrugged, as though it was a possibility, which made me wish I hadn't joked about it.

I looked back and forth between the two men at the table. Nick, in a camel hair blazer, white shirt, plaid scarf. His curly brown hair was slightly disheveled which made him look younger than he was. Eddie sat across from him, in a nylon windbreaker over a Green Lantern T-shirt. He'd shaved the side of his head on one side, not unlike his yearbook photo. Both looked comfortable in their own skin even though they couldn't have appeared more different.

"Have you two been formally introduced?" I didn't wait for an answer. "Nick Taylor, Eddie Adams. Eddie, Nick. You guys should chat. You probably have a lot in common." They looked at me like two men who didn't know they'd been set up on a blind date. I grabbed the folder off the booth and shoved it into my handbag. "I gotta go."

I drove out of the parking lot and turned right on Perkiomen Avenue. The address on Michael's application wasn't far. I passed a couple of diners and gas stations, one roller rink, and a beverage distributor before the numbers on the buildings came close to Michael's address. I slowed down until I spotted a small shed that sat back from the road. The mailbox out front said MD Designs in black plastic letters.

I parked next to the mailbox and got out of the car. The shed was the kind you could buy at Lowes and place on the back of your property line to store your lawnmower and tools. It wasn't a residence. I knocked on the door but no one answered. There were no cars around. Not one to waste a perfectly good opportunity I walked around to the back. A small blue Gremlin pulled up behind my car and Michael got out. I clutched my keys tightly and walked back to my car. There was no way to hide myself now.

"What are you doing here?" he asked.

"As you may know, I've stepped into Patrick's role for the competition."

"I don't believe you."

I thought quickly. His response, though argumentative, was not the same as saying he knew I was lying. I ran with it.

"Patrick had your name on his calendar for today along with your address. I think he wanted to review your ideas?"

"That's not Patrick's role. He was a judge. The judges don't get to see the collections until they're done."

"So who sees them first?"

"Ms. Ingram, the consultant."

"Florence? From Pins & Needles?"

"If you really were part of this competition you'd know that."

"Michael, we both know Patrick must have seen your collection. You worked for him and you're a finalist. I have a hard time believing you were able to keep everything secret from your boss."

"I knew someone would say I cheated! That's why Patrick didn't want me to know about the bank account or the sponsors, so nobody could accuse him of favoritism."

"But you do know about it, don't you?"

"I'm not telling you anything." He looked at my fist holding the keys.

"Keys." I raised my hand and spread my fingers with the key ring hooked over my thumb so he could see I wasn't hiding anything from him. "You told Eddie your keys were missing, but I found them in the office."

"They were missing. After I get to work I always put them in the bottom drawer of my desk. Always. When I couldn't find them I told security. I told the detective too."

"What-who-when?"

"When he questioned me about you being at Tradava."

"What did you tell him?"

"That I never heard of you."

"But you were Patrick's assistant! He had to tell you about me!"

Michael's deer-in-the-headlights stare relaxed into a very small smile. "You would think so, wouldn't you? But he's not around anymore so it looks like you're on your own."

"Michael, I'm not the person the police are looking for."

He snapped his fingers. "The police, that's right. Detective Loncar asked me to call him if I saw you again." He walked past me and unlocked the door of the shed.

I didn't stick around long enough to find out if he made that call. I hopped into my dirty car and drove home.

Unfortunately, I wasn't alone.

19

"I don't remember inviting you over," I said.

"You didn't." Nick rose from the porch swing in front of my house and followed me into the house after I unlocked the front door. I headed directly to the freezer and pulled out a half-gallon of ice cream. "Make yourself useful," I said, and pushed the carton and a couple of bowls toward him. When he wasn't looking, I shoved the *Style Section* into the trash and hid the computer. Nick tore a paper towel off the roll and wiped up a blob of ice cream that fell to my counter, then carried it to the trash.

"Hey, you threw out the newspaper with my picture in it." He held out a copy of the *Style Section* with the model in the red suit on the cover. Immediately I snatched it from his hand. "I find that personally insulting. I'll forgive you if you tell me you didn't know my picture was in it."

Play dumb? Yeah, sure. I could maybe stall him for oh, about ten seconds at best. "I didn't know your picture was in it," I recited dutifully.

He snatched it back. "Let me show you. It's not every day the paparazzi takes my picture."

"Here it is." He opened the paper and pointed to his picture. You would think for all of the times I'd looked at that picture I would have had a hard time faking surprise, but it came pretty easily. Largely because I wasn't faking.

The picture was unmarred by black ink. Amanda Ries' eyes stared directly into mine as she stood in the photo next to Nick. I gasped when I looked at the picture, which Nick misinterpreted as mild infatuation with celebrity.

"I had no idea you'd be so impressed."

Where were the black teeth? Where were the horns? Nick watched me with more than a little curiosity, so I filed my confusion away for later.

"When was this taken?" I asked.

"A couple of months ago at a benefit. I was lucky to step in front of the press photographer, to get some exposure."

I wanted to ask him about the caption that identified Amanda but after his recent warnings to leave her alone, it felt as though I'd be commenting on the elephant in the middle of the room. We stared at the newspaper spread out in front of us, scooping ice cream into our mouths. I tried another approach.

"Do you attend a lot of benefits?"

"Not really. Now that I'm opening my own boutique it's going to be more of a priority to attend industry events. You know, see and be seen. You never know who you're going to run into, or what could potentially be discussed at events like this. A lot of times it's just food, drink, and some entertainment but sometimes you get lucky and end up seated next to a CEO or a magazine editor who is wearing your shoes, and you have a natural conversation waiting to happen."

"Has that happened for you?"

"A few times. I've had my collections in major retailers for a while. I already have connections in the industry but now that I'm limiting my distribution, I need to have a different set of relationships. It's not all about market week and potential department stores anymore. Now it's about editorial coverage in magazines, a loyal client base, and capital."

"How exactly did you go about getting the funding to go solo?"

"It wasn't easy and it's still not a done deal. Getting referrals from people in the industry, especially at a store like Tradava, helped. Without Patrick's endorsement, I might have been looking at an entirely different set of circumstances. You have to find financial backers who are willing to invest in your collections and ideas and business plan but hopefully let your vision stand. Sometimes these backers have ideas of their own, and your vision gets lost. Best case scenario, you find a way to get the money with no strings attached."

I thought about the hundred large attached to the design competition and wondered again about the strings Patrick had pulled to get the funding. "So a large windfall could make a real difference to a new designer."

"For designers starting out, yes. Being in the right place at the right time doesn't hurt, either. Publicity, getting people to know your name, that can make all the difference in the world." He gestured toward the newspaper picture. "That's what Amanda was hoping, at least."

"Could winning the design competition help you?" I asked tentatively, immediately wondering if I'd just blown the only opening I had to get him to talk about Amanda. But Nick had never mentioned his connection to the competition, and I didn't know if there was bad blood there.

Nick looked at me sharply. "Why would you ask something like that? I'm not in the competition."

"But you entered. I saw your application."

"Amanda entered me without asking. Technically it's a design competition and I'm a designer. A couple of interns processed the paperwork and I got lost in the shuffle. When Patrick saw the candidates, he was afraid it would look bad to say there had been a mistake so we agreed he'd disqualify me. Stop guessing at things that have rational explanations, Kidd.

If that's what's been bothering you, you should have asked me."

My mind wandered to the money. The contest. The contacts. The guaranteed order from Tradava. It would have been easy for an insider to gain favor from the judges by being closer than the competition. Amanda would already have friends on that judging panel. If her history with Patrick was less than favorable, his vote might not have gone in her favor. That might be something worth killing for. And Nick's behavior, while temporarily explained, was still off. There was a reason he'd told me to stay away from Amanda and I still didn't know what it was.

Suddenly I wasn't feeling so great. I carried our empty bowls to the sink and ran cold water over my wrists. My thoughts raced.

"Do you know how I can get in touch with Amanda? If I want to ask her some questions?" I asked.

Nick's spoon clinked against the bottom of his bowl. "I don't think that's a good idea," he said without looking up.

"Why not? She used to work at Tradava. Maybe she can give me some tips."

He pushed his bowl away from him with a shove. "I'm warning you, Samantha, keep Amanda out of this."

It was like a slap in the face. "Keep Amanda out of what?"

He leaned back against the kitchen counter and his stare drilled holes into my gaze like root-beer barrel shards. "She's moved on and you should too."

"Yeah? Well I'm trying to but the world, life, isn't cooperating!" I leaned forward and waved my arms around. "That's what this whole move to Ribbon was about—moving on. Only I can't, Nick. I can't move on because there are walls all around me, locking me in and not letting me move forward or backward, or even sideways."

He was startled by my response and a part of me couldn't blame him. An instant later his face softened. "Come here," he said, and opened his arms. I kept my distance. His arms dropped to his sides. "I guess the transition to Tradava has been tough on you."

"Things at Tradava are fine," I snapped.

"Are they?" He stared at me for too long. Long enough for me to wonder how much he really knew about my predicament. Long enough for me to crack under the pressure of his direct eye contact and look away. Long enough to realize how that must have looked to him and to look back.

He stood from the table and picked up his jacket. Our eyes connected, but I stayed behind the counter. "Okay, if that's how you want it, I guess I'll be going now."

I followed him to the front door, my nerves fraying as we walked. When we reached the door, he turned around, catching me off guard. "You're not as alone as you think you are, Kidd. You're the one who's building those walls." The sweetness of his smile was disarming. "Everything's going to be okay."

I stared into his deep brown eyes, this time not breaking the connection. A few seconds later he pulled away and left. I shut the door behind him and triple-locked it.

I didn't waste time pushing the sofa in front of the door. I raced to the newspaper on the table to figure out what was going on. I checked the cover, then flipped through the pages one at a time. When I got to the page with Nick and Amanda, a round stain on the opposite page, probably from the base of my wine glass, stared back at me. No horns. No blacked out teeth. No nothing. That meant there were two newspapers. That meant I wasn't the one who had marred Amanda's image in a fit of wine and jealousy.

That could mean only one thing.

Someone else disliked Amanda more than I did.

20

I slumped against the duct-tape-patched booth at the restaurant where Eddie and I arranged to meet. Three of the letters on their sign were burnt out and an A was on the fritz. Eddie lined up packets of sugar, not saying a word. I'd called him and demanded a meeting when I realized there were two newspapers and he had the one with the incriminating artwork.

"There's a killer setting me up," I said in a low voice, and leaned forward. "And I might have information that could end all of this. But I'm afraid to go to the cops, even though they might be able to use what I know and my life can go back to normal."

"What do you have that you could actually take to the cops?" His attention remained focused on his sugar packet masterpiece while he spoke.

"I have two newspapers, one with the ring of a wine stain on it from the other night and the one with the doodles." I ticked items off on my fingers. "I have the empty wine bottle in the recycling bin too. Don't they have some kind of tests that can show that it's all the same wine, to prove something?"

"What do you want them to prove, Sam? That you drank a bottle of wine while reading a fashion newspaper? All that would prove is that you're a stylish lush." In a sweeping gesture he pushed the delicate grid of sweeteners off to the side of the table.

"What about Red? I saw her buying the same kind of seam binding that killed Patrick."

"How do you know it's the same kind? Besides, didn't you buy some yourself? A search of your house would turn it up as evidence."

"I don't know how many different kinds there are. I just want to find something that can lead the police in another direction." I didn't like to admit that, in my efforts to remain clear of a murder investigation, I was unintentionally fabricating clues against myself. I put my elbows on the table and buried my face in my hands. Eddie dumped a couple of packets of sugar into his coffee and stirred aggressively.

"Here's my reality," I said from behind my hands. "I have a file on Patrick's computer that I broke into with a password I happened to find. The file has reviews of the finalists' collections and a list of Italian fashion designers, and neither one means anything to me. I have two copies of the same newspaper, one with a marked up Amanda, one not. An EMT jacket was put into the bottom drawer of the file cabinet sometime between my first day at Tradava when I found Patrick in the elevator and the night I spent at the store when someone dumped his body in the trash." I buried my face in my hands again.

"Anything else?" Eddie asked.

I peeked at him from between my fingers. "This whole thing definitely has to do with the competition. Nick's covering for Amanda. Michael stole something from Patrick's office. Maries Paulson is scared for her life. Red demanded a meeting with Patrick the morning he died and it turns out she doesn't even like him. Maybe there was no meeting. Maybe she did that so it looked like she had a reason for being at Tradava besides killing Patrick." We were both silent, absorbing our recap. "I need to get into that gala," I said, not for the first time.

"Too bad I RSVP'd no," Eddie mumbled.

"You were invited?"

"Of course. All of the management at Tradava was invited."

I sat up. "Why didn't you say something?" Things were looking up. "Call them. Tell them you changed your mind. I'll be your date."

"You're not exactly my type," he said. "No offense."

"Is that your reason?"

"No." He set the spoon down and pushed his hands away from him, rejecting my idea. "I'm saying no because I think it's a bad idea. I don't think you should be at the gala. If you're right about the killer being there, it's going to be dangerous. Not that I'm not enjoying the gossip aspect of all of this," he waved his hands in big circles, "but gossip is one thing and murder is another. You're in a jam and I'll help you out when I can, but I'm not going to put you in the line of fire."

I tuned him out halfway through his diatribe, hearing only things like "jam" and "line of fire." My mind, in top revise-your-game-plan mode, had already moved on.

"Okay, new subject. Now that I know I didn't black out Amanda's picture, who would?"

"If you hadn't finished a bottle of wine yourself you would have known that before now."

"This is no time to pass judgment. Who would black out Amanda's picture and why doesn't Nick want me talking to her? Did she have any enemies at the store?" I asked, sitting bolt-upright.

"Not that I know of."

"Did she get along with Michael?"

"No. They barely spoke."

"Would Patrick do it?"

He rolled his eyes at me. "I hardly think it's in character for the fashion director to draw horns on his assistant and leave the picture lying around the office."

"Okay, so if Patrick didn't do it, who would? Why would someone want to black out her picture?"

"Jealousy, anger, envy, annoyance, bitterness, to name a few reasons."

I didn't comment but realized Eddie was listing the reasons I would have done it. *Mental note* ... nah, don't bother.

A snippet of conversation between Nick and me floated around in my head. "Amanda was the previous trend specialist at Tradava," I said.

"Yes."

"But she's one of the designers in the file. Not just one of them but a finalist."

"So?"

I closed my eyes in concentration, straining to retrieve mental transcripts of last night.

"Nick was talking about going to different benefits and said something about her hoping to gain some exposure, to 'see and be seen'."

"Did you ask him about her?"

"Yes but all he did was warn me to leave her alone."

"Which obviously had little effect on you."

"I think he's somehow connected."

"To what? The competition? The murder? Amanda?" Eddie asked.

"That's what I need to find out."

We went our separate ways. Eddie had the best of intentions, but he was wrong. Avoiding anything connected to the murder and the competition wasn't going to help me. I had to return to the fundamentals. I needed to learn more about Patrick.

Aside from my observations during our interview, what did I actually know about him? Were there people who missed him? Did he leave behind family? Was anyone sorry he was dead besides me? Was there going to be a memorial service? What kind of person was he? To find the real killer, I had to know more about the victim. More than I'd learned from our interviews. I had to study his life, his patterns, his history, like I was following a seam to figure out how best to alter a dress. If I followed the stitches I'd eventually come to the starting point and ending point, hopefully without fraying my nerves in the process.

Back at home I went to work, writing up notes. *Who was Patrick? Critic. Mentor. Judge. Boss. Tastemaker. Famous. Fashion Insider. Powerful.* I scribbled over the preprinted blue lines on the blank page. Next: *Eliminate clues that lead to me.* That made me sound guilty. I lined through it and wrote *Find other suspect(s). Why kill Patrick? Career advancement. Blackmail. Revenge. Inherit his 'power of the pen'. Falsify his recent reviews. Information on laptop. DESIGN COMPETITION.* Other thoughts poured from my mind and covered the page. *Strangled with seam binding? Seam binding—fabric store—Florence. How does she tie in?* I wondered about the ally I thought I had in Nick and realized with chilling awareness I wasn't completely sure about his innocence. *What is Nick hiding?* He had a relationship with Amanda, who had a lot to gain by Patrick's untimely death. *Find out truth about Amanda.*

Who can I trust? followed finding out the truth about Amanda, and right about there I decided that, like it or not, I was going to have to take some covert action.

I didn't need Nick's permission or blessing to talk to Amanda, I had her contact information in the file of applications. I hit *67 to hide my return number then called her. She answered on the third ring.

"Could I speak to Ms. Amanda Ries, please?"

"This is Amanda."

I paused and scanned the bookcase. "This is Donna Parker calling from the *Style Section*."

"Donna Parker? Like the books?"

Crap. "Um, no. Donna Poker. Like the card game." *Stop babbling!* "I'm checking some facts for a story we're running on Patrick." I let my voice trail off. "I understand you worked for him at Tradava?"

"That's correct."

"And you're a finalist in his design competition?"

"That's true too."

"Can you tell me anything about your competition?" I asked in a sudden bolt of ingenuity.

"There's only one person who poses a threat. The others are still doing the work of students. Even Patrick thought so."

Mentally I ticked off the names: Amanda, Michael, Nick, Clestes. I knew all of them but one.

"Aren't you worried about Clestes?" I held my breath, waiting for her response. When she spoke, it was in a conspiratorial whisper.

"Ms. Poker, if you're really interested in talking about this, we need to meet face to face to talk. I know a few things that might help you out."

21

I made arrangements to meet Amanda at the public library. I didn't care what Nick had said. I wasn't letting this opportunity go to waste.

The library stood in the downtown district, and since childhood, it inspired happy thoughts and an overwhelming fascination with the concept of trust. I was mesmerized by the thought that the information coded in a little plastic card told the woman behind the desk to trust I would return the books I checked out. The library had always been a building of answers and innocence. Upon entering it, I had always felt empowered. I could use the safety of its walls and the knowledge that it offered to somehow better my life.

An eerie silence, more so than the usual library quiet, cloaked the building. Scruffy men in need of a shower read the newspapers and magazines to the left of the circulation desk, but the research terminals to the right were empty. I wandered the aisles and found a copy of *Who's Who: Fashion Edition*. Balancing the book on my knee, I flipped to the R's. There was nothing where Ries, Amanda should have been. I shut the book harder than intended and a puff of dust fluttered in the sun's rays. I mouthed an apology to the librarian.

A brief search of the library's database led me to several back issues of fashion magazines that referenced Patrick. I keyed the articles up, one by one, and read through *Mirabella*, *Mademoiselle*, and *Glamour*. *Vogue* carried a featurette on him as part of their "People Are Talking About ..." series. It was the cover that was blown up to poster size and hung on Patrick's wall. The Patrick that smiled at me from the article was a much younger man than I'd interviewed with weeks ago. One picture showed him standing next to Halston. The caption read, "Jersey? Sure!" Another showed him clinking champagne flutes with a radiant woman with white hair and trademark black glasses. The caption read *Celebrating Carrie Donovan's "29th" birthday*. Patrick had hung out with fashion royalty, that was for sure.

After reading the articles from the magazines, I moved my attention back to the *Who's Who*. Patrick's reputation blew me away. Reading about his start in the business, how he had an eye for talent that helped him identify new designers who went on to emerge as major contributors to the fashion world. He was credited for being one of the first American tastemakers, calling attention to stateside artisans once anonymous but now common knowledge. Article after article called him a friend to the unknown designer, encouraging those with talent to go out on their own and not let their careers be defined by the powerhouse labels that gave them their start. I began to see what Maries had meant when she said the competition was Patrick's legacy. Establishing a forum for new designers was a big deal, and the success of the first competition would allow for subsequent contests.

I read on. These journals painted a picture of someone who had impacted the lives of young creative students of fashion. He had been in the industry for decades, so it was possible his encouragement could have motivated a newcomer to go solo years ago and now be successful. Tradava was probably filled with assortments from people Patrick discovered, those indebted to him for providing a foot in the door opportunity. Recipients of glowing reviews had probably moved on to bigger and better collections, leaving behind nothing more than a few leftover markdowns on a clearance rack. Perhaps the merchandise hanging in Catnip. Merchandise with the labels removed. Someone who didn't want anyone to know their collection hadn't sold.

Patrick had a reputation for exposing new talent; that was his legacy. But from what I'd read, he hadn't discovered anyone recently. The changing face of the fashion industry had left critics like him behind while reality shows and celebrity endorsements claimed to discover the next big thing. It appeared the industry he loved had moved on without him. But then, he had decided to create a local competition.

This year.

Coincidence?

He had joined Tradava years ago because there he was a big fish in a small pond. Was that all there was to it? A high profile fashion director could exist comfortably at Tradava, in the industry but not be at risk of stirring up trouble. A family-owned department store wouldn't challenge him, an industry legend, to make or break anyone's career but rather would hope he would lend them credibility. It was the perfect co-dependent relationship, until Tradava pulled the plug on Patrick's plans for the competition, or determined he had outlived his promise. When Patrick turned elsewhere for funding, he said to the store and the world that he would not be turned out of the industry. If only I knew where he had gotten the money. Or where it was now.

Other than this particular competition, Patrick seemed to have been living a relatively normal, under-the-radar life. He had no enemies. Greed seemed to be the best motive for murder I'd discovered, and my research solidified the fact that the finalists in the folder at home represented those with the most to gain.

"Would you prefer this copy? It was returned while you were reading. I gave you an older version." I hadn't heard the librarian approach and I jumped, then noticed she was holding a different *Who's Who* than the one on my table. Met with my confused silence, she continued. "That patron just returned it."

"Thank you," I said automatically, while I craned my neck to see the figure who had left the library. The windows were smudged, restricting my view. A flash of red punctuated the gray figure but from this distance, I couldn't make out the details. Was that red hair peeking out from under a hat, a red scarf knotted around someone's neck, or just a red herring?

I turned the new volume of *Who's Who* to the 'R' section and looked up Ries, Amanda. There she was.

I devoured the information. Amanda Ries was indeed listed as a new designer. She had schooled at I-FAD, the Institute of Fashion, Art, and Design, had won a few design awards in local competitions, and had shown a capsule collection from a hotel room in New York a few years ago. It was the only collection cited.

There was nothing about her time at Tradava, which didn't surprise me. Our position was an assistant to the director, so it wouldn't merit a mention in *Who's Who*. The thing that stood out to me was even though she had been the trend specialist at Tradava for a few years there were no unaccounted for years on her design history. The journal wrote of her graduating years and her scheduled collection debut this year.

I reread the last line.

A collection debut this year.

The same year Patrick had decided to launch a competition.

Patrick's endorsement might have made a difference in her success, but an unflattering review would have killed those opportunities. She was a finalist in the competition that he would have reviewed, and he wasn't around to give his opinion. The timing seemed awfully suspicious.

I flipped to the T's to look up Nick, though my motivation lay somewhere closer to attraction than suspicion. His bio was fascinating:

Instead of following the well-trod path of most designers, design school and internships, Taylor interrupted his schooling to gain experience working for local cobblers, to understand how to construct footwear like a couturier constructs a garment. He spent his nights pursuing a double major in fashion history and business, graduated with honors, and licensed his name.

While his schooling could easily have landed him a sought-after position as creative director to a number of fashion houses or director of fashion at a respected retailer, he chose instead to partner with financiers to produce his shoe collection. His knowledge of the ins and outs of fashion and the business acumen gained in college put him a clear step ahead of other designers vying for editorial attention and orders from retailers. Uncredited, he collaborated with several designers to produce shoes for their runway shows, building a solid network in the business, and believes these contacts led to his early success. After several years of successful partnership between Taylor and his financial team he stunned again in a bold move to buy back controlling interest in his name, scale back distribution of his collection, reposition his line at a more attainable price point, and launch Nick Taylor Boutiques. At publication it is unknown if this risk will pay off.

The article went on to mention details of his graduation from the same fashion institute Amanda had attended. Same year. And knowing he and Amanda met in college disturbed me more than that photo in the *Style Section*. There was something about college friends that allowed them to drop in and out of each other's lives. Those bonds withstood just about anything. I wondered if the same applied to Eddie and me. Could I count on his loyalty if I needed it, or was I really on my own?

I approached the librarian at the checkout desk. "Can you tell me who returned this?" I asked in what I hoped to be a conversational tone. She looked at me suspiciously, then shook her head.

"Nobody returned it. It's reference material and can't be checked out." She reached out and took the volume from my hand and set it on a shelf behind her.

"But when you brought it to me, you said it had been returned."

"Another patron had been reading it, much like you were."

"Who?" I asked. "Was it a man or a woman? Can you tell me anything about them?"

She stared at me for a few seconds, and I got the distinct feeling she was memorizing my face, in the event she was asked to make a positive ID. "That would be a violation of privacy. Why are you so interested?"

"I'm new in town and just started a job in fashion. I thought maybe I'd find someone with the same interests as mine."

The librarian fingered the glasses that hung on a chain around her neck. "Fashion, you say?" She bent down and pulled a manila file folder from the trash. "A man called a couple of weeks ago and asked me to run copies from a few of our stacks. He said he'd be in to pick them up, but he never did. I threw the file away this morning while I was cleaning."

I flipped the folder open and discovered copies of magazine articles from back issues of *Vogue*. The top one was "People are Talking About ...Patrick." The following articles were on each of the designers listed in Patrick's protected file. Each copy was dated on the upper right corner in cursive handwriting.

"Are you sure it was a man who asked you to make these copies?"

"Quite sure."

"May I have them?"

"Five minutes ago they were in the trash, which is where I'll return them if you don't take them with you."

I doubled the folder over and stuck it into my bag. As if to prove she was telling the truth about the trash bit, a smudge of ketchup smeared across the corner and left a red residue on my thumb. I looked around for a tissue box but found none. Instead I found myself standing face to face with Amanda Ries.

Perfectly straight jet-black hair, a lilac wool tunic belted over brown tights and boots, and a stunning lavender handbag. While I would have known her anywhere, it struck me that the recognition wasn't two-sided. I put on my best poker face, fitting, for more reasons than one, and held out my hand. "Amanda Ries? Donna Poker. From the *Style Section.*"

"You—you asked me here to talk about Patrick?"

"Yes." I took a few steps away from the librarian who had evidence in the form of a library card application that I was lying about my name. "Can I buy you a cup of coffee?" I asked.

"You can stop the charade, *Ms. Poker,*" she said. I didn't like the way she emphasized my pseudonym. Made it sound fake. She glared at me and I forced myself to maintain eye contact. Looking away would have been too obvious of a tell.

"I don't buy your cover story for a second. Are you some kind of a spy for Clestes?"

"Clestes?" I blurted. "Your competition?"

"You might want to check your facts a little better." She leaned in toward me and I smelled peppermint on her breath. "I don't know who you are or what you want, but you work for the *Style Section* about as much as I do. If you're looking for facts, let me tell you one thing." She flipped a long black lock of hair behind her shoulder, glanced toward the librarian, then back to me. She leaned in, well into my dance space, and I pulled back involuntarily, then immediately regretted the move and leaned forward too. I had the feeling that, to anybody watching, we were acting like a couple of chickens in a cage fight.

"Patrick and Maries have given me consistent feedback and Florence has been impressed with everything I've done so far. Don't get in my way. I *will* win that competition." She stormed past me and pushed against the heavy wooden doors. I followed her.

"Florence Ingram was attacked at the fabric store," I called out behind her. "You know anything about that?"

Her hand reached out for the banister and her knuckles went white as she gripped it. Her left foot dangled over the step long enough for me to notice, then she continued her descent down the concrete stairs to the sidewalk.

More slowly, I descended the stairs too, then unlocked my car and flipped through the articles in the folder. I could think of only one man who would take the time to have a file of articles copied and never pick them up. The same man who had a list of those designers on his computer in a protected file. The man who couldn't make that trip to the library because he wasn't alive. Patrick. Not for the first time, I felt I was walking in the footsteps of a dead man. I only hoped while looking for answers, the same fate would not befall me.

I started the car and drove to Tradava. I needed to get in to the gala and the Tradava connection was my best shot. It wasn't until I sat in the parking lot outside of the store that I questioned my motives. Was this one in a string of very bad decisions? Was my judgment completely in left field, or was I getting closer to figuring out who killed Patrick? I didn't know, but now didn't seem like the time to question my thoughts. After all, I'd recently bought a purple fedora. Clearly, my judgment was fine.

The Indian summer heat had broken, leaving an abrupt change in temperature. I found a driving glove in the glove box, and dug its mate out from under my car seat. After snapping them on and disguising myself with the pashmina

I'd swiped from Patrick's office and an oversized pair of sunglasses, I went into the store and headed straight to the trend offices.

There was a strip of yellow tape across the glass door, but it had already been sliced through. I pushed on the door and it swung open easily. Someone else had been here. Recently.

The desk had been cleared of Patrick's inbox and the papers I'd left behind and set up with a sewing machine. A mess of fabric cuttings, lace, and trim covered the purple sofa. A bust form stood half-pinned with origami folds of taffeta in shades of lavender, orchid, and black. Pieces of chartreuse lace lay scattered on the floor along with a long strip of lilac seam binding. The color combination was rich and sophisticated.

I crossed the hallway to Michael's desk and called Eddie. A black and white photo peeked from the base of the phone. I freed the picture, immediately recognizing the two people in the photograph, even though one of them had been covered with horns and a mustache. It was a picture taken outside of the diner Eddie and I frequented. The Devo logo was legible on the front of Eddie's T-shirt. But the person he was talking to, the person with a knife drawn stabbing her in the heart, with blood droplets drawn falling down her gray tweed cape, pooling around her purple patent leather pumps was me. The words *GET HER* were scrawled on the side of the picture, and the handwriting was undeniably the same as that on Michael's calendar.

I slipped the picture in an envelope and put it in my pocket. Eddie's machine picked up. "Eddie, it's Sam. Listen, I'm at Tradava, and I'm freaking out. I think I stumbled onto something—" I heard noises from the hallway. I had to get out of there, before someone discovered me. "Call me." I hung up and grabbed my handbag and hurried into hallway. Just as I rounded the corner, something crashed down on the back of my head. I fell to the floor and blacked out.

22

"**K**idd? You with me?" asked a voice that sounded like it spoke from the other end of a tunnel. "Yo, Kidd, come on, wake up." Somebody jostled my shoulder repeatedly. "Samantha?"

I moved a little. My head pulsed with pain that radiated from the back. The voice saying my name got closer, and when I was finally able to open my eyes my unfocused vision rested on Nick. We sat side by side on a sofa outside of the men's and women's lounges.

"You okay?" he asked.

"What happened?" I tried to remember. "Why are you here?" I looked at him again. I wasn't supposed to be seen at Tradava. I had to get out of there before someone recognized me, but I didn't think I could stand up yet. I touched the back of my head, felt a lump, and dropped my hand to my lap.

"I found you sitting here by yourself. I said hello a couple of times and you didn't answer me. I came over to give you a hard time. When I sat down you slumped against me. You gave me a scare, at least until I felt your pulse. What are *you* doing here?"

"I-I don't know." Details of the past few minutes escaped me. I had been in Patrick's office, but now I wasn't. My fingers returned to the lump at the back of my head. I'd been knocked out. But how had I come to be sitting on a bench outside of the little known ladies lounge on the fifth floor?

"Work," I said. Paranoia was back and I was in a distrustful mood. I needed more time to think, more time to concentrate on what had happened when I was in the office, what I remembered. "Get away from me," I said, pushing his arm.

"Kidd, calm down." Two short, round ladies in hats walked out of the ladies lounge and smiled at us. Nick put his arm around me and smiled back.

"Let go of me," I hissed.

"Kidd, I don't know why you're mad at me, but I didn't do anything." We faced each other and he had a hand on each of my upper arms. He smiled his eye-crinkling smile, and I wanted to believe what he said more than I didn't.

"I'll be right back. Wait here."

"Okay," I lied. As soon as he turned the corner, I stood up on shaky legs. Dizziness overcame me and I reached out to the wall to steady myself. I could leave, I could go right now, before Nick returned.

I fingered the envelope in my jacket pocket then pulled it out. On the back was a hastily scribbled note. *You are wasting your time. I can prove you murdered Patrick if you get in my way.*

I sank back into the sofa. Someone had been in the trend offices. Someone had deliberately knocked me out. The envelope was empty, the photo was gone. If I had any doubts about being watched, set up, or knocked out, they'd just been erased. I'd been assaulted by the killer.

The magnitude of the situation hit me. Was I scared? Sure. But I was pissed off too. Someone was making a mockery of my fresh start in Ribbon, tearing out the seams of my carefully planned new life and throwing bleach on the vivid colors of possibility. And everyone around me wanted to stop me from discovering who that person was.

But I wasn't ready to pack it in. My whole life I'd worked for someone else and excelled and it was time to put myself first. No matter what happened, I'd leave here knowing I didn't go without a fight. Some crazy killer out there was about to learn one thing. You don't mess with the Kidd.

Nick returned. I stuffed the envelope back into my pocket before he could ask about it and stood back up.

"I thought you would have left by now," he said.

"I told you I'd wait."

"I naturally assumed you were lying. Come on, I'm getting you out of here." I wasn't sure I liked the directness to his tone. I didn't know if it stemmed from concern, irritation, or something darker. After I took a few unstable steps I begrudgingly accepted his offer.

When we reached the parking lot he directed me toward his white truck, against my constant claims that I was capable of driving myself home. "I don't know what happened to you back there, but you're in no shape to drive. Get in."

"I don't want to leave my car here."

"You don't have a choice."

"I'm not drunk."

"Exactly. But you were passed out on a bench at Tradava, and you won't tell me why. I'm taking you home so you can get some rest." Our standoff ended when Nick picked me up and threw me over his shoulder.

"Put me down!" I said, and pounded on his back with a gloved fist. He ignored me until we reached his truck. I could have elbowed him in the ribs and tried to run away, but even I knew I wouldn't have gotten far.

Nick drove to my house in silence. Our relationship had taken a weird turn a couple of days ago and was still in uncharted territory. I didn't know if we were better or worse for all of the changes. By the time we reached the house I was too tired to function. I tossed my coat on the sofa. The envelope fell out of the pocket and landed on the floor by Nick's feet. He bent down to pick it up and tapped it against his thigh a couple of times before tossing it on the table. A nagging voice at the back of my head kept telling me I needed to get him out of my house. I think it came from the same area as the bump.

"May I have that?" I asked, nodding at the envelope.

He folded the envelope in half and thrust it at me. "You're not going to the gala, are you?"

"Of course I'm going. It's an industry event, right? I work in the industry."

"I don't think it's going to be worthwhile for you to attend. Anyway, I'll be there so I'll let you know if anything exciting happens."

Heat flared up around my neck. "Look, Nick. If you're trying to string me along while you date your girlfriend, that's not going to happen. I appreciate you being nice to me and helping me out today, but don't think you can tell me what to do and where to go. I'll go wherever I want to, whenever I want to. Got it?"

He leaned forward, his arms resting on his thighs, and dropped his gaze to his hands. "I'm worried about you," he said. He looked up at me. I remained silent and waited to see what he would say next. He leaned back against the cushions and smiled. "Doesn't matter what I say. You're going to do whatever you want. Right?"

I was confused again, not knowing his motivations. On one hand, I wanted to show him the threat, tell him about the suspects, and ask if I could be a third wheel to his date with Amanda. On the other hand, he knew something, and was keeping it from me. And if Amanda was the one guilty of murder, that made him an accessory, and not the kind you coordinate with your shoes. I wasn't sure how to treat him.

"You look like you want to talk about something."

Fight the temptation to tell him what you're thinking, I coached myself. "I'm tired, that's all."

"Then get some rest." Unexpectedly, he kissed me on the forehead, then stood up and left. I threw the locks shut behind him too tired to push the sofa to the door. I turned off the lights. As I pulled the curtains shut, I saw the outline of a person detach themselves from a bush in front of my house.

Someone was outside of my house right now.

And I was alone.

A flashlight would have been handy, but I was unprepared for this kind of emergency. *Mental note: leave flashlights everywhere.*

The last time I was in this house and had to rely on my senses in the dark was when I was ten years old, playing hide and seek with my sister. She'd turn off all the lights and give me a head start to hide. In the pitch black house, she would try to find me, while I either stayed hidden, or moved from spot to spot to stay unnoticed. In hindsight, it was kind of a creepy game for a ten-year-old to play.

But creepy or not, it had left me with the knowledge of how many steps it took to get from one room to another. The statistics were burned into my memory. Nine steps would get me to the kitchen. Eleven would get me to the counter, and twelve would get me to the phone.

At the ninth step, I ran into the stool tucked under the counter and knocked a stack of metal mixing bowls onto the floor. They rolled in a circle, sounding an aluminum alarm to anyone in a five-block radius. The phone fell to the floor, an insistent beep replacing the dial tone.

I guess my legs were a little longer than when I was ten.

A shadow approached my front door. I pressed my body to the base of the counter. A rap on the door triggered a burst of adrenaline. Slowly I extended my right leg, pointing my toes like a prima ballerina toward the phone on the floor, trying to pull it to me.

The man moved from my front door to my bay window. He reached inside his coat for—what? A knife? A gun? A lead pipe?

From the living room, my cell phone ring pierced the silence. The man out front returned to the front door again. I moved, fast, scrambling to the living room, fishing my hand between the green velvet cushions like a dog searching for a previously buried bone. The ringing stopped. I had to get away from sight. A few seconds passed and the buzz sounded again. As my hand closed around my phone I sent silent messages to the caller. *Leave a message. Come over and check on me. You should think it's weird I'm not answering the phone.*

The man out front rapped his fist against the living room window. "Samantha, I know you're in there, I just saw you. Let me in." Click.

Eddie.

The body moved back to the front door and the fist raised and pounded again. I unlocked the padlock and pulled the door open.

"Took you long enough. Your neighbors were looking at me like I was some kind of stalker. It was like someone told them to look out their windows at that moment to check up on you."

Apparently my telepathic message travelled far enough to leave the house but didn't make it past the block. Good to know the limits of my powers.

"Where have you been? I've been calling you since I got that message from you at Tradava. What happened?"

"Follow me," I said. In the kitchen, I righted the phone and restacked the metal mixing bowls. I poured two glasses of water and handed him one. "There was a photo on Michael's desk, a picture of you and me, outside the diner. Someone drew a knife stabbing me in the heart. And blood droplets and a pool of blood around my boots. It said 'get her' along the side of the picture. I put the picture in an envelope and took it but someone knocked me out. I woke up on the fifth floor, next to Nick. Empty envelope, bump on my head."

Eddie gulped half of the water then burped. He leaned back against the kitchen table. Logan buzzed around his ankles, purring within seconds. "You have to call the cops, dude. This whole thing has gotten over your head. This is beyond detective games."

"You think that's what I'm doing? Playing detective games?" I drained my glass and considered refilling it with vodka. "Think about it from my perspective. Someone is out to get me."

I picked up the driving gloves I'd worn to Tradava, lined up the fingers, and set then in a neat pile on the countertop.

"Can I see the envelope?" Eddie asked.

I tossed the envelope on the table between us. He turned it over and read the threat, then tossed the envelope back on the table. "Dude, I'm telling you, go to the cops."

"I don't think so."

"Sam, don't be stupid. That's a threat. I mean it's a clue. I mean, it's both."

"Is it? Loncar hasn't believed one word of what I've said so far. If I take this to him now, what's to make him start believing me now? I could have written this myself. And it's not just Patrick anymore. A woman was attacked at the fabric store. The owner. She was the consultant to the finalists. She might have been killed too, if I didn't show up. But Loncar doesn't believe that either!"

The phone rang. We stood in the dark staring at it until the machine clicked on. "This is Brittany Fowler from Full Circle Mortgage. I've been trying to reach you with no luck. If you don't call us back about your mortgage we're going to start foreclosure proceedings." She hung up.

"What am I going to do?" I said.

"If you don't go to the cops, I will," Eddie said, his green eyes as sharp as a broken Coke bottle.

"Give me a day. Let me get through the gala, let me see what I can find out."

"Sam, I don't feel good about this." He stood up and crossed the room to the front door, then turned back around. "Twenty-four hours," he said before leaving.

23

ddie didn't understand my reasoning for not calling the police, and I didn't waste time trying to convince him. Instead, I'd shuffled him out the door, then filled two bowls of vanilla ice cream: one for me and one for Logan. He sniffed at it, patted it, then licked his paw. I lowered myself to the floor, opposite him, and scooped a mound of ice cream from my own bowl into my mouth. After it melted on my tongue I swallowed, then reached a hand out and stroked Logan's black fur. "If the cops take me away, who's going to take care of you?" I asked him. He turned his yellow eyes toward me and yowled. Traces of ice cream coated the tips of his whiskers. I pulled my hand back, took another scoop, and let him eat in peace. My mind, hopped up on Breyer's, wandered to Nick.

His presence at Tradava. The ride home. The right place/right time coincidences.

When I was a buyer and Nick was a vendor, he'd needed my relationship—the professional one—to ensure his success. From the moment I met him, years earlier, I'd felt an attraction to him, but getting involved with one of my vendors was strictly verboten. I'd had to remind myself of it on more than one occasion, especially on those nights when he took me to dinner after a long day of appointments. From that first night, when he offered to walk me back to my hotel before learning I lived in the city, to the night in May when we capped off the evening with lemon meringue pie, I knew I'd been keeping myself in check for fear I'd ruin our work relationship by trading it for something fleeting. I had always suspected he felt the same way but now, I wasn't so sure.

Had the chemistry I'd felt all been an act? Had the flirtation been all about orders? He didn't need anything from me anymore. I had absolutely nothing to do with the success of his solo venture, unless you counted future shoe sales. What I'd read in *Who's Who* detailed a talented designer driven enough to stand out from the pack. What I didn't know was the depth to his drive.

Nick was on the verge of jumpstarting his career, without the benefit of financial backers. Could that make him go from the normal, charming person I had been attracted to in the past—hell, was still attracted to—to a person with homicidal tendencies? I couldn't see it. But was he willing to look the other way if someone he knew did? *College friends*. What did Amanda know about Nick that I didn't know? He was telling me to leave her alone for a reason.

As much as I wished they were, Nick and Amanda weren't the only two people on my radar. There was Red. And there was Michael. And there was Clestes, the mystery entry to the competition. One of them was hiding more than a runway collection. It really came down to one thing. The person who killed Patrick was either the one person with the most to gain by him being dead, or the most to lose by him remaining alive.

The attack on Florence from Pins & Needles was just as baffling, unless she knew something about the competition. If she did, her attack could have been a message ...or a warning.

There had to be more. I knew by now Patrick had taken measures to tell the world something was wrong. Going to the police. Loaning me the laptop with the protected file and hiding the password in the case. Leaving his Rolodex open to the card for Pins & Needles. But as charming as his cryptic methods might have appeared once, now they frustrated me. I thought back about our last meeting.

"As arbiters of fashion we have an obligation to honor the past and encourage the future. Every piece of fashion before us was important. Claire McCardell. Pierre Cardin. Steven Sprouse. Every fabric means something too."

"Even double-knit polyester?" I joked.

"We are not here to judge but to guide and educate."

"Patrick, I'm excited about this job."

"I see that in you. You'll make a fine addition to my team, Ms. Kidd."

"Is there anything else I need to know?"

"I don't email." He thought for a moment. "When you want to say Thank You, send a note. When you want to communicate, come to my office. And always remember, in our business, it's important to look the part. I expect you to be on time, but if you must be late, I'd prefer it to be because you were putting on lipstick before reaching the office or taking an extra thirty seconds to find the right shoes. When all else fails, Ms. Kidd, look *en vogue*."

At the time, I liked that expression. It was like a moment lifted from *Working Girl*. I liked knowing my sense of style would help me do my job. But now, I was as frustrated as ever. I looked at the ceiling.

"Patrick, why did you waste your time telling me how to dress? Why didn't you tell me what was going on? This business, your trend Department, was not as important as your life and now you're gone and I'm the only one trying to figure everything out. Why couldn't you just tell me?" I stared at the ceiling for a few more moments, wishing he really would speak to me from beyond the grave. Logan jumped up on the table and padded across the folder I'd brought home from the library and head butted me. I nuzzled his face for a second before scooping him up and flipping open the folder.

There was one article for each designer listed in the computer file. Patrick wanted to make sure someone paid attention to that file. I planted myself in front of the computer screen and stared at the list of designers. And again, nothing seemed out of the ordinary.

. Until now, I'd been approaching the mess of my life in reactionary mode. The killer had been one step ahead of me, destroying the life I was trying to create for myself. But what about those years of experience I had, the problem solving, the analytical sense? What about the ability to walk into a showroom filled with samples and edit a vast collection into a cohesive assortment for Bentley's? What if I used *that* skill set to figure things out?

My years of working in a buying office had left me with above-average skills when it came to manipulating a spreadsheet, and I couldn't get past the idea the one thing I needed to know was staring me in the face.

I clicked around the other pages in the workbook.

Nothing.

I scrolled down.

Nothing.

I hit control/ end, to go to the last cell used on the page.

The cursor bounced to v61472. Patrick's copy had ended on row 657.

It seemed like I'd stumbled upon something.

I clicked the button between the row numbers and column letters and set the font to black. Cells that had appeared empty now filled with data. Patrick had set the text to white on white so the page appeared blank to the naked eye. Virtual invisible ink.

I scanned the list of names. I'd seen them before but not formatted like this.

Rucci	Ciccone	$10,000
Cavalli	Costello	$10,000
Gucci	Corleone	$10,000
Gabbana	Louchesy	$10,000
Missoni	Liotta	$10,000
Armani	Tanzini	$10,000
Pucci	Marcello	$10,000
Piana	Gravano	$10,000
Miuccia	Maria	pending
Donatella	Castellano	pending
Entry fees		$10,400
TOTAL		$90,400

It wasn't a passing knowledge of fashion that helped me recognize the second set of names. It was a passing knowledge of quote/unquote business men. Names that had been in and out of the papers for years. I didn't know what they had to do with the list of designers or why Patrick had hidden the info. With the exception of the names by Donatella and Miuccia, each designer's corresponding entry indicated a ten thousand dollar deposit. The names by the two women of fashion were marked pending.

But that wasn't all.

Below the names was another section of text. It was addressed to me.

Dear Samantha,

I'm wracked with guilt over my recent behavior. This is not what this business is about. New talent needs a proper home. I cannot sit by and watch anymore. I leave it to you to Look in Vogue and correct my legacy. I won't be around. This is not about the money, it is about the creativity. Friendship and loyalty do not have a price. If this is the new business of fashion, it will go forward without me; my only regret is that I did not take the time to properly train you to succeed me. I hope I am right about the instincts and tenacity you've demonstrated up to this point in your career.

I felt an ice cold blast, as though someone had opened a freezer behind me. It was like Patrick had sent me an answer. I was on the right track, but it was a track that scared me. What did a list of known Mafioso have to do with Patrick's murder? Had he gone to them for the money? How had he planned to pay it back? Why had he used my name, why had he identified me in this file?

I didn't know what to make of it, but it was clear this was more than the minor leagues and Eddie might be right. The cops needed to know about this, although they didn't need to hear it from me. After working up my nerve, I placed an anonymous call to the police station.

"Loncar," he answered.

"I have infor—" I panicked, fearing he'd recognize my voice. I dropped it lower and disguised it. "Invormazon. Deeteective, zhere ist more to ze Patreek case zan designers," I continued, immediately embarrassed. Instead of reporting important information to the police, I sounded like I should be plotting big trouble for Moose and Squirrel.

"Who is this?" he asked.

"You need not know my identitee." This was going poorly. I had to get him the info and get off the phone. "Ze monee ist from ze mob." I dropped the accent but kept my voice low, then quickly rattled off a list of the names in the file. When I reached the last one, I paused for a couple of seconds, considering the least suspicious way to disconnect the call. I finally hung up without saying good-bye.

Patrick had reached out to me, and telling the police what I found was the right thing to do, even if I hadn't done it the right way. Loncar had the information now. He had to investigate it. Whatever it meant, he'd figure it out. That was his job.

The phone rang and I jumped and knocked over Logan's bowl. He scampered into the living room. My heart pounded as the rings continued until the machine picked up. "Ms. Kidd, this is Detective Loncar. I need to talk to you about some information we received from a call made from this number." He paused, as though he knew I was standing there screening his call, then left his number and disconnected.

That was impossible! I'd dialed *67! Unless ... unless the police could see my number regardless of the covert actions I'd learned back when I was a kid making crank calls at a slumber party. But *of course* they could see my number. They were the police.

What was wrong with me? Why was I unable to fully embrace my situation, to act like an adult, to turn what I knew over to Detective Loncar and move on with my life? Because being back in Ribbon, back in this house, made me feel like a kid despite any professional success I'd achieved in New York.

I wandered the living room, straightening pillows on the green velvet sofa, rubbing the toe of my shoe against the tracks in the carpet from moving the sofa. I wasn't the only person dealing with the situation, either. Maries Paulson was too. I went to the kitchen, searching the piles of paper on the dining room table for the interoffice envelope she'd dropped by. When I found it, I dialed the number she left inside.

"Ms. Kidd? I assume you're calling me because you have information that can help me?"

My chest heaved and fell with a deep breath of courage. "Ms. Paulson, I don't think we're going to find the money. I think Patrick went outside of the fashion industry to get the get it."

"What are you suggesting?"

"I found some password protected files on Patrick's computer and I think—I mean, I'm not sure, and I don't want it to sound like I'm accusing him of something, but—"

"Get to the point, Ms. Kidd."

"I found a list of, um, businessmen."

"It's quite possible that Patrick did approach a team of businessmen. Financial types are often looking for a return on their investment. This competition, if it discovered a great new talent, would be worth much more than a hundred thousand dollars in publicity. Plus, it could give someone a foothold in the fashion industry, instant status as part of the new wave of tastemakers."

"Ms. Paulson, I don't mean businessmen like the kind who look at portfolios and crunch numbers. They're all ..." I stopped talking. What were they? They were all Italian. I'd been so busy proclaiming my innocence in the murder, when had I become guilty of racial profiling the same nationality credited for bring the world Pizza? Regardless of my instincts, of the familiarity of the names, and the conclusions I'd drawn from their collective associations, I had nothing. "Maybe I'm wrong," I finished quietly.

"My dear, Patrick's reputation in this industry is spotless. If I understand what you're implying, no one would believe you."

Once again I found myself twisting the phone cord around my finger. This time when I reached the kink I kept winding. The tip of my finger turned purple.

"That's what I thought you were going to say."

"Tell me some of the names," she said.

"Louchesy, Costello, Maria," I said off the top of my head. She laughed, at first a low throaty laugh that grew. Uneasily, I waited, wondering what was so funny.

"My dear, those are *garmentos!*" Her laughter continued.

"Garmentos?" I repeated.

"Businessmen, like you said. In the garment district. Of course Patrick would have turned to them. Fabric wholesalers depend upon the fashion industry's success in order to thrive. Oh but you gave me a laugh."

"Ms. Paulson, these men each gave a ten thousand dollar donation, and the entry fees to the competition amounted to ten thousand, four hundred dollars. How would that be collected? Would those men have cut Patrick a check? And where would he have deposited the money?"

"I don't know. At least now I know where he obtained it. I'll make a few phone calls and figure it out."

I thought about what Michael had said. "Ms. Paulson, I'm not so sure the money *is* safe. I think he might have kept it in the office and one of the designers in the competition found out."

"I highly doubt Patrick would have kept the money in the office."

"If he caught someone in the act of stealing it, he would have tried to fight them. That might be how he died."

"If someone stole the money they wouldn't be pressuring me to deliver it to the gala, now, would they? No, I don't think anyone has gotten their hands on the money. Not yet. This can all be over if I make it be known I'll deliver the money as requested. You haven't called the police about any of this, have you?"

"Not exactly," I said. The room felt hot, and I opened the sliding doors behind the kitchen. A breeze caught the long vertical blinds and blew them into the room, then sucked them out as quickly, snapping the plastic against itself rapidly. "Ms. Paulson, are you still planning to attend the gala?"

"Of course."

"And you're taking the money?" I asked in a tentative voice.

"I've already met with my financial advisors and made the withdrawal. I see no other choice," she replied. Too many lives, including your own, are at risk. I can't see how I can ignore the request."

"And the police?"

"I've followed the instructions given to me, in deference to you, but I have asked the museum to make arrangements for heightened security. I have a few trusted people who will be monitoring everything. If all goes as planned, this will soon be over."

"Someone killed Patrick over that money. If someone believes you have the money, you might be in danger too," I said.

"Ms. Kidd, I have a plan to draw out the murderer at the gala, but it will only work if he or she thinks I am complying with the instructions left to me. That is imperative. Now, my dear, it is your turn to do as I say. Keep this information to yourself. I'll speak to the executives at Tradava this afternoon, and we'll turn the event into a memorial for Patrick instead of a competition. If one of the designers is the guilty party, this change in plans will cause them a misstep, one that might give the police the break they need."

"Ms. Paulson, the police think I'm involved in Patrick's murder," I said.

"My dear, when this settles down, let me see what I can do about finding you a position in my showroom. I like your style."

If it wasn't so bittersweet, it would have almost been funny.

I showered and looked at my closet to see what to wear. There was no chance of me going far from the house, short of lugging the recycling to the corner for pickup the next day, so I pulled on a pair of lavender cashmere pajamas and started wandering around, tidying up the messes I had been leaving behind all week. As I tucked several errant shoes into the closet I rediscovered the pinstriped suit I'd bought at Catnip. Now seemed as good a time as any to try it on.

The pants slipped on easily, with a low-slung waistband and a flared leg. I turned around and checked out the fit from the back. The flattering cut concealed evidence of my recent comfort eating. But the suit needed shoes, and I had a good idea where to find the perfect pair.

Back when I landed the job as senior buyer for Bentley's, Nick had sent me a package. Nestled snugly in the cardboard shipping container were four crisp white shoe boxes, all marked in my size. It was against company policy for me to accept a gift of this value from a designer, and I wasn't the type to break policy. Yet there was something about his generosity that touched me, and I didn't have the heart to make the phone call to tell him to take the shoes back. Instead I folded the flaps of the shipping container inside of each other and tucked the box away in the back of my closet. I had never thanked him for the shoes. Never acknowledged his gift. Never worn them.

I'd rediscovered the carton when I cleaned out my closet before moving from New York. No longer an employee of Bentley's, I figured I owned the shoes outright. I'd packed them up with the rest of my wardrobe and put them where they'd been all along, into the back corner of my closet, sight unseen.

I knelt on the floor, reached past my turquoise suitcase, and found the box. With two hands I lifted it over the suitcase and set it in front of me. I tore it open. Inside were the four white shoeboxes, labeled in black with Nick Taylor's logo.

I eased one of the boxes out of the packing crate and lifted the lid. Inside the tissue was a pair of black and white Dalmatian-printed mules. I held one shoe in my lap and traced my finger over Nick's signature like I had that morning at Tradava, the morning before I saw Patrick's body. There had been so much hope and anticipation that morning. I had been on the verge of something new. I had been energized by the idea of working for Tradava in their trend office. And then, in seconds, it had all ended.

I slipped the shoe onto my foot and held it up. A perfect fit. I stood, slipped into the other, and looked in the mirror. My reflection showed the image I wanted to project at the Gala. Confident. Stylish. Someone who has every right to be at the event. But looking the part was only a portion of my strategy. Knowing the details, as many of the details as I could, before arriving on that red carpet was part two. I was going to attend that gala and figure out a few things or my name wasn't Samantha Kidd.

24

The doorbell rang while I was admiring my outfit. "Kidd? It's Nick. I have food."

The scent of tomato sauce and mozzarella trumped the warning bells ringing in my ears. I stripped off the suit and pulled my cashmere jog suit back on, then descended the stairs and let Nick inside. I did not comment on the carryout bag in his hand and the bottle of wine tucked under his arm. He set them both on my kitchen table and handed me a couple of paper towels, then poured two glasses of wine. After he unwrapped a pair of meatball sandwiches, I pulled one over to my placemat and started without him. He eased himself into the wooden chair across from me, watching with an amused expression on his face.

"Are you going to stop and come up for air?"

A meatball dislodged from inside the roll and fell to my lap, leaving a round stain on my thigh before it rolled off and landed on the floor. I scrubbed at the stain with the paper towel, turning it into a trapezoid.

"So, are you in for the night?" he asked.

I was going to the event, whether he thought it was a smart idea or not, so I decided to avoid the subject and the lectures of the Samantha-be-careful sort. "I'm going to relax tonight, forget my worries, and find something totally superficial to watch on TV." Usually I was pretty good at vaguely answering questions and not committing to actual lies, so I started making mental notes to make sure I relaxed sometime that evening, and to make sure I took in at least thirty seconds of mindless television. Aside from a frontal lobotomy, there wasn't much I could do about the forgetting my worries part.

"Good. I was afraid you were still thinking of going to the museum."

I glanced down at my stained pajamas. There was no way my cover was going to be blown. "Do I look like I'm still planning to go to the museum tonight?"

"No, you look like you're ready to sit this one out." He refilled my wine glass, though it was far from empty. "Good girl."

I cringed. I really can't stand that kind of language.

"I need to tell you something," Nick said, ignoring his own sandwich.

"Mkayf," I replied, which was supposed to be "Okay," but I was chewing a particularly large glob of mozzarella. He picked up the oregano shaker and spun it around in his hands, then set it back down on the table.

"I'm taking Amanda to the gala tonight."

I wasn't sure where he was going with this but the timing, when coupled with the golf-ball sized amount of meat and cheese and in my mouth, was unfortunate. I swallowed a too-big lump and, with no other options, guzzled from the glass of wine to force it down my throat.

"You're telling me this, why?"

"I don't know why I'm telling you this. There's absolutely no reason in the world I should worry about telling you this, only ..." His voice trailed off, and I would have paid good money to get him to finish that thought, if I didn't need all of my good money to pay the mortgage. Somehow, though, it didn't seem like a good idea to interrupt him while he thought through his words. "Only, I can't get you out of my head."

His brown eyes were the colors of melted Milk Duds, all chocolaty and caramelly and sweet, and ....*STOP IT, SAMANTHA!*

Nick said nothing more, waiting for my response, I assumed. Only, I didn't know what to say and, for once in my life, that translated into not saying anything. Go figure.

"I've got to leave so I can get ready for tonight. You sure you're going to be okay by yourself?"

"I'll be okay. This is one night where I'm happy I'll be on my own."

"I brought you a movie," he said, and set a DVD case on the sofa. *How to Steal A Million.* A movie about a woman who plans a museum caper and some undercover work. Perhaps a glimpse into Nick's sense of humor, or worse yet, an indication he wasn't buying my angelic act.

I ignored the reference. "One of my favorites. Thank you." I held the door open for him and leaned against the frame. "Don't have too much fun tonight. I don't want to hear about the great party I missed."

"Deal." He stared into my eyes again, and I felt a serious moment coming on. "I'm glad you're being smart."

Nick may have had my best interests at heart, but a part of me, the paranoid part that felt like my ankles were being pulled down into a pit of quicksand, still wasn't sure who to trust.

I caught my reflection in the living room mirror and realized I hadn't needed to do much to convince him I wasn't planning to leave the house. I looked and smelled like I'd spent the past few hours in a pizza oven and I had only about half an hour to get ready. I called information and got the number for a taxi company, then reserved a pick-up in thirty minutes. Time to get glamorous.

Twenty minutes later I stared at my reflection. Designer pinstriped pantsuit. Designer Dalmatian shoes. Designer attitude, marked down to half price. If ever there existed a reason to wear an outfit I couldn't afford, this was it. I knotted a vintage black and white silk scarf over my head like a sixties film star and topped off the look with the purple fedora. A spritz of perfume masked any lingering meatball sandwich smells. I twirled in front of the mirror. Not bad for an unemployed ex-fashion industry employee suspected of murder.

From the driveway, the taxi driver laid on the horn. I yelled out the front door I'd be ready in a couple of minutes. The taxi driver yelled back he was starting the meter.

Nick's visit put me behind schedule, allowing me no time to think about what I was about to do. I grabbed my already assembled handbag filled with essentials for the evening, locked the door behind me and pulled on a pair of gloves. I slid into the back seat of the cab and told the driver where to go.

The day had moved from dusk to dark, helpful for my undercover activities. My nerves rose in direct proportion to the distance we were from the gala. I asked the driver to drop me off at a coffee shop within walking distance of the museum. He pulled over and I held out his fare, plus a nice tip. "If anyone asks, you never saw me. Got it?" I said. I didn't know if it was the fedora or the pinstripes making me act like Humphrey Bogart.

He eyed me up and down and took the money from my outstretched hand. "If you don't want to be remembered, you shouldn'ta worn that hat."

I guess it was the pinstripes.

Inside the coffee shop I bought a bag of chocolate covered espresso beans and a latte while trying to ignore the fact that everyone in the shop was staring in my direction. Not for the first time since returning to Ribbon I was reminded it was much more than a distance of a hundred and twenty miles that separated us from the fashion capital of the country. Here, I was a roadside attraction in the middle of Starbucks.

I finished half of my latte and stood to leave. On my way to the door, a few high school boys asked where the costume party was and I succumbed to the pressure of conformity. I took the hat off and gave it to a little girl playing on the floor by her parents. "Enjoy it, honey," I said, and patted it onto her head with a silent good-bye.

I popped a few espresso beans in my mouth and trudged through the fallen leaves scattered across the sidewalk with the early evening breeze. The air was crisp and cool, and if it wasn't for the fact that I was out looking for a murderer, it would have been a perfect September night. Shiny luxury cars pulled onto Museum Drive; people in eveningwear mingled outside. I sat on a bench by the duck pond, close enough to watch but maintaining a distance of anonymity. I was looking for something—anything–unusual. I just didn't know what. In a fashionable crowd, unusual was defined more by the poseurs than the socialites. Many women who had taken care to dress for the event shivered in the evening air, unprepared for the drop in temperature. They looked out of place next to women in full-length fur coats. A flash of red hair caught my attention, and I watched the boutique owner move through the crowd.

She cut a chic picture in a black pencil skirt and a fitted jacket with a nipped in waist. Reminded me of the outfit I'd worn that first day at Tradava less than a week ago. Silver chains dangled from the lapels of her jacket, which coordinated nicely with the long silver earrings she wore. She ascended the steps next to a man in black: black tux, black shirt, black hair, black tie. A silver leather clutch, flat as a pancake, was tucked under her arm.

I followed her figure until she entered the museum, passing a large black and white portrait of Patrick displayed on a wooden easel. A woman blocked my view but when she turned, I recognized Amanda Ries. Her dress, a high cut halter with a plunging back, fell to the floor like black oil and oozed onto the ground around her feet. Light from the almost-full moon bounced off her creamy skin. Her hair was held back with chopsticks, and a beaded handbag rested in her left hand. She waved at someone on the steps. Nick.

Even though I knew they'd be attending together, I wasn't prepared for the sight of them as a couple. A pang of jealousy trumped the other, more practical, emotions I felt. I watched their body language: her laughter when he whispered in her ear, his hand casually resting on her arm. Her tucking her hand into the crook of his elbow as they spoke to another couple on the balcony, him putting his hand on the small of her back to guide her inside the building. I felt played with, like a cat plays with a mouse. Nick's admission earlier amounted to little more than a ploy to keep me home. This was clearly the body language of a couple in love, or a couple of conspirators, not a couple of college chums. Whether he wanted me waiting in the wings or not, I wasn't about to find out.

The crowd had thinned drastically. A few smokers lingered on the balcony but the festivities were about to begin. I didn't care I was missing out on dinner and a bad cover band for the night, but I did want to know what was going on under that roof. I wished someone would show up with a banner that said "I killed Patrick and am prepared to frame Samantha Kidd if necessary so I can get away with murder," but if that banner existed it seemed to have been traded in for satin evening clutches and beaded shoes. Even murderers cleaned up well, I thought. I blindly accepted someone connected to the crime would be at this event but once the crowd disappeared behind the heavy wooden doors I was as in the dark as I'd been all along.

A limo pulled up to the steps. The driver hopped out and circled the front of the car, opening the passenger door. Maries Paulson stepped out, and the driver handed her a small, flat briefcase. Bursts of camera flash illuminated her lavender fur stole and the dark aubergine lace dress fit so well it appeared to have been sewn on her body. The pile of shiny curls atop her head had lent a regal quality. She moved like a movie star on the red carpet.

She paused at the bottom of the stairs, allowing the media to capture her better angles and I knew this was my only chance to speak with her. "Ms. Paulson!" I called out. Her head turned toward me and a thousand flash bulbs crackled. She shielded her gaze and scanned the individuals clamoring for her attention. I stepped toward her, not sure she had heard me. "Maries?"

"You have no right to be here," she said in a low voice.

"I'm here to represent Tradava, like I told you," I said, confused by her unexpected animosity. I dropped my voice. "I didn't say anything to anyone."

She pointed a finger at me, her manicured plum-black fingernail like a self-defense pistol ready to fire my direction. "Don't pretend to know me or to be my friend. More than one person has contacted me about you. I trusted you and put myself in danger. Patrick hired you as the trend specialist at Tradava no more than I've become the Queen of Sheba. I don't know what role you played in his murder, but I intend to find out."

I searched her face for signs she was acting for someone else's benefit, but Botox injections had made her face unreadable. I didn't know what had changed from earlier that day when we'd spoken. I looked at the briefcase she held, then, realizing what was inside, stepped forward again. "Ms. Paulson, wait!" I reached out for her arm and she flung off my touch.

"Don't—*Don't!*" her fingers fanned out in an aggressive manner and her voice dropped to a whisper. "I would rather throw this money in the river than give it to a manipulative bottom feeder like you." She turned away from me and advanced up the stairs.

"But you said—I thought we—I'm trying to help—"

"Approach me one more time and I will make sure you never work in this industry again." Halfway up the stairs she turned back and scanned my outfit from head to toe. "On you, that's a waste of six yards of fabric." She turned back toward the crowd and it parted, giving her room to ascend the stairs. She paused by a security officer standing by the door and pointed one finger my direction. He leaned in and looked straight at me.

25

I jogged to the bench and ducked behind it, watching the conversation between Maries and the officer. She handed him the briefcase, then lit up a cigarette. He disappeared inside. Her burning ember marked her presence, until it went out. A high voice, from the bottom of the steps, pulled me out of my thoughts. "Ms. Paulson!"

The designer stopped in the doorway and looked down. A scrawny figure in a purple velvet tuxedo bounded up the stairs after Maries. Michael Dubrecht, Patrick's assistant and self-proclaimed designer. Was this it? I wondered. Was this the moment when someone demanded a hundred thousand dollars from Maries, no police present, in exchange for my safety?

You're no more the trend specialist than I'm the Queen of Sheba.

If Maries no longer believed I was the trend specialist, she was no longer concerned with my safety. Which meant, I was on my own.

Michael's chin jutted from side to side as he spoke, in a manner befitting a two-hundred-pound diva with attitude, not the ninety-eight pound weakling he was. I half-wanted Maries to kick sand in his face. She smiled and shook his hand, then turned away and left him behind. He jumped to grab the handles before the doors closed and narrowly slipped inside.

I swiped on another coat of lip-gloss and took a deep breath. With caution, I approached the museum, looking for an opportunity to enter. There was too much at stake to leave, but I couldn't risk being identified. Not now. I avoided the main doors and walked around the perimeter of the imposing building to look for a back door.

I circled the museum, my heels puncturing the ground with every step. I made slow progress, avoiding the dry leaves that begged to be crunched underfoot. I popped a few more espresso beans into my mouth and continued. The darkness cloaked me and I dropped my guard. That's probably why I jumped when a beam of light shot through the darkness and a voice called out asking me what I was doing.

A groundskeeper held a giant flashlight in my direction. *Think fast, Samantha, and don't worry too much about telling lies or telling the truth. Say something to make him go away.* My heart raced and my hands grew sweaty inside my gloves.

He stood there waiting for me to talk. His flashlight cast about two thousand degrees of heat in my direction. Like Detective Loncar's office, it wasn't the best circumstance for thinking under pressure.

The wind bent the branches overhead, which inspired me to speak. "My cat ran up one of these trees and I'm trying to find him."

He flashed the light up into the trees and we heard a few birds fly away. "Up there? Where'd he come from?"

Keep talking. "I live over there," I motioned to the houses behind the Museum. "When I got home from work he bolted out the door and ran over here. I think he might have chased a squirrel or something and now I can't find him." I almost believed the words as I spoke them. In their own strange little way they sounded plausible. Cats escaped and chased squirrels up trees all the time, I was sure of it.

He flashed the light around while I silently begged him to stop. He was drawing attention to the exact spot where we stood, and all of my efforts for undercover work were starting to feel hopeless, until some rustling in one of the nearby trees endorsed my lie. I held my breath for a few seconds, not sure if he bought my story or not.

"I think he's up there," he said, motioning toward the tree beside me. "I have a ladder inside the shed. I'll help you get him down."

"That's okay, Sir. I can get him."

He looked me up and down, scarf-wrapped head to Dalmatian-printed toes, then looked me straight in the eye. I knew the jig was up, and thought it might have been better to abandon my quest instead of lying, because he was going to be pretty mad if I told him the truth now.

"Little lady, how do you think you're going to get a cat down out of a tree dressed like that? I don't think those shoes were made for scaling maples." He shined the light on the path and walked toward the building.

I couldn't believe my luck. I tried my best attempt at cute, helpless female. I normally hated that routine, but it was the only thing to keep this charade going.

"Thank you so much. I don't know what I was thinking." I followed him to the building, hoping against hope he would lead me to a door that would get me inside. Instead we reached a separate building where he had the necessary tools and machinery to maintain the grounds, and my hopes fell.

"Try to be quiet, though, because there's a big event going on in the museum tonight."

"I noticed. But they can't hear us out here, right?"

"This shed has an underground passageway that connects to the museum. If we make sounds out here they might echo through the passageways and someone might come to check it out. I was supposed to be out of here long before this thing started tonight, and as much as I want to help you, I don't want to lose my job over a lost kitty."

His comments explained why he was speaking so quietly, and I think he attributed my newfound silence to what he'd said but really I was thinking over phrases like "underground passageway that connects to the museum," and "I was supposed to be out of here long before this thing started tonight." I thought for a second about trying to pull the pins from the hinges on the door, but that might be an actual crime since it was on public property and I was not currently chaperoned by someone who could approve such an act. My newfound comfort with danger notwithstanding, I thought it best to avoid actively breaking the law.

He handed me a rope net. "Hold this." He gently closed the door to the underground passageway and inserted a key into the door to relock it. I tried to hide my disappointment. He then walked to the wall of the museum where a ladder leaned along side of the building. I wondered how I had missed it earlier.

"Don't just stand there, missy, grab an end and help me move this thing. I can't do it myself."

I tossed my handbag down on the dewy grass and grabbed the other end of the ladder, juggling it with the net. We maneuvered to get it propped up against the tree. I knew we weren't going to find a kitten up there but was obligated to go along with my story.

"Do you see him?"

"No. He might not be up this tree." I was getting antsy, wondering how I was going to ditch this guy and continue my search now that he had decided to do his good deed for the day.

"Look. It's this tree or nothing. If the little guy isn't up here, you ain't gonna find him tonight."

"Okay, maybe he *is* in this tree."

"Well? You gonna climb up and check or not?"

"I'm not so good on ladders."

The look on his face told me I didn't really have a choice. "You said the little guy ran out the door and took off this direction up a tree. He probably climbed too high and now the little fella is scared. I got a couple of cats at home myself. Once they're scared they won't come running to anybody, they want to hear a familiar voice. I don't plan to let you call out to him from down here while I go up and chase him up further. You better get up there and call him. Take your shoes off first. You'll have better luck on these rungs." He pointed toward the net. "Once you get him, put him in the net and hang it down to me. He'll hang on tight until he's down, and you can come down to get him. Hurry up 'cause I don't have all night."

I had no choices left but to climb. The ladder bowed in the middle and might as well have been a hundred rungs high, neither of which strengthened my waning confidence. I kept climbing, soon becoming hidden by leaves, wondering if I would be lucky enough to find a random kitten trapped thirty feet up in a maple tree. Probably not.

"You see him?" The groundskeeper called up to me.

"Not yet."

"Call his name a little."

I couldn't subject Logan to my lie, so I named my fake kitty. "Max, here Max," I called softly, and made kissing noises in the air. The stupidity of the situation was not lost on me.

Ten minutes and no kitten later I climbed back down. "No luck. I think it's another tree."

"I can't stay here anymore." He looked up at the sky for several seconds, moonlight bouncing off of his full face, then looked back at me. "It looks like it's gonna be a clear night tonight. The ladder will be fine if we leave it out, I'll be back in the morning. I'll help you move it to another tree but then, you're on your own."

I became the ultimate Johnny on the Spot, carrying the ladder to the next tree, nearly bounding over him in my enthusiasm to get the fake search over. The groundskeeper made his apologies and left me alone to conduct my rescue mission, ignoring the thanks I called to his back.

Again I climbed up the ladder. With a little maneuvering I positioned myself in a fork in a branch. I gingerly sat, praying for it to hold me. I was temporarily distracted from the danger of looking for a murderer by thoughts of being found, unconscious, outside of the event, because the branch where I'd sat had broken under my weight.

I strained my eyes to take in every detail of the event. Round tables covered with white cloths took up much of the ballroom. Each table held an elaborate floral centerpiece arranged around a miniature bust form. Along the side of the room, on a raised, lighted platform, stood three mannequins draped, toga-like, in black fabric. Next to each mannequin was a sign holder that held a capital letter: A, B, C. Four spotlights shone down from the ceiling, three illuminating the mannequins and one shining on an empty pedestal next to the letter D. This event was called the Designer's Debut. My suspects were all present and accounted for, representing their collections. But the mannequins draped sloppily in black cloth lacked the originality expected in fashion.

I looked for familiar faces in the crowd, scanning the audience systematically, left to right, clockwise around the table, then moving on to the next seating arrangement. This would have been a whole lot easier if 90 percent of people in the fashion industry didn't choose to wear black.

Empty seats peppered the ballroom. I guess when nature calls, you have to answer. Better change that train of thought. I was trapped in a tree with literally nowhere to go. Three tables back along the far side I recognized Red's hair. I didn't recognize anyone else sitting at her table. I continued my search of the crowd. On my way back up the second row—I was snaking right to left on every other row to keep track—I spotted Nick and Amanda at the back of the room. Off to the side I spied a small figure in purple, crouching in the shadows.

I drew my attention back to Nick and Amanda. Watching them get along so well made me feel all kinds of alone. Alone and up in a tree. What was I doing? This was crazy. I wasn't going to discover anything.

At that moment the band stopped playing and a speaker came up on stage. I couldn't hear what he said but watched as the crowd entertained polite applause. He looked to the side, as if expecting someone to appear. A few awkward moments passed as he leaned into the microphone again but didn't speak. Heads in the crowd twisted at varying angles, looking around.

Something was wrong.

I started to lose my balance and grabbed a branch in panic. It snapped off in my grip and my earlier fears became a reality. I reached for another limb. Several leaves snapped off in my grip and fluttered through the air. The caffeine had made me jumpy. When I felt I'd regained stability, I looked into the room and swore Nick was looking right at me. Was that possible? I was pretty far away from him, and he really had no reason to be looking for me in a tree outside of the event.

Wait a minute. He was starting to know me pretty well. He had lots of reasons to look for me in a tree. He looked at the empty stage then back up to the window. I froze, hoping to blend in with the background and seem like a figment of his imagination. Anger shaped his face, with a crease between his brows and a firm, hard jaw line. He stood abruptly, pushing his chair toward the table so hard the seat back bounced when the two collided.

Maybe he was going to check on Amanda, who now that I thought about it had been gone for a long time. Maybe he was going to come outside and check on what he thought he saw in the tree. He looked side to side before pushing through the swinging doors that led to the exit.

I wasn't going to stick around and let him find me. I fled down the rungs of the ladder. It was dark. And something—

someone—stepped away from the shadows close to the back wall of the museum, then receded into darkness.

I wasn't alone. Someone had been watching me while I watched the gala.

For a moment I was as rooted to the ground as the tree I'd been sitting in. I heard the crunch of leaves under a foot—close. Closer than the shadowy figure had been. Someone grabbed at my arm. I tried to yell but no sound came out. I twisted my torso and ran past the museum to the road. The heel of my left shoe stuck in the ground, but I kept running. I jumped into the first taxi in a line of several and pounded my open palm against the back of the driver's seat.

"Go! Go, go, *GO!*" I shouted frantically, slapping the plastic partition with each word. He peeled away from the curb with a squeal of tires. I turned around at the first stop sign and squinted through the dirty rear window. A man stood in the middle of the road.

If he had wanted me dead right now, I would be.

It was close to midnight when I got home. I triple-locked the front door, pushed a folding metal chair under the lock and angled the sofa up against it. I carried Logan with me to the bathroom where he sat outside the sliding shower doors while I stood under a jet of hot water. As the spray pummeled my head and pooled around my ankles I knew what I should have known all along. There was only one way out.

I turned off the water, turbaned my hair, and walked, naked and dripping, down the hallway, to the phone. The number was easy enough to remember.

"This is Samantha Kidd. I'm done playing games. We need to talk about Patrick's murder." By the time I hung up the phone, I wondered if I'd just sealed my fate.

26

The rapid-fire assault on the front door jerked me upright like a limp puppet about to perform. Between stints of pacing and regret that had lasted until close to three in the morning, I'd tried, unsuccessfully, to fall asleep. Whenever I closed my eyes I felt the touch of the man who had grabbed for me at the museum. Exhaustion had kicked in somewhere around four thirty and I'd crashed on a makeshift bed of cushions from the sofa that was pushed up against the front door. Now, foggy from being pulled out of a sleep I never thought I'd find, I fought to wake up.

The pounding persisted. I pushed my feet into slippers and moved the sofa away from the door. By the looks of the sunshine, it was well into morning. Two men stood on my doorstep. One I recognized, the other I didn't. Neither looked pleased.

"Detective Loncar, come in," I said.

"Ms. Kidd, we need you to come with us."

"Let me make some coffee. I have a lot to tell you, but I'm not quite awake yet."

They looked at each other. Logan buzzed my ankles while we stood in the front corner of my living room, the sofa in the middle of the room, the blanket and pillows on the floor beside them.

"Ms. Kidd, I'm serious. "

"Let me go upstairs and put some clothes on. If you want I can follow you to the station—wait, no I can't, because I don't have a car. Give me five minutes to get dressed."

"Ms. Kidd, this is no joke."

"I'm not joking. I really can be ready in five minutes." I turned around and let go of the door, thinking they would catch it or come inside or maybe didn't want to intrude and would stay on the porch. Detective Loncar reached out and snatched my thin wrist in his bear grip and everything about the moment felt wrong.

They weren't there to give me news about Patrick's murderer. And they weren't there to listen to what I had to say. They were there to take me in. As in, *IN*.

I looked at the wrist the detective was still clutching, thinking he would realize I needed the wrist before starting that five-minute routine. He looked down at my wrist too, and the next thing you know he clamped a handcuff on me. What the hell was going on?

"Ms. Kidd, you are under arrest for suspicion of murdering Patrick ...Patrick ..." said the new guy. He looked at Detective Loncar.

"He only has one name. He's like Cher," Loncar said, looking directly at me.

"There have been some new developments in the case," said the unnamed man.

"Do I have the right to know what they are?"

"No. But you do have the right to remain silent."

Dizziness hit me. Breathing became difficult and my knees went weak. To make matters worse, I was still in my bathrobe. The officers maneuvered me to the car with a yank on the handcuffs and a nudge between my shoulder blades. It was a black and white, standard issue cop car. The detective opened the back door, I slid in, and he clamped the other cuff to the door of the car. It wasn't like I was looking for a breakout or anything, but a girl likes to keep her options open. At the moment, I didn't have any options to speak of.

Thousands of questions circled through my head, but I sensed it wasn't the right time to ask them. Maybe if I'd listened to Eddie and turned over what I knew a few days ago, I wouldn't be in the back of a squad car.

Or maybe the police didn't have any new details. Maybe the person who threatened me had hung me out to dry after all, or maybe I had been on their radar all night. *Gather your thoughts, Samantha*. Plus, being new in town, I didn't have a lawyer to speak of so I was left trying to reason this out on my own, like the rest of this mess. And still, one question nagged at me. *What possible motive could I have?*

By the time we reached the station I knew there was no one to count on but myself. Despite the best intentions I had last night, I wasn't going to tell them a word until I knew what was going on.

Ignorance had been on my side that first day I'd gone with Detective Loncar to the police station from Tradava. But now, I knew too much. As we walked from the car to the stationhouse, I tugged at the neck of my robe, painfully aware that underneath I was next to naked. It was a metaphor for the situation. Clothing was my armor. Without it, I was vulnerable to attack.

The dynamic duo led me down a narrow hallway to a small room. Two chairs sat, facing each other. A white laminate table sat next to the chairs. The walls of the room were the color of smog, with a harvest gold floor. Corners of the linoleum tiles had since come unglued and chipped, leaving murky pockmarks underfoot that matched the paint on the walls. Aside from a camera mounted in the corner above the door, the room was a box: no windows, no art, no distractions. Nothing to take me away from the fact that I was about to be questioned by the cops.

Detective Loncar unlocked my cuffs. The new officer introduced himself as Officer Smoot. I watched and waited. I was torn between keeping my mouth buttoned up and exposing everything I'd discovered. I thought about things like unflattering orange jumpsuits and ankle monitors that would make me rethink my choices in footwear and decided right there to let them direct the conversation while I played it safe.

"Where were you yesterday?" Smoot asked, flicking his thumbnail against the underside of his wedding band.

"Home, most of the day. "

"What'd you have for lunch?"

"Meatball sandwich."

"From?"

"B&S."

"Did you do anything else?"

"Watched a movie."

"What movie?"

"*How to Steal a Million.*" I paused. "It's a classic."

"Rented?"

"No. I mean, yes, I think."

"You don't know?"

"I own it, but the person who loaned it to me didn't know so I don't know where he got it."

"He?"

"The person who brought me the food. Is that relevant?"

"In the afternoon?"

"Yes."

"But you said you ate at B&S."

"No, I said the food was from B&S."

"And you've seen this movie before?"

"It's one of my favorites." Until I knew the score, I kept my answers short, contained. It was the only way for me to function.

"Did you go out last night?" Loncar asked, drumming his fingers rhythmically on the splintered wooden table while perspiration marks appeared under his arms. When I didn't answer he repeated the question. Dangerous territory.

"I went to the museum last night. To the Designer's Debut Gala."

Smoot stood up and leaned against the wall. Arms crossed, he jumped in where Loncar had left off.

"You just said you didn't have a car."

"I took a taxi." I perked up a little. "My car is at Tradava, I was stranded. Can you tell me what this is about?"

They exchanged another look. Loncar spun his watch in a circle around his wrist. I wanted to reach across the table and tighten the band so he'd have to stop, but that was close to assaulting a cop, and considering my situation, I refrained.

"Why is your car at Tradava?"

"Two nights ago I was knocked out in the store. Someone gave me a ride home, and I left my car there."

"You were attacked?"

"Yes!"

"Did you file a police report?"

"No."

"Why not?"

"Because I wasn't supposed to be there in the first place."

"Are you confessing, Ms. Kidd?"

"To what? Being knocked out at Tradava two nights ago? Yes, I guess I am."

"What were you doing there?" asked Smoot.

"I was—" I didn't want to admit to rifling through Patrick's mail looking for the museum invitation. "I can't say. Will you please tell me what this is all about?"

"Why can't you talk about Tradava?" Loncar asked.

"I was with another woman's boyfriend," I said dramatically. If this were a Lifetime movie it would have gotten a reaction. "He drove me home. I didn't want anyone to find out. End of story." Telling the truth wasn't so hard. That was probably the most honest thing I had said since I'd arrived.

"Who's the guy?" Loncar asked, flipping through a file.

"What?"

"Who's the guy who gave you a ride home?" He shut the folder and looked at me. Smoot watched me closely too, gauging my reaction.

"Why does that matter?"

Loncar suggested this mystery guy might corroborate my story. That suggested to me someone was planning to tell Nick what I said. And *that* suggested I might want to clam up.

"I don't want to say."

"Who are you protecting?" Smoot said, leaning forward on his palms.

Duh. I was protecting myself.

Loncar sat back and stared at me. "Let's take a break. You want anything? Need to go to the bathroom? Want some coffee?"

I looked back and forth between their faces, hard lines etched in flesh that gave away nothing.

"No, thank you," I said automatically. The two officers left the room, presumably, to make me think about my situation. A couple of minutes passed. I grew restless. More time passed. I went from restless to nervous. When I'd gotten home from the gala I was ready to confide in them but now something was off and I didn't know what. I wasn't sure how long they left me alone with my mounting paranoia. All I'd wanted was a chance to get on that other path in life, the road peppered with dreams and hope and imagination. But who was I kidding? Even if I found that road, the entrance ramp would probably be closed for construction.

The door reopened and Detective Loncar came back in, this time alone. My hands were locked together in my lap. I tried again to read his face, and again I got nothing. He set a bottle of water on the table next to me. After a couple of seconds, I reached for it and took a sip, then screwed the cap back on.

"Ms. Kidd, you work in fashion, right?"

"Yes."

He lowered himself into the chair in front of me.

"What do you think of my outfit?"

"Excuse me?"

"My wife says I shouldn't wear plaid."

I shrugged one shoulder, tipped my head to the side, and crossed my arms over my chest. "You can pull it off."

"What about these shoes?" He pushed a foot out in front of him, giving me a clear view of a pair of thick, round toed black sneakers with black soles and black laces. Standard issue orthopedic.

"Do you have foot problems?" I asked.

"No. Why?"

"They're not particularly attractive."

"What would you suggest?"

"Tell me what you do in the course of a day," I asked. I uncrossed my arms and leaned forward. He stared at me a couple of seconds, like he didn't understand my question. "Do you walk a lot? Drive? Run? Sit?"

"All of the above. This isn't about work. My wife has been nagging me to update my, um, style."

"You want to know what I think?"

He nodded.

"She's right. Lose the plaid shirts. Go for something with a vertical stripe. Definitely a collar, and never ever *ever* wear a V-neck T-shirt. Keep the jeans dark. And you have to do something about those shoes."

"They're that bad?"

"They tell the world you've given up."

He looked down at his feet for a couple of seconds, then nodded. "I guess you're right."

As we sat there, him staring at his ugly shoes, me staring at the top of his head, working up the nerve to suggest a different hairstyle, I realized how easy it was to say what needed to be said and how hard it was to keep it all bottled up.

"Detective?" I said tentatively. "I'm ready to tell you about yesterday."

He looked up from his shoes and nodded, once. Details poured out of me. I told him about Nick and the meatball in my lap, and the threat on the envelope. I told him about Patrick's computer and the password, the file of quote unquote businessmen. I described the sewing machine set up in Patrick's office and the bump on the back of my head, and the person in the shadows outside of the museum, the photo under Michael's phone that said *GET HER* with an arrow pointed to me, and the note I'd found in Patrick's office that had been taken from me, that I'd discovered again on the laptop.

It felt good to clear the air. There was no stopping me, and I wondered for the briefest moment why I'd been so scared to talk to the police, why I had ignored the voice of common sense that should have prompted me to confide in Detective Loncar days ago. I told him about the fabric store and my conversations with Red, Amanda, Michael and Nick when he cut me off.

"What about the attack?" Loncar prompted.

"At Tradava? I told you all I can. I didn't hear anybody, didn't see anybody, but I was knocked out."

"Not that attack."

"The attack on Florence? I told you what I know about that too." I leaned back in the chair and crossed my arms over my chest, then immediately uncrossed them. I kicked my heel against the metal leg of the chair.

Loncar leaned forward, one elbow resting on the table to the side of us. His face was inches from mine. "We know you were at Tradava when the break-in happened, and we found your fingerprints all over the office. We want to know what you were looking for. We have enough to connect you with Patrick's murder, the fabric store, and last night's attack."

"What attack?"

My chest tightened, my palms were sweaty, and the air I gulped didn't seem to reach my lungs. The room spun. I bent down to try to control the nausea.

Loncar picked up the water bottle and held it out to me. I waved it away. *Where were they getting their information?*

I dug deeper into details that twenty-four hours ago I had hoped to conceal. About the taxi to the museum, the walk from the coffee shop, the surveillance by the duck pond. I told about hiding in the shadows and enlisting the help of the groundskeeper by looking for a nonexistent kitten.

For every detail I provided he asked for something concrete to corroborate my story. I had paid the taxi driver off to forget I was his fare. I ditched the purple fedora so as not to draw attention to myself. I had no hope with the groundskeeper, since he had already said he was going to deny helping me. There was no kitten named Max; there was no taxi reservation to take me home. The chances of finding the high school kids from the coffee shop were slim to none.

I described the clothes I had seen at the event. I begged him to do the research to see if I was right. I personally thought the detail with which I described some of the outfits should have proven the accuracy of my story, but he seemed to think anyone could identify black tie ensembles with such precision. If only there was a way to prove I had been at that benefit—

"Talk to Maries Paulson," I begged. "She knows I was there."

"Oh yeah? You talk to her last night?"

"Outside of the museum. She was mad at me."

"You two fought?"

"She accused me of—" Loncar leaned forward and instantly I knew it wasn't wise to finish that thought. "Ask her. She'll tell you I was there."

"We would ask her if we could. Only, she's definitely not talking. She's lying unconscious in a hospital bed."

27

Before I could ask any more questions the door opened. A young woman in a white shirt and navy blue Dickies motioned Loncar into the hallway. I was in the middle of a very real, very scary crisis, and I only wanted things to get better. Nothing had gone right since the day I'd left Bentley's. I wanted to go back in time. I wanted to go back to New York, back to the sixty-hour work week and the monotony of prime time TV as my social life. I may have lived between muggers and crack heads in New York but at least I'd known what to expect, every second of every day. Here? Not so much.

By the time the detectives reentered the room I was beyond exhaustion. Loncar's thick fingers were wrapped around an old, creased mailing envelope bulging with contents, a stack of well-worn file folders, and a couple of videotapes. He dumped the pile on the table next to my elbow. I closed my eyes. It must have been hours since we'd arrived, though time had become an abstract concept that mattered less than it ever had in my life.

"Tell us about Nick Taylor," said Detective Loncar.

"We used to work together, when I was a buyer at Bentley's department store in New York. I was the designer shoe buyer and he was one of my vendors."

"You still consider him a friend?"

"I don't know what I consider him," I answered truthfully.

"Do you consider him an enemy?"

"No."

"How did your relationship with Nick Taylor impact what you did yesterday?"

"Nick knew I wanted to attend the Designer Gala at the Museum but he thought it was a bad idea. He showed up with dinner and a movie and I pretended I was in for the night. As soon as he left I changed clothes and took a taxi to the museum."

"What were you planning on doing at the museum?"

"I don't know. I was looking for something suspicious. Someone wants me to look guilty and I'm trying to figure out who. Maries Paulson said someone was extorting money from her, that she was supposed to hand it over last night. Whoever it was warned her not to go to the cops."

"How long have you known this?" Loncar asked. I looked at my hands in my lap and didn't answer. "Ms. Kidd, if you had cooperated with us all along—"

"They told her they'd kill me," I said in a small voice. "Somebody made a grab for me last night when I was leaving. If I cooperated with you all along I might be dead now." I hung my head down, my chin touching my chest. I didn't sob. I didn't wail. No one said a word for several minutes.

"Ms. Kidd? You've told us a lot of crap today."

"No, I haven't. I told you the truth. I even told you the truth about your outfit." Smoot's face scrunched up and he looked at Loncar, who continued to look at me. "I didn't do anything wrong," I said. "If I'm guilty of anything, it's of being in the wrong place at the wrong time, and if there was a way to prove any of this, I'd do it."

Slowly, Loncar unwound the string on the envelope and pulled out a dirty, Dalmatian-printed shoe. He held it between his hands for a second, then handed it to me.

"Put this on," he said slowly.

I set the shoe on the floor and slid my foot into it. Despite the clumps of mud caked to the heel and sole, it fit perfectly. I looked up at the detective, who scratched the side of his balding head. "Freakin' fairytale around here." He looked in a ratty brown folder that had been recycled once too often, then turned to the door. Before he left the room again, he turned back to face me. "Thank you for your cooperation. The police would like to offer you an apology."

"That's it? I can leave?" I wiped the last of the tears away from my face. The woman in Dickies reentered and told me to follow her. We walked down a narrow corridor to the front desk. The clock on the wall read ten forty two. Nick leaned against the wall, talking to a couple of officers. When he saw me, he stood straight. I couldn't read his face. He picked up a sweatshirt and pants from the desk next to him and held them out to me.

"Put these on in the restroom and meet me out front. I'm taking you home."

I hobbled to him, off-balance since I was only wearing one shoe. I couldn't read his expression. I put a hand on the desk to balance myself before taking the clothes. He put his arms around me and I leaned against his chest, too tired to laugh or cry. He slowly pulled away and held me steady by my shoulders. I didn't know what strange trick of Fate had brought him there at that exact moment, and I honestly didn't care.

His low voice whispered in my ear. "We'll talk when I get you home. Right now you need to get dressed. Your robe is coming open and there's a pool going on whether or not anybody's going to see you naked."

I tugged at the collar of the robe and went into the bathroom to change. When I came out, Detective Loncar was waiting for me.

"Detective, why did you ask me about your outfit?"

"Ms. Kidd, you were all over the place in there, and you haven't exactly been honest with me so far. I had to figure out what you were like when you were telling the truth so I could figure out what you were like when you were lying."

I leaned in closer and dropped my voice. "And what about Nick Taylor? What's he doing here?"

"What, him?" He jerked a thumb toward Nick's truck in the parking lot. "Prince Charming's been working with us from the start."

28

"What did the detective mean, you're working with him?" I asked Nick as we walked to his truck.

"Get inside."

"Not until I get some kind of explanation. You owe me that."

He unlocked the door to his truck and held it open for me. "Do you want to do this here, in front of the police station, or at your house? Because I can go either way, but I'm not the one wearing borrowed clothes of questionable origin."

I climbed into the truck and waited a whole half a block before I asked the question again.

"Remember when you asked me about being in the competition?"

"Yes," I answered. "You said Amanda entered for you, the application got processed and went too far and Patrick disqualified you instead of admitting what happened."

"I wasn't entirely honest with you."

"Meaning what?"

Nick merged from Penn Avenue onto the highway. He didn't speak until after he passed a large truck with a grocery store logo on the side.

"I knew Patrick fairly well. He took an interest in me way back, when I was producing footwear for designers' runway collections. He introduced me to a couple of financiers who put up the money for my first collection, and encouraged me to get out from under the hem of apparel designers, so to speak, and let my shoes stand on their own."

"When was this? "

"Ten years ago? Fifteen? I don't remember exactly. Before I met you, before you started buying the collection for Bentley's."

"So you knew him. So what?"

"He knew there was trouble with this competition. He asked me if I'd pose as a finalist, to check things out from the inside."

"What did you find out?"

"Nothing. The morning I saw you at Tradava, the morning we found him, I was there to go over his concerns."

"But you're listed on his files as disqualified, and those files are from before he was murdered."

"One of the designers made a stink about me. Said I didn't meet the eligibility requirements since I already had achieved full collection success on my own."

"Do you know which one?"

"Clestes."

"Who *is* Clestes?"

"A brother-sister design team. They do some interesting work, but she's a real fire cracker. She threatened to go public with the news the contest was rigged if I wasn't disqualified."

"She—she who?"

"The redhead. Catherine. Patrick, Maries, and I all knew I was a bogus entrant but there wasn't anything else I could do, and once I was disqualified, I lost my inside angle."

"But you didn't. Amanda is your—Amanda kept you connected."

Nick exited the highway and turned right onto my street. Two blocks further he turned into my driveway and cut the engine.

"I don't want to bring Amanda into this any more than she already is."

"But she did, didn't she? Be honest, Nick. Because if Amanda isn't your connection to the competition, then she could be as guilty as any of the other designers. What does she say about last night?"

"I haven't talked to her yet."

"Maybe you should. I bet she has a couple of secrets she's not telling you too."

"Kidd, listen to me. The police are handling it."

I got out of the truck and slammed the door. Nick got out too. "Where do you think you're going?" I asked.

"It seems like every time you tell me you're going to be safe, I trust you. But then you go out and something happens and everything gets worse. I'm trying to keep you from making things worse. Now go inside and take a shower, then lay down and go to sleep."

"Are you going to tell me what's going on with you?" I asked with a yawn.

"We'll talk more when you wake up."

Hours later I awoke and stretched as far as I could, savoring the peaceful post-sleep state. Memories of the previous night, of the gala, the cops, and of Nick assaulted me and I sat up and looked around, expecting not to be alone. But the room was empty, the house was quiet.

Maybe I dreamt the whole thing.

I pulled myself to the corner of the bed, ignoring the clothes now folded and sitting outside of my bathroom. They strongly resembled clothes I dreamt I wore home from the police station. That's why I was ignoring them.

I approached the window and looked outside, not sure what I'd see in my driveway. Surprisingly, I saw nothing. Maybe I dreamt the drive home too.

Satisfied I was alone, I opened the bedroom door. A thunderous crash came from the hallway. Footsteps sounded downstairs. I shut the door and leaned against it. Who was here? Where was I to go? Someone knocked on the door. I froze. Footsteps walked away. I opened the door and tiptoed into the hallway and looked down the stairs.

At Nick. Surrounded by several dozen books, scattered in messy piles around his feet.

"What was that crash?" I asked, while he bent over and stacked the hardbound tomes.

"I booby-trapped your door so I would know if you planned to escape without my knowledge."

"You *what*?"

"You have a habit of lying about your whereabouts, and I wanted to make sure I knew if you got up and tried something funny."

A rope had been knotted around the brass knob to my bedroom door. I followed it with my eyes, down the stairs, to the floor by Nick's feet. "This rope is rigged to my door. What if I tried to go out the window?"

"I had a different booby-trap for that."

I stomped down the stairs until I was directly in front of him. "I don't need a baby sitter, Nick."

As we stood in the living room, having a stare-off, a green VW Bug barreled down the street and swung into the driveway behind Nick's truck. I looked past Nick to the window and saw Eddie, clutching a greasy paper bag to his white Frankie Say Relax T-shirt. He jogged to the front door and let himself in.

"What are you standing around for? Burgers are getting cold." He looked back and forth between us.

"What are you doing here?"

He raised an eyebrow. "I picked up food since it is a well-known fact you are much more forgiving about people dropping by your house when they bring you food and honestly, how much pizza can one person eat?"

"I'm not talking about the food. Why are you really here?"

Eddie looked at Nick. "You want to tell her or should I?" Nick shrugged. "Dude, it was your plan."

I didn't like what I was hearing but the scent of onion rings from the greasy bag distracted me long enough to get past my annoyance. Eddie thrust the bag at Nick and let him pass us, then pulled me in to a conspiratorial whisper. "Here's the deal. Nick doesn't want you to be alone. I'm here to get your car keys, so I can go get your car from Tradava." He followed Nick into the kitchen and sat down at the table.

"Your burger is getting cold," Nick said from the kitchen. I rounded the corner and watched him bite into his hamburger. A blob of mustard remained on the corner of his mouth.

"Get out of my house," I commanded.

Nick stood up with his burger in one hand. He took another bite, then set it on the table. "I can see there's no way you're going to eat while I'm here, so I'll go. Eddie, can I count on you?"

"No problem," Eddie answered between chews.

Nick wiped his mouth and headed toward me. I turned around and he followed me to the front door and tugged on my ponytail.

"Take it easy, Kidd."

I locked the door behind him. When I returned to the table, I stuffed two onion rings into my mouth and bit into a burger before swallowing. With a full mouth, I asked Eddie what Nick meant about this plan of theirs.

He toyed with the onion rings on his plate. "Who knows? He could have meant anything. It's an expression."

I smelled something that didn't blend with dinner. "What's with the baby sitter routine, anyway? It's all over.

Right? I spent the day at the police station and now they know everything I know. What time is it? Five o'clock? We should go celebrate."

"You seem to be the only person who doesn't realize how dangerous it was for you to go to that gala. Nick saved you today, and he's worried you're going to go out and get in more trouble, so he wanted to make sure you stayed put, at least for now. He knew about everything: the threat on the envelope, the missing money, the notes in Patrick's file."

"I can't help I keep ending up in the wrong place at the wrong time. And the police didn't believe me. I was *that* good at covering my tracks. You wouldn't believe how hard it was to convince them I didn't do anything wrong. But you're right. Even though the cops are on my side now, I still don't have a job, and I'm still going to lose my house. I'm right back where I started, except the Patrick thing is over. Why are you looking at me like that?"

"Sam, listen. The Patrick thing is definitely not over."

I lowered myself into one of the wooden chairs surrounding the kitchen table.

"Nick wasn't sure I should tell you this but you need to know about it. There was another incident last night."

The burger and rings turned over in my stomach. "Maries Paulson, right?" I asked, not sure I wanted to hear the answer.

He nodded. "At Tradava."

"But she was at the gala."

"She must have left or been taken to the store. I don't know why she was there. She was pretty badly beaten, and was bound with seam binding."

"Just like Patrick and Florence," I muttered. "The three people who controlled the outcome of the competition."

"She was found unconscious in his office. When the police swept the room, they found your fingerprints all over."

I didn't know what to say. The threat I received on the invitation said I would be set up if I kept digging, and sure enough, that's what happened.

"What are you thinking?" Eddie prodded.

That the real killer was still on the loose. That going to the cops hadn't finished anything. That trying to do the right thing had made things worse.

"My car was at Tradava. It still is. Nick left it there when he drove me home."

"That's why the police immediately thought they could place you at the scene of the crime. Someone said they knew you were there. Turns out they only saw your car. When they talked to Nick, he told them he gave you a ride home the other night, and that you left your car at the store."

"Nick saved my ass."

"He also told them you were at the museum event."

"Nick didn't see me at the museum event."

"Well, he may have made a few assumptions on that one. He saw a person outside of the event perched in a tree." He paused at this statement, closed his eyes and shook his head at the idea and continued. "And he found a shoe stuck in the ground. A Nick Taylor shoe he claims he gave you years ago."

"I was saving them for a special occasion," I said.

"It's a good thing you wore them because they might have kept you out of jail. You know, another thing you might want to consider is Nick left the gala early and spent the last twelve hours making sure you were safe."

"So Amanda was left on her own," I said. "I'm telling you, it could still be her."

"Whoever it is, they're still out there."

"They found Maries at Tradava. Patrick's body was at Tradava. And I was attacked at Tradava." He looked at me, and I looked back at him, and then I continued. "It's not going to be over until we figure out why everything leads to Tradava."

Wordlessly, we formed our own plan. It was time for another overnight stakeout.

29

Undercover Fashion Chic, I might have called it, if I were writing editorial coverage instead of preparing for a date with doom. Phrases like "death wish" and "bad idea" filled my mind. Eddie ran home to change then returned to my house, giving me ample time to change my mind. I didn't.

We had agreed on a uniform to keep me from being recognized. Black knit hat, black sweater. Black cargo pants, though his were canvas and mine were satin. We matched down to our Doc Martens, his buffed to a high polish, mine coated with a layer of dust. I zipped on a motorcycle jacket I'd owned since college and followed Eddie to his car.

We arrived at the store shortly before closing time and planned to meet up in the trend office.

"If anybody asks, you're a freelance visual stylist. Don't get into a conversation. Just say you're new and you're working for me," Eddie instructed. He unscrewed the cap from a bottle of tomato juice and took a swig, then tucked it into the side pocket of his cargo pants and got out of the car.

He used the employee entrance and I used the door by Juniors. I took the stairs, all seven flights, back to our corridor and arrived first. Using the key I had lifted from Michael's desk days ago, I let myself in.

Following the beam of a pencil-sized flashlight I had remembered to bring, I headed straight for Patrick's office. It was in complete disarray. The framed cover of *Vogue* hung crooked on the wall above the purple sofa. The oversized *Harper's Bazaar* sat on the floor, the frame and the glass broken in the ransacking. The sewing machine was on its side. I tried not to disturb anything, tiptoeing through the mess to the back of Patrick's desk. Several sheets of white paper were scattered over the floor. I picked them up one by one and assembled them by page number.

It was Maries' speech, a fitting tribute from one legend to another. She started by acknowledging the lackluster mannequins draped in black, explaining her last minute decision to use the display platform to indicate the designers' mourning for Patrick instead of showcasing their runway creations. Before I could finish, Eddie's voice interrupted me from outside of the office.

"Michael's desk has been cleaned out."

He passed the desk in the hallway and entered Patrick's office. He went directly to the mini fridge and poured himself a glass of lemonade. "He took everything." As he took a gulp he spun the knob on the side of the empty Rolodex on the corner of Patrick's desk. It appeared as though someone had pulled every card from the spinner and left the stand behind.

A red scarf, the same one Michael had worn around his neck the day he picked up his portfolio, was caught in the hall closet. I touched the wool and let the scarf trail through my fingers.

"Odd that he took everything but left his scarf."

"Do you think it's been him?" he asked.

"He knew about the money and he worked close enough with Patrick to maybe even know his password. He said something to Maries to make her distrust me. He was here all along and he had access. But still, I don't know."

Eddie drained his glass of lemonade and crawled behind the desk with me. "How did you do this? It's not exactly comfortable," he complained. After a few minutes of watching him try to find the best position, I crawled over to help him figure it out. I was a little curious how I had slept there myself.

We sprawled out, side by side, staring at the bottom of Patrick's desk. It was a pretty big desk but with the two of us there, it was close quarters. I folded my hands over my hips and made a steeple. Eddie drummed his fingers on the bottom of the desk drawer above us, a close approximation of "We Got the Beat."

"Why are you so willing to help me?" I asked somewhat tentatively. He stopped drumming. I wasn't sure how far I wanted to push the boundaries of our friendship. And I didn't realize it when I'd asked but the longer the question hung in the air, the more vulnerable I felt.

"That thing, in high school, that could have changed the entire path of my life. If you hadn't come forward, I would've been expelled. I had a scholarship to art school lined up. It would have disappeared. And that's what everybody, the principal, the teacher, the other students thought. That I was the new kid, the troublemaker from another high school. Nobody would have been surprised."

"But you didn't cheat."

"Until you spoke up for me, nobody was on my side. I still don't know why you did it. We weren't friends before it happened, and we didn't become friends after that."

"That's because we graduated."

"Why did you stand up for me?"

"Because I saw it happen. Somebody was trying to get away with something, and it wasn't fair. Not to me, who stayed up studying all night. Not to you, the person who really knew the answers. Not to anybody in that class who was being graded on the bell curve."

"It was high school. People don't go around sticking up for strangers."

"It wasn't right." I bounced my knees against each other and stared at the bottom of Patrick's desk drawer. The office was silent. "You work hard to make your own opportunities. You don't get to make your own breaks by stealing someone else's hard work. That's not the way life is supposed to go."

"After college I landed this job. I've pretty much stayed in Ribbon since then. A few years ago I had the opportunity to move to New York and take a risk. It was a great job, and I thought about it long and hard. But I didn't go. And here you are, you had that career and it didn't make you happy."

"What are you saying?"

"You're where you're supposed to be. Only you can't appreciate it, because someone's making you doubt yourself. You probably would be good at this job if you stick around long enough to get a chance to do it."

"Help me figure out who killed Patrick and I'll stick around long enough to tell you all about what you missed by never moving to New York."

I didn't use the words *I promise* because I wasn't sure I could. But I *was* sure I couldn't keep trying to figure things out on my own.

Eddie reached over and thumped his fist against my hands. I thumped him back. The seriousness of the moment hung in the air for a couple of seconds. "How did you manage to sleep under here?"

"I think my body shut down that night. Between moving here, then finding Patrick's body, the cops, the mortgage people, I don't know. I think something took over. I just kind of collapsed and slept."

"Was this your view?"

"Pretty much." I pointed out the wad of Post-its, cold medicine packets, and old crumbled business cards that belonged to employees who at one time occupied the chair in the trend office. I worked one of the business cards loose and looked at the name. *Cat Lestes. Trend Specialist.*

"Let me see that," Eddie said and snatched the card from my fingers. "This is an old card. At least six years. We changed our logo five years ago and this has the old one on it."

"Cat Lestes—Clestes. She must be the person Amanda was talking about. Did you know her?"

"Six years ago I was on staff. Visual didn't move up here until three years ago, and even now the staff still works out of the office on the first floor."

"Wait here," I said. I writched my hips until I was out from under the desk, then flipped over and crawled away on all fours until I had the space to stand up. I went back to the trend specialist office.

Only days ago I had entered this space and it felt void of personality; I had assumed the person I followed had left on poor terms. Today I knew that wasn't true. Amanda had been my predecessor, and I wanted to explore a little more. There was something here in the trend offices, a connection somewhere I was missing.

I scanned the vacant office, looking at it through the eyes of a stranger. The office still held little more charm than a high school gymnasium the day after the prom, with remnants of life swept into the corners. I opened up the file cabinet drawers and flipped through the plastic tabs on the top of the folders until I found the one I was looking for. Seasonal Recap, filled out by LESTES.

It started to make sense. The visit to Tradava, that very first day. The collection I'd seen in the designer boutique. The label cut out of the pinstripe suit. I booted up the computer and launched the Internet, then did a Google image search for 'Cat Lestes'. It was Red.

"Eddie, I think I found something," I called out as I rounded the corner back into Patrick's office. I froze as a dark puddle oozed out from under the desk and slowly stained the carpet.

My heart jumped into my throat. I put out a hand on the door and gulped deep breaths. Eddie's arm stuck out from under the desk, palm up, fingers curled. Before I had a chance to act a hand clamped itself over my mouth to keep me from screaming.

30

I bit down on the hand, hard. It let go. I whirled around and faced Nick Taylor.

The same Nick Taylor who had arranged for me to be at home, under Eddie's watch. The same Nick Taylor who claimed to be looking out for me, who claimed to care for me. This time, there were no comforting crinkles surrounding his eyes.

This time I was scared to death.

"What were you thinking, biting me? Who did you think I was?" he asked sorely.

"Stay away from me. I don't know why you're here, but I'm calling the cops." I stepped backward, one hand out front, keeping him at bay, the other in back, waving in the air, feeling for the desk. He reached his unbitten hand out to me and I smacked it away.

"Don't touch me! What did you do to Eddie?"

"What happened to Eddie?" he asked, looking confused.

I pointed toward the desk, to Eddie's feet jutting out from underneath.

"Eddie's—he's lying under the desk. You—you—while I was in the other office."

Nick looked first at the desk, then back at me. "Keep talking," he ordered, moving toward Eddie. The stain on the carpet grew.

"I didn't—didn't hear anyone. I d-d-didn't even hear you. I came back to t-t-tell him I f-f-f-found C-c-c-lestes."

The sound of a snore from under the desk brought a halt to my babbling. Eddie's legs, the only thing visible other than his limp arm, repositioned themselves as his legs rolled to their side. An empty tomato juice bottle rolled across the carpet, bumping up against Nick's foot. He picked up the bottle and held it by the lid with two fingers. Dribbles of thick red liquid ran down the outside of the bottle. A fat droplet hit the carpet and seeped in. Nick set the bottle on the desk behind me and wiped red tomato-juice handprints on his jeans. He led me to the purple sofa.

"Tell me why you two are here."

My words still poured out in a rush. "The trend specialist b-b-before Amanda is tr-trying to frame me." I said. I was shivering uncontrollably but not because it was cold.

"Have you learned nothing?"

"It's the only way to get on w-w-with my life. I c-c-convinced Ed-d-die because he c-c-could get me in here. I didn't think he would be in any d-d-danger." I didn't know if I was making any sense, but I couldn't stop talking.

"So you saw a large puddle on the carpet and assumed he was dead. Then you saw me and thought I was the killer. That's why you bit me?"

"You clamped a hand over my mouth." I took a few deep breaths. "All in all I think biting you was a n-n-natural response." I took a breath and tried to get control of the stuttering. Nick started massaging his palm again. For all I knew he was wondering if I had rabies.

I lowered my voice to a reasonable level. "I know you want me to leave all of this alone, but I can't." Considering how loud the voices in my head were, my own voice was coming out quiet and more than a little shaky. "I'm sorry you're wrapped up in this, and I'm sorry people keep getting hurt. I just," I paused to take a deep breath. "I want to get on with my life."

"I called you at the house. You didn't answer. I called Eddie. I could hear enough background noise to know he was at Tradava. It wasn't hard to put two and two together, even if it doesn't add up to anything wise." I braced myself for the lecture Nick was gearing up to deliver. "Samantha," he said. He reached out for my hand and held it between his. "Look at me." I slowly raised my gaze from his hands to his face. "Amanda is my friend. She is mixed up in this, and I've been trying to help her."

"But how?"

"She was about to debut her first solo collection under her name. It was an important step. She had a good chance of winning the design competition and the hundred thousand dollars. For an emerging designer, that's a lot of money."

It *was* a lot of money. It was the kind of money that would solve my problems, at least temporarily. I'd get the mortgage company off my back, tear out the shag carpet, and buy the best kind of gourmet cat food they made for Logan. But those were my problems, and this wasn't about me.

"Aside from the money, the contest came with connections. A guaranteed order from Tradava. Plus, Patrick met with the buyers regularly to advise on trends and emerging talent. His connections and endorsement could have opened a lot of doors for her. She needed him to validate her designs, otherwise it would have been too difficult to move from assistant to designer. Stores are like little worlds. You get a job, and that's who you are. There's not a lot of room for someone to reinvent themselves, and for Amanda to have any kind of credibility, she needed this. Something big to endorse her talent."

"But wouldn't there always be questions about her winning, if she did win?"

"That's why she quit her job. She had to sever ties and distance herself from Tradava and Patrick before the competition got underway. She had solid feedback from everyone who saw her samples. Including Patrick and Maries. It was at Patrick's encouragement she left."

Eddie rolled over again and knocked his head on the desk. He cursed, sat up, and looked around the room with glazed eyes. After he mumbled some unintelligible words he stood up, the tomato juice caked to the side of his pants. He refilled his lemonade and drained the glass in several gulps, then squinted at us as though he couldn't make us out clearly. He stumbled to the sofa, plunked a pillow from under my arm, and returned to the floor behind the desk. The even breathing resumed.

"Morning people," I scoffed, shaking my head.

"I wouldn't criticize too much. Didn't you fall asleep in here too?"

He had a point.

"Tell me about the gala. Something happened inside that room. And what happened to the money?"

"What money?"

"The money Maries Paulson took with her."

"Why would she have the money with her?" he asked.

It was my turn to pick up the explanation. "Someone was extorting the money from her, or was trying to. Someone who knew about the money and the competition. Only, she didn't know where Patrick kept it. I found a list of investors on Patrick's computer, and it looked like he had collected eighty thousand dollars, plus the entry fees. That was ninety thousand, four hundred. He was short. But Michael told me the money was safe, and the right person would get it."

"Michael Dubrecht?"

"Yes. He was at the gala too. I saw him talk to Maries. All the suspects were there."

"All?"

"The designers. Michael, Red—I mean Clestes, Amanda, and you."

"Me?"

"You. You were there, the morning Patrick was murdered. You were there, when my house was broken into. You had access to the computer, I found it in your store. And you tried to keep me from going to the gala."

"For your own good. I tried to keep you away for your own good. This is a murder investigation, Kidd, not a game. People have been hurt."

I jumped up from the sofa. "Then why are you here now, Nick? If it's so dangerous for me to be here, why isn't it dangerous for you?"

"Because I suspected you were going to pull a stunt like this. Patrick is dead, Kidd. Two other people have been attacked. And you haven't learned anything, have you?" Nick stood up and gathered his jacket in his palm. "There's one way for me to prove to you I have nothing to do with this, and that's to leave. Wake Eddie and let's go. This isn't business for us. It's for the cops." He walked to the doorway before turning around. I stood rooted to the spot next to the purple sofa. I had no intention of following him.

"Come on, Samantha. It's time to go home."

"No," I said, surprising both of us.

"You haven't learned anything, have you?"

"I learned having a home to go to only means something when you feel safe there. Until this is over, I won't feel safe."

"I'm not going to let anything happen to you."

"I learned something else too. I learned I don't need you to save me."

"You sure about that?" he said, and, for a second, I thought about Nick helping me with the flooded basement, about Nick driving me home after I was knocked out at Tradava, and about Nick saving me from the police interrogation. I thought about how often he'd been there to save me, and how it really was time I learned to save myself.

"I'm not leaving."

"Then you're on your own." He turned around and walked out. Seconds later, I heard the heavy glass doors that separated our offices from the store clunk into place.

How much truth was there to what Nick said? More than I cared to admit. In one week I'd lived through some of the worst experiences of my life, and most of them were of my own doing.

I shook Eddie's leg until he woke up. "Dude, let's get out of here."

He sat up and scratched the left side of his head. "Where am I?"

"Tradava. Here. Take the keys, meet me in the car. There's something I have to do before I leave."

He pulled himself out from under the desk. He opened his eyes as wide as he could and blinked repeatedly. "I'm not driving."

"I'll be down in a sec. Hang tight." I checked the clock. The store would be closing soon. This was it, my last chance to stand in these offices. Once I walked out that door, I'd be done with Tradava. This job had worked out for me about as well as a root canal performed by a sadist. I'd shown up and someone had done the kind of number on me that exposed my weaknesses, my nerves, my doubts to the world. Then they'd drilled.

It was time to say good-bye to my fresh start.

Eddie took the keys and stumbled out of the trend offices. I rounded the corner from Patrick's office and turned into what should have been my office. Michael Dubrecht lay slumped in a corner.

His spiked black hair, gelled into a Mohawk, pressed into his forearm, leaving small red welts. His red scarf, the one I'd seen in the closet when we first arrived, was knotted around his neck.

I rushed to him and loosened the scarf. His eyes, unfocused and dilated, peered out of his face, then closed. His mouth remained open. I pulled off my gloves and felt along his neck. My fingers found a piece of seam binding knotted around his neck, under the scarf. With shaking fingers I fumbled with the knot until I was able to loosen it. I pressed on his neck and found a faint pulse.

"Help!" I called, but no one was there to answer.

"Michael, Michael, can you hear me?" I asked, shaking him by the shoulders. His eyes opened slightly, like small slits of a cat. "Vogue," he choked out, then coughed a couple of times. "Water," he said next.

"There's no water. Stay with me, focus on me. There's lemonade. I have to leave you to get it."

"No!" he said, his hand gripping my wrist, tightly. Panic flooded his face like an electrical current that had been suddenly switched on.

"I have to, you need the liquid. I'll be right back. There's not a lot of time."

"Not alone," he said.

"We are now. Nick and Eddie were with me, but they left. I'll be right back, and I'll get you out of here." I raced to Patrick's office for a glass of lemonade.

I flipped the light switch a couple of times, but it didn't work. I grabbed a glass and filled it. There was a heavy *ka-chunk* in the hallway, like a lock falling into place. Store security had taken to locking the doors, to keep people like me out. I looked to the ceiling in vain. We had to get out. Michael might not make it otherwise.

I raced back into my old office, sloshing lemonade over the brim of the glass. He hadn't moved. I tipped his head back so I could pour the lemonade into his mouth. When I let go of his head, it lolled to the side, his neck muscles apparently too weak to hold it up.

Footsteps sounded in the hallway. "Help! Help! We're locked in here!" I hollered. I reached for the phone and clicked it repeatedly, trying to get a dial tone. There was nothing.

Before I could turn something brushed against me. I pivoted around. If only I'd been faster to figure it all out, so much could have been avoided. I should have known from the beginning, but still, she was the last person I was prepared to see.

31

I watched the designer push a stray lock of brilliant red hair from her eyes. Then, in a sudden gesture, she pulled a vibrant wig from her head and shook out her own black locks. A sheath of glossy black hair fell to her shoulders and I stared directly into the eyes of Maries Paulson.

"You? I thought you were in the hospital."

"That's what you were supposed to think," she said. "It's that Ries girl in the hospital, not me. It only took a couple of bruises to her face to make her unrecognizable and a blow to her head to make her unconscious. I planted my ID on her and called 911. She wasn't conscious enough to tell them they'd made a mistake."

It had been easy for Maries to copy the signature hair of one of the finalists, as easy as it had been for her impersonate an EMT or a grieving friend. It was a testament to the aging icon's natural beauty, or at least an expensive moisturizer, that with a two-hundred dollar wig, she could pass at a glance for Red tonight, a woman almost half her age.

"You have a real talent for doing exactly what I want, don't you, dear?" Maries joked. "It might have been fun to work with you, if you didn't keep getting in my way. Now, where's the money?"

Any surgeries she'd undergone had been successful if success was judged by a vacant expression that gave away nothing. It was her eyes, that had seen too much, that belied her true age. The dark sunglasses she frequently wore had been the best defense she had against the truths her eyes revealed.

"I don't have the money. I don't know where it is!"

"How predictable. Predictable people are nice to have around, until they wear out their usefulness. You helped me figure out what Patrick had done. I didn't know about the file on his laptop, or that he'd gotten the money from the garment district. You told me all of that. And you made it very easy for me to make you look guilty. Things couldn't have been easier if you were following a script. It's too bad you're going to wear out your usefulness in one night, sweetie," Maries cooed. Her attitude was pissing me off, but she was right. I might as well have been following a script.

The gloves I had so carefully worn to avoid leaving fingerprints were on the desk next to Michael. I looked around the office for a way out while the walls felt like they were closing in.

"Who do these kids think they are, entering a contest to get money to back their collections? That's not how it used to work. It took talent. Passion. Vision. And hard work. I've been designing clothes since I was seventeen. I witnessed the beginning of American Design. I watched Dior launch the New Look when I was a child and realized how famous he would become—he'll live forever because of that! That's the industry I wanted to be a part of. And I was. I dated Halston, for Christ's sake!"

The woman was clearly delusional. Everybody knew Halston was gay.

"But the industry is changing. I've seen the genius of Correges copied so much people think he's a boot and not a designer. I've seen true talent retire because the industry became less about creativity and more about marketing. This contest, this whole farce, is part of the problem, not the solution. Dangling a contract and money in front of a bunch of small town designers is not the way to discover the future of fashion."

"But you're a judge, you were part of the contest all along," I said. "You're gaining as much publicity as any of the contestants."

"I don't need the publicity. I owe money, too much money to pay. My debts run deep. When Patrick said Tradava pulled the funding, that he had to raise one hundred thousand dollars to see the competition happen, I thought it was over. But when he secured the money, quickly, I had to know how he had done it. He wouldn't tell me details. That's when I knew I had to get at the money myself."

Her eyes glowed with rage and insanity, accented by the reflection of the fluorescent tube lighting that lit the room. "He caught me going through his files. I suspected he knew, but he pretended not to. I discovered the bank and the account number. All I needed was the password on the account and I could have transferred the money to my own bank and vanished."

"Patrick was a better person than you. He went to businessmen who had a stake in the success of future designers. He remained true to the industry while you wanted to steal from it," I said.

"Don't be a child. Those men were loan sharks. I should know. I turned to them myself when I first had financial trouble. There's no getting away from them once you're in bed with them. This was my way out. Patrick knew I had turned to them once. He was the one who reopened that door, not me. And he wasn't going to stand in my way after the door was open."

"But you said—"

"Such naiveté. It's almost charming." She ran a gloved finger down the side of my face. I sat still, achingly still, clenching and unclenching my jaw. My temples pulsed with the motion, but I was powerless to stop.

"When I came here, that morning, I wanted to give him one last chance. But he refused. He said he would find another judge and that I was no longer a part of the competition. When he hired you, he planned to train you to be the second judge. I couldn't allow him to do that. I couldn't allow him to tarnish my name, to cut me out, and I couldn't let you take my place. He put up a good fight. I didn't expect that." Her pupils dilated and her spittle hit my cheek. "I'll ask you one last time. Where is the money?"

"I don't know where the money is," I said. "I don't know anything about the money."

"That's not true. You've been snooping around here for a week. You figured out so much you must know. You're the only one who had access to his files."

"There's nothing in the file about where the money is hidden!"

"Patrick may have discovered me, but he was going to ruin me too. He thought it was in our best interest to start this contest, to become judges, in this small city, with these small talents. I'm not a small town woman, and my career is far from over. These children wouldn't know what to do with a hundred grand, but my debts are too numerous to list. That money would buy me out from under the men I owe. I have to have it. Patrick knew what it would mean to me, but he wouldn't tell me where he kept it. Don't you understand? I have to have that money!"

"*You're a killer!*" I shouted at her. She smiled, as if she was heavily medicated. It was like she didn't even realize what she'd done.

"I'm sure the police will be interested in knowing how you stole Patrick's computer and violated his privacy, how you extorted a hundred thousand dollars from me at the gala."

"There is no money!" I yelled. "The police found your briefcase, empty. Nobody ever threatened you, and nobody demanded cash from you."

"Are you sure about that?" she said. "Maybe *you* demanded the money from me, money that would help you start over. If anything happens to me, maybe I've left enough evidence to lead everyone back to you." I moved away from her and bumped into Michael's foot.

He made a gurgling sound. Maries stood up and we both looked at him. "I know where the money is," he whispered.

"Where is it?"

"Water," he choked out.

Maries grabbed the back of my jacket and yanked me up. "Get him something to drink."

I picked up the glass of lemonade and held it to his head, beads of condensation transferring onto his bluish skin, running down the side of his face. My mind raced. I needed time to figure things out, but time might be the one thing Michael couldn't spare. I raised my eyes to the ceiling and silently prayed to the gods of footwear and designer clothes and everything I found holy. Who was the patron saint for fashion? *Yves St. Laurent, I need your help! Are you listening?*

Lemonade sloshed over the opening of the glass, down Michael's cheek. Maries shot a gloved hand out and caught me by my wrist. The glass dropped and shattered against the floor. I jumped at the crash. Maries picked up a shard with her other hand and dragged it across my cheekbone. My skin burned like someone had set it on fire and I saw the blood out of the corner of my eye.

I tried to pull away but she was stronger than I'd imagined. I realized with sickening certainty my prayers were not being answered. She twisted my wrist around until my shoulders and neck followed. The pain had doubled me over and my face was inches from the broken glass. She bent over behind me, pinning me down.

"Get more lemonade," she hissed in my ear. She let go of me and I tried to stand. My legs were shaking so hard I could barely walk. I couldn't speak. I leaned against the walls in the hallway and guided myself to Patrick's office.

I pulled the delicate glass pitcher out of the mini-fridge. It was half empty.

Before all of this happened, I might have said it was half full.

My eyes darted wildly around the office. To the desk. To the sofa. To my reflection in the glass on the framed magazine covers that had fallen off the walls and now littered the floor. My cargo pants were disheveled from sitting on the floor. My undercover chic look had been replaced by Goth cheerleader from hell hours ago, but what difference did it make now?

"I don't think he has a lot of time left," she called in the singsong voice of a murderer.

I walked back to the horror scene. Lemonade sloshed over the sides of the pitcher and spilled on the desk and the floor. Maries had moved Michael into the chair behind the desk. She was perched on the corner, close enough for me to see the roots of her hair.

She was crazy, of that I had no doubt. But unlike me, she had managed to keep her gloves on all of this time. She looked like she always looked: elegance personified. And here I was, sweating profusely and barely able to stand. But I would not let her see my weaknesses.

My mind swam with information. The design competition, the night I spent locked in Tradava, and the museum event. I thought of Eddie, asleep in the car out front. Of Patrick's password, Livo72, of Michael's promise that the money was safe, of the protected file, and the two contributors who still had pending payment. I watched Maries face as I tipped the pitcher to Michael's mouth, the look of anticipation on her face reaching climax.

And then it all became clear.

32

She'd doped the lemonade.

Maries Paulson had called me predictable, so now I did the most unpredictable thing I could think of. I smashed the pitcher against the desk, crashing it into a thousand pieces and splashing the remaining lemonade on her. She jumped back, startled. Score one for me.

The door to the offices rattled. I heard my name called from far in the distance.

Maries lunged for me. I jumped back, one step, then two, then turned around and raced for the door. She grabbed a fistful of my sweater and threw me sideways into Patrick's office. I stumbled across the floor, ricocheting off the desk, hands in front of me to soften the blow when I fell. My left hand connected with the arm of the purple sofa, but I was off balance. My right hand slapped against the wall. She grabbed the back of my head and pushed it forward, into the corner of the framed *Vogue* cover. A sharp pain exploded behind my right eye and spots blurred my vision. The glass shattered, then fell to the floor in a shower of shards. The poster curled from the frame, exposing neat stacks of hundred dollar bills.

"The money!" Maries gasped.

I spun to face her and swayed with dizziness. I grabbed a long blade of broken glass. Blood dripped from my palm. Maries lunged at me, her hands clawing on either side of my body at the money that had been hidden in the office all along. I closed my eyes and screamed. Her body fell against me, knocking me backward, into the wall, and onto the pile of cash on the floor. I kicked at her, screamed, and tried to move her off of me. She went limp. I pushed out from under her arm and raced back to Michael.

"We have to get out of here," I said, trying to help him stand. "Now."

"But Maries—" he squeaked out.

"Maries Paulson is dead," said Detective Loncar from behind me.

He stood in the middle of the doorframe and held out a hand. I took it and stood, then walked to the doorway of Patrick's office. Through my tears and sweat and matted hair I saw Maries Paulson lying on the floor, face down, on a pile of money. The large shard of glass had pierced her neck. A pool of blood seeped over the bills and the *Vogue* poster, dented and torn, lying next to the sofa.

It was the first time I'd seen her not look glamorous.

A blonde woman in scrubs offered me a cup of water and a rose-colored blanket while a medic checked my pulse. "Michael," I said, and pointed to the other room. "He's hurt worse than I am." I held the blanket around me while they went to check on him. Minutes later the blonde pushed a wheelchair into the office, then Michael was pushed out.

Detective Loncar directed a team of police officers around the office. Two men in navy blue windbreakers pushed a gurney covered with a sheet out of the office. I looked away.

"Ms. Kidd, you want to tell me what happened here tonight?" the detective asked. He ran the palm of his hand over his short crew cut while he looked around the room. A skinny man in a black leather jacket snapped photos of the money, the glass, the blood.

"Somewhere else," I said. My voice had turned raspy, despite the water. He guided me, alone, away from the trend offices, to the sofas by the ladies' lounge, and I told him the story of Maries Paulson, Patrick, the design competition, and the hidden money that had led to a murder.

It might have been the birds chirping or the sun shining. It might have been the soft, fluffy down comforter on my bed, or Logan by my side. It might be the peace and quiet I'd earned after the night at Tradava when I'd narrowly escaped with my life. Whatever it was, I didn't care. The drama was over and I was free.

Tradava had been given enough information to exonerate me from wrongdoing, but no offer of employment had been extended. That meant I was probably going to have to interview for the job all over again. If I still wanted it.

My mind wandered to Cat—Catherine—Lestes, the owner of Catnip. In a parallel universe, she and I might have been friends, her owning a boutique that could fuel my passion for fashion. Everything she'd ever told me had been true. Clestes was a collection of one of a kind items co-designed by her and her brother, a textile designer. She sold the collection at her store. Together, they'd been a legitimate finalist in the design competition. She had never believed the competition was a level playing field, and had approached her chances with a watchful eye on anyone who might have had an unfair advantage. My own actions, my own appearance at Tradava and misguided partnership with Maries Paulson had done little other than lead Cat to believe I had something to hide.

The bags from my shopping spree were still lined up along the wall, ready to be returned. I didn't need a collection of unique choices I couldn't afford to endorse who I was. Fashion was in my blood. I'd land on my feet and demonstrate my abilities to the world, yet.

But not today. I pulled out my T-shirt drawer and stuck my hands into the back. Under the stack of neat white Hanro tank tops I found it. A faded black T-shirt that said The Kid. The adult XL had once hung to my knees now fit like a security blanket, softened with repeated washings. The black had turned to gray and the metallic iron-on peeled up by the bottom of the decal. I pulled it on over Union Jack pajama bottoms and shoved my feet into a pair of white Moon Boots for warmth. Downstairs, I retrieved the newspaper and the mail from the front porch. There would, no doubt, be yet another account of the events at Tradava, as there had been every day since the showdown. It had been over a week, and the paper was still going strong. I carried the still-bundled newspaper from the porch to the trashcan.

Nick's truck turned into my driveway. I looked down at my outfit and sighed. I was tired of trying to impress people. The boss who'd been impressed by my resume was dead. So was the designer who would have appreciated my taste level. My closet was half-full, but this was me too, Moon Boots and all. I held the door open for Nick. He set a pile of mail on a side table inside the door and followed me to the sofa.

"How's the hand?" he asked.

I held it up to show off the clean application of gauze across the cut on my palm. "I won't be playing handball anytime soon, but I'll survive." Logan padded into the room and jumped onto the window sill, staring outside.

"Have you read the papers?"

I shook my head.

"Do you want to talk about it?"

"I don't know."

We sat side by side on the green velvet sofa. It was back in place along the wall, facing the large bay window. I had stopped pushing the sofa up against the door the day after the police brought me home from Tradava. Now that Maries was dead, I finally felt safe.

"Patrick wanted this competition to be his legacy. He believed, completely, that design talent doesn't have to come from a big city. He wanted to find someone with vision and put them on the map."

I flipped my wrist over and stared at the gauze, then flipped it back and set it on my thigh. "He asked Maries to be his partner. I don't think it ever occurred to him what would happen."

"What happened when you were in there with her? Why did she snap?"

"She owed a lot of money. Money she had borrowed to relaunch her collection, that she couldn't repay. When she learned Patrick had raised the hundred thousand dollars, she saw a way out of her debt. Add in that Patrick had turned to questionable loaners, the same people she owed money to, and she freaked."

"But why did Patrick keep the money in the frame?"

"That wasn't him. That was Michael." It made sense, after the fact. Michael heard Patrick talking to people about investing in an undiscovered talent. He knew where the money was coming from, and where the account was kept. Maries Paulson had asked to be a co-signer on the account, but it never happened. Michael thought Patrick was being secretive about the money because he was a finalist. But when Patrick died, Michael had all of Patrick's passwords, and moved the money out of the bank and hid it. What he really wanted was the validation. He wanted to be announced the winner.

When Patrick and Maries first conceived of the competition, they both had ulterior motives. Patrick wanted to be relevant again. A new generation of designers barely knew who he was, and he wanted to be a part of the future of fashion.

"Patrick's password. Livo72. Look in Vogue 72. I misunderstood him. The note he left told me to 'Look in Vogue', but I didn't get it. It was all right there. His password was more than a password, it was a clue. If I'd figured it out, if I had listened, maybe he'd be alive. Now two people are dead."

"Kidd, Maries made her bed and now she's lying in it."

Nick reached his hand to my face and cradled my cheek, his thumb lightly tracing the almost-healed cut Maries had inflicted. I tapped the toes of my Moon boots together.

"How's Amanda?" I asked, trying to change the subject.

"She's still recovering from injuries. Doctors say there will be no long term damage, but she's shaken up. Terrified, actually. I think she's taking an extended break from the runway circuit. Women like Amanda don't get over things like this too easily."

"Women like Amanda? What about women like me?"

"Women like you are a lot more rare. That's why I'm here."

Truth be told, I wouldn't blame her if she did take that extended break. I considered taking a break myself. My image of the fashion industry was somewhat tarnished.

A few minutes lapsed and Nick stood. "I should be getting to the store." I followed him to the door. "So what's next for you, Kidd? Are you going to stay here?"

I didn't want to face how much those questions had been plaguing me over the past week. Had this all been a sign I should never have moved back here and started this new life? Was the house too much for me to handle? Would I be able to get my job back—or officially get it in the first place? Did I want that job? Or the one in New York that I'd left? Was I anywhere closer to knowing what I wanted to do with my life?

I'd changed. I wasn't the same person who had left Bentley's with the hopes of starting over in my childhood home. I'd grown up more in the past two weeks than I had in the entire time I'd spent growing up in this house. I'd been interrogated by the cops. I'd risked my life. I'd watched a woman die.

"Kidd!" Nick's voice snapped me out of my mental inquisition and back to reality. He reached his hands out to me, touched my arms and let his fingers trail down until our hands were entwined.

"I don't know what's next," I said. It was the most honest thing I could say.

He pulled me with him so we were facing each other but didn't let go of my hand. The gesture was both innocent and intimate.

"I don't want to say anything that's going to affect your decision but as long as I'll be hanging out here, I wouldn't mind having you around too." He took a step back and scanned me from head to Moon Boots and back. "You bring a certain *je ne sais quoi* to Ribbon."

I pushed him away. He pulled his keys out of his pocket, then waved as he walked down the driveway to his truck.

"Call me if you need anything. You know where to find me." He revved the engine of his truck and backed out of the driveway.

I closed the door behind me and picked up the stack of mail. Absentmindedly I flipped through the envelopes. A postcard from Mom and Dad. Another form for customized stationary, like the one I'd received days ago. A threatening letter from Full Circle Mortgage.

I carried the mail to the kitchen table. So much had happened in the past month. I'd given up a job and lost a mentor, but I'd gained so much more. I gained a direction. I grabbed a pen, and filled out the form. *Name: Samantha Kidd. Address:* I paused.

I looked around at the walls of the house I'd remembered so well, the seventies shag carpet and built-in bookcase in the living room, the avocado green appliances in the kitchen. For all of my recent questions, I had one answer. This was where I wanted to be.

My decision was made. A couple of phone calls were in order, to straighten out the mortgage and the job. I'd do what I had to do and it would be fine. Logan appeared from nowhere and jumped on the sofa next to me, paws on the mail, nuzzling his head around, hoping for attention. It felt right, sitting on the sofa with my cat in my parents' house.

No. In my house.

Maybe I wouldn't call anyone yet. Maybe I'd hang out with Logan for a little while, enjoying the silence.

Read on for a sneak peak
at the second book in the
Style & Error Mystery Series,

Buyer, Beware

(COMING MARCH 2013)

EXCERPT

This wasn't how I'd planned on spending my Saturday night. It was one thing to be alone, waiting for the phone to ring. The man I wanted to call had spent the last month in Italy, and I'd gotten used to Saturday nights by myself. Maybe that's why I was hiding in a bathroom with a naked man. He quickened my pulse, sped up my breathing, and inspired thoughts that would make a more innocent woman blush. Never mind that he was made of wood and tucked inside my handbag. Never mind that five minutes ago I'd stolen him from his place of honor in the admissions hall of the local design school.

I'm not a thief, my inner monologue cried out. *I'm not a crook, or an opportunist, or the kind of person who breaks the law.*

Well, maybe, on occasion, I *was* the kind of person who broke the law, but only in very specific situations.

If I make it out of here safely, I promise to never wear sweatpants in public, my inner monologue bargained with the patron saints of thieves and fashion.

From the hallway, I heard the resonant strike of leather soles on the marble floor. I promised myself if I could make it fifteen more seconds without breathing I could have two bowls of cherry vanilla ice cream when I got home. If I got home. If I didn't get caught. Not the best strategy for not breathing.

The footsteps faded and I exhaled. The naked statue shifted lower in my handbag. I relaxed for a moment and rooted around, making sure my wooden companion was hidden inside the slightly worn Birken handbag I bought from eBay back when I had a disposable income. At least if I was hauled off to jail, it would be locked up with the rest of my outfit, patiently awaiting my release. How long do you get for stealing art? Ten to twenty years? Good thing the Birken was a classic.

The door to the bathroom slowly creaked open. Before I could scream, climb through a vent, or adopt a really cool fighting move, a man in a black turtleneck, black knit hat, black gloves, black cargo pants, and black Vans grabbed my wrist and pulled me toward the exit.

"Did you make the swap?" Eddie whispered.

I nodded.

"Good. The security guard is on the other side of the building. We have to go. Now!" He shoved me into the bright hallway of the admissions building. We raced past closed classroom doors and bulletin boards filled with bright slips of paper that announced campus activities. We charged out the front doors, down the concrete stairs, to the parking lot. I dove into the back of the waiting getaway car, otherwise known as our other friend Cat's Suburban, and pulled an open sleeping bag over my body. Eddie disappeared into the night on foot. I snuggled against the backseat and remained in the fetal position while Cat drove to the edge of the lot.

The car stopped. Why did the car stop? There was no way we were out of the parking lot. It was too soon to stop.

"Can you tell me how to get back to the highway?" Cat asked in an innocent tone. I pictured her flipping her red hair over her shoulder and tipping her head to the side. A male voice described a series of exits and turns. She thanked him. A set of tires peeled out of the lot past us, the voices ceased, and off we drove, me clinging to the naked man in the backseat like it was our third date.

And that describes my first premeditated robbery.

The night was a success, if success can be measured by things like theft and clean getaways. Somehow we'd done it. My careful planning had taken us from concept to execution, but success was a team effort. Eddie, visual manager for Tradava, Ribbon, Pennsylvania's oldest retailer. Cat, owner of Catnip, a discount designer boutique in the outlet center, and Dante, Cat's brother, had made it happen. We'd pooled our collective resources and talents and swiped a statue from the Institute of Fashion, Art, and Design, or I-FAD, as it was known in fashion circles. Even more impressive than the success of our mission was the fact that I'd planned the whole thing less than a week ago.

Things had been quiet around Ribbon, Pennsylvania. Life was normal, or as normal as it can be when you're in your early thirties, out of work, trying to figure out how to pay the bills. Six months ago I'd given up my glamorous job as a buyer for Bentley's New York for a chance to move into the house where I grew up. Things hadn't turned out exactly as planned, thanks to a murder investigation. I lost my job, lost a mentor, and came darn near close to losing the house. I'd taken to obsessively reorganizing my ample wardrobe, first by color, then by silhouette, and finally by decade. With my savings account rapidly dwindling thanks to things like the new mortgage payment and cat food for Logan, I was a starving fashionista, living off the contents of my closet.

And then the contest had been announced in the *Ribbon Times*.

Interested in a Heist?

Ribbon's hottest new store opens on July 14. Join us for the Pilferer's Ball to get a sneak preview of our unparalleled assortments at criminally low prices. The daring are challenged to arrive with one of the following items in tow, "borrowed" from their current place of residency. Should you successfully lift said loot without notice, you can win a $10,000 shopping spree at HEIST. Rules and regulations listed below.

It was right up my alley.

Eddie, a high school friend I'd reconnected with during the aforementioned murder investigation, seemed the perfect person to help me. Plus, safety in numbers and all that.

"The best time for the theft is in the early morning, like three or four o'clock. It'll be dark, the night guard will be tired, and there will be minimal traffic on the campus since the bars and parties shut down at two. Anyone wandering around will probably be drunk and not a credible witness," I had said to Eddie, while we hung out in my living room, discussing my plan.

When I first moved in, the house was a study in post-college hand-me-down. I'd painted an accent wall with a gallon of aqua paint from Home Depot's "Oops" rack, then decorated the wall with fabric cuttings framed in black plastic document frames from the dollar store. Three rows of nine frames each filled the wall opposite the large bay window. A white afghan, crocheted by my grandmother, covered the back of the gray flannel sofa Eddie bought me from a prop sale at Tradava. Two black and white chairs sat opposite the sofa, set off by blue tweed fabric I'd found in the markdown bin at the local fabric store and fashioned into curtains.

"We need to not look suspicious around the campus, because people might remember us if we seem like we don't belong," I added. "I think you should pretend to be a security guard. That way the real guard won't spend too much time watching the areas where you already are."

Eddie sat sideways in one of the black and white chairs, his knees bent over the arm, his checkered Vans bouncing on the outside of the fabric. His pencil flew over a pad of drawing paper, making sketches.

"I don't think I'll make a very convincing security guard."

I ignored him. "My new neighbor is the head of the fabric curriculum at I-FAD. I'll volunteer to talk to one of her classes or something."

I was interrupted by a knock on the door.

"Hold that thought," Eddie said. He spun to a sitting position and pushed himself out of the chair.

"You invited someone to my house?" I asked, shoving incriminating plans and schematics under the sofa. I followed him to the door.

Standing on my porch were a man and a woman. I recognized the woman as Catherine Lestes, Catnip boutique owner. The last time we'd spoken we shared a couple of not very nice words. She'd accused me of murder, and I don't take well to that. Next to her was a man in a black leather jacket. He had jet-black hair and sideburns like Elvis in the 1968 comeback special. A white T-shirt, faded denim jeans that were frayed at the hems, and black boots finished his outfit.

"Are you Samantha Kidd?" he asked.

"Yes."

"I've heard a lot about you." He held out a hand. His jacket sleeve rode up, exposing flame tattoos around his wrists. "I'm Dante. You know my sister, Cat." He tipped his head to the side.

Not sure of the protocol to welcome a formerly hostile fashionista and a strange biker dude on my doorstep, I took a half-step backward and looked at Eddie. He stepped to the side and held the door open.

"Glad you guys could make it. Come on in," he said.

Not what I'd expected. I glared at him, communicating thoughts that he appeared able to tune out.

"I get the feeling you didn't know we were coming," Dante said.

"Eddie invited me. We're here to help with the theft," Cat added. "I invited Dante to join us. You don't mind, do you?"

"Sure, fine, no problem." I turned to Eddie. "Can I see you in the kitchen for a moment?"

Logan, my frisky feline, slinked into the room. I turned to Cat and Dante. "Watch out for my cat. He's very selective about the company he keeps," I said. Logan crossed the room and sniffed the toes of Dante's boots. Fickle cat.

In the kitchen, Eddie said, "Before you say no, think about it. We can't pull this thing off by ourselves."

"Cat doesn't like me."

He waved my protest away like the scent of stinky cheese. "She didn't like you when she thought you were a murderer. Things change. Let them stick around and listen what they can do. Cat has connections at I-FAD so she can easily be our person on the inside. And she tells me her brother has all kinds of hidden talents."

"Like what?"

"I don't know, sneaky stuff, by the looks of him. But listen, we might need another man besides me."

The problem was, I already had another man besides Eddie: Nick Taylor. Only, I didn't. Nick was a shoe designer I'd worked with in my former life as designer shoe buyer at Bentley's New York department store. When I gave up that job for a lifestyle makeover and moved from the Big Apple to the small town—Ribbon, Pennsylvania—Nick's name moved from the "colleague" column of my life to the one labeled "you've got potential." And then, like all good shoe designers, he left for Italy, where he'd been for the past month. I was pretty sure that, in addition to keeping the secret about our planned theft at the museum, keeping the secret of the hot tattooed biker who had experience in all kinds of hidden talents might be a bit of a challenge.

"Fine," I said, though it was anything but.

We returned to the living room. Logan was curled up next to Dante on the green velvet sofa. Cat sat on one of the black and white chairs, flipping through the Halston coffee table book I kept on my glass and chrome coffee table. Her legs were crossed, and she bounced one patent leather lime green pump against her calf.

I sat next to Dante and retrieved the plans and schematics from under the sofa. I outlined my general plan to get them caught up.

"I'll come up with assignments for both of you tonight. In the meantime—"

"Dante will make a better fake security guard than I will," Eddie said. He pulled a piece of paper from his manila folder and held it out to Dante. "Plus, that will give me more time to work on the fake."

Cat chimed in next. "I'll set up the guest professorship with the college, Samantha. I've done it before and already have the contacts. The college probably won't respond to your offer since you're currently unemployed." She brushed a stray lock of vibrant red hair behind her ear. "Now we just need something for you to do." She leaned forward, her elbows on her olive pants, her fingertips tapping against each other in a pulse while she thought.

"I got it!" Eddie said, spinning to the front of the chair and leaning forward. "You can go undercover as a student."

We all turned toward him. Expensive moisturizers and a box of Miss Clairol could only do so much, and I think the ship had sailed on undercover student ten years ago.

"Undercover *grad* student," he clarified. "What? She could do it. Get her into a sweatshirt and jeans and she'd look like half the students on campus." He looked at me and cocked his head to one side. "A tan, less eyeliner, no lipstick, some highlights ..."

"We get the point," I said.

"So to make sure I'm up to speed," Dante said, "Eddie's going to make a fake sculpture. Cat's going to use her contacts to get inside the college and look around. I'm going to pose as a security guard. And you're going back to school."

Everyone nodded but me.

"Eddie, how long will it take you to make the replica?" Cat asked.

"Not sure. I need measurements, pictures, specs. I need to conduct recon."

Dante pulled a folder of his own out from inside his motorcycle jacket and tossed it on the coffee table in front of Eddie. Cat leaned forward and Eddie opened the folder. I watched out of the corner of my eye. Eddie fanned a series of photos across the table. They featured every angle of the statue, along with newspaper clippings describing the material, installation, security, and measurements.

"Is that what you need?" Dante asked.

Eddie's eyes went wide. "Where'd you—"

"You guys aren't the only ones who read the newspaper. Just seemed easier to be part of your team than try to steal it on my own. How long?"

"With this info? I'll review it tonight and work on materials tomorrow. I'll take a couple of days off and can probably have this ready by the weekend."

"Good. So we all know our assignments?" Dante asked.

The heads around the table bobbed. I pushed my chair away from the table and walked into the kitchen. Dante followed. I pulled a Fred Flintstone juice glass from the cabinet and filled it with tap water, effectively keeping my back to him.

"You don't like that we changed your plan."

"Doesn't really matter. It's not my plan anymore."

"Sure it is. The players may have changed, but the game is still the same. Just because people swapped parts doesn't mean you didn't design it. Besides, it's best that everyone take the role that they're most comfortable in."

I turned around and faced him. "You really wanted to try to steal it on your own?" I asked, leaning against the counter.

"The thought occurred to me. I like a challenge."

"How do I know we can trust you?" I asked, swirling the water around in the glass. "I know nothing about you."

"You can keep me under surveillance if you'd like."

"What do you mean?"

"I've got nothing to hide. Spend the next couple of days with me."

"I—I can't," I said, cursing my shaky voice. "I have to stay on task," I finished.

He shrugged. "I have to split. If Cat wants to stick around, tell her to call me when she's ready for a ride." He took my hand in his and flipped it so it was palm-side up. He picked up a pen from the counter and wrote a series of numbers across the fleshy part. "That's my number."

"You're her brother. I think she knows the number."

He capped the pen and set it back down on the counter. "I know *she* knows the number. That's for you."

He walked to the front door, calling good-byes to Cat and Eddie, who were flipping through the Halston book. As much as I wanted to dive in and show them the outfit on page 157, I followed Dante because it was the hospitable thing to do.

"You sure you can keep them focused?" he said. "Because this won't work unless *everyone* stays on task."

"I'll do my best."

He reached down, tipped my chin back, and stared at me for an uncomfortable couple of seconds. "This turned out to be a pretty good night," he said. He turned and left.

Turns out, Eddie was right. Rarely do professionals move as quickly as beauticians who hear the phrase, "I need to look younger," and the professionals I'd chosen from the back of the yellow pages were no exception. My brown hair had been highlighted and layered into a tumble of curls that hadn't been allowed this kind of freedom in a decade. My blue-green eyes stood out against sun-kissed skin, the result of a week's worth of spray-on tanning and bronzer to achieve a post-spring break glow. I traded foundation for tinted moisturizer, lipstick for lip-gloss, and fought my eyeliner habit. Cat bought me an I-FAD sweatshirt, laundered and dried a dozen times to give it a lived-in look. I drew the line at matching sweatpants, pairing the sweatshirt with a plaid, pleated skirt.

It was uncanny to look in the mirror and see a face that only slightly resembled my own. It was even more uncanny to spend the next week wandering the college campus. Surprisingly, that's all it took. One week of surveillance to figure out what we needed to know to pull off our plan. The most uncanny part of all of it was that it worked.

After the theft, out hodge-podge team had regrouped at my house for a celebratory drink. It was close to two in the morning, but we were hyped up by the fact that we'd gotten away with thievery. Dante popped a bottle of champagne and we toasted our success. At least, Cat, Dante and I toasted our success. Eddie was upstairs getting the shoe polish off of his face.

I pulled the bundle out of my handbag and unwrapped it. A wooden Puccetti statue on permanent loan from the Philadelphia Museum of Art to I-FAD. It was one of the few known works by Milo Puccetti, a student of Brancusi. It had resided on the college campus for the past five years, and we'd managed to swipe it, all because of a contest in the newspaper.

"Who's going to be in charge of Woody until the party?" Dante asked.

"Woody?" I asked.

Dante pointed toward the Puccetti. "Woody."

Cat rolled her eyes. "You can't call him 'Woody.'"

"We can't call him Puccetti," Dante countered. "What do you suggest?"

"Allen. Get it? Woody Allen." Cat said.

"What about Steve?" I asked.

"Steve?" they answered in unison.

"Woody Allen—Steve Allen. Steve."

"We're naming him? Can I get in on this?" asked Eddie, towel drying the side of his bleached blond hair.

"We went from Woody to Woody Allen to Steve Allen. Where do you want to go? Tag, you're it. You seal the final name."

Eddie repeated after me. "Woody ... Woody Allen ... Steve Allen ...." He dropped the towel and shot two fists in the air. "Steve McQueen!"

I dipped two fingers into my champagne glass and dabbed the base of the statue. "I hereby dub thee McQueen."

We stared at him, all twenty-four inches of him. It was the figure of a well-sculpted man, and I know size doesn't matter but his twenty-four inches were awe-inspiring. Now we just had to get it to Heist and present it to the judging committee. That was the last detail on our agenda, and it would happen tomorrow night at the Pilferer's Ball, the store's opening party.

Cat yawned. "Time for me to get home and go to bed. Dante, you want a ride?"

Dante looked at me. I was still wearing my college-girl outfit, and even though it was a unisex sweatshirt, it felt a little like he was seeing me in my underwear.

"Yes, Dante wants a ride," I said.

Eddie walked down the stairs. He was back to his usual shade of surfer-dude with his towel-dried hair sticking up in all directions. He tossed the towel on the end of the sofa. "You're leaving already? Don't you want to keep celebrating? Did I miss something?"

And that's when we heard the sirens.

About the author

Diane Vallere is a fashion industry veteran with a taste for murder. She started her own detective agency at age ten and has maintained a passion for shoes, clues, and clothes ever since.

You can find her at www.dianevallere.com

If you liked this book, you might like these mysteries:

Pillow Stalk
A Mad for Mod Mystery
October 2012

Interior decorator Madison Night has modeled her life after a character in a Doris Day movie, but when a killer targets women dressed like the bubbly actress, Madison's signature sixties style places her in the middle of a homicide investigation. The local detective connects the new crimes to a twenty-year-old cold case, and Madison's long-trusted contractor emerges as the leading suspect. As the body count piles up like a stack of plush pillows, Madison uncovers a former spy, a campaign to destroy all Doris Day movies, and six minutes of film that will change her life forever.

Buyer, Beware
A Style & Error Mystery
March 2013

Out-of-work fashion expert Samantha Kidd is strapped. But when the buyer of handbags for a hot new retailer turns up dead and Samantha is recruited for the job, the opportunity comes with a caveat: she's expected to find some answers. The police name a suspect but the label doesn't fit. Samantha turns to a sexy stranger for help but as the walls close around her like a snug satin lining, she must get a handle on the suspects, or risk being caught in the killer's clutches.

CPSIA information can be obtained at www.ICGtesting.com
Printed in the USA
LVOW13s0100140913

352438LV00015B/980/P